Dirty Puck Buddies

Hamilton Steelhawks
Book 4

A C Sheppard

Dirty Puck Buddies is a work of fiction. Names, characters, places, and incidents are the products of the author's imagination or are used fictitiously. Any resemblance to actual events, locales, or persons, living or dead, is entirely coincidental.

Copyright © 2024 by A C Sheppard

Primary Logo Artist: Sempiternal

Secondary Logo and Cover Designer: Patrisha Badalo of Art Muse Graphic Designs

All rights reserved.

No part of this book may be reproduced in any form or by any electronic or mechanical means, including information storage and retrieval systems, without written permission from the author, except for the use of brief quotations in a book review.

Hamilton Steelhawks Roster

Max Ducharme (#13) *Dirty Charmer*
Jayden "Killer" Kelly (#17) *Dirty Lover*
Colby "Top Cheddar/Ched" Shelton (#10) *Dirty Heartbreaker*
Jamie "Eddie" Edwards (C) (#6) *Puck Around and Find Out*
Laurent "Gilly" Gill (#1) *Dirty Puck Buddies*
Michael "Presto" Prestifillippo (#55) *Getting Bodied*
Ryan "Rocky" Rocque (#19) *Getting Rocked*
Chase "Chaser" Barrett (#26) *Getting Chased*
Raphael "Biz" Bisson
Jordan Dougherty
Lukas Gustavsson
Corey Jennings (A)
Dmitri "Kovy" Kovalenko (#30)
Alex Labrie
Jesse "Yes-Man" Makinen
Logan "Sauce" Marinaro (A)
Jan Novotni
Alexei Petrov

Chapter One

@HamiltonSteelhawks Happy birthday to our favorite goaltender, Gilly!! #GoHawksGo

@Eddie4prez Happy birthday. Don't do anything I wouldn't do

@timmytank man, he sucks. We could have made the second round if he didn't let in softies

@lilygilly Go be a fan of another team.

Port Carling, Ontario, June 30th

Lorelei Wescott would hardly qualify walking through a forest with a backpack slung over her shoulder as an adventure. Ontario cottage country was far too tame, and anyway this path was actually a driveway. The wildest thing she might run into was a raccoon or a deer or a local who had already downed a two-four.

Australia—now there was an adventure. Spiders larger

than her own hand didn't faze her. She'd just spent a year there, and every off day had served as a chance to explore the coast or hike in the Blue Mountains. Hell, she'd even driven through the Great Victoria Desert in a minivan.

Still, when she'd parked her Rent-a-Wreck next to some Mercedes, her nerves had jangled. Sure, she'd been invited to this party—same as every year, even when the birthday boy knew full well she was nowhere near Ontario—but she hadn't exactly RSVPed or anything.

One, she'd had no idea ahead of time if she'd be in the area that day. She was more of a spur-of-the-moment type of gal. And two, when it turned out she could come... Well, why not make it a surprise?

Her oldest friend, Laurent Gill, wasn't even aware she was back in Canada. She couldn't wait to see the look on his face when she strolled into his party.

She hitched her bag up her shoulder and took a moment settle her breathing. Damn, why was she even nervous?

That time at the club in Hamilton. Yeah, not one of her favorite memories. She'd just been passing through, and Laurent had insisted on her joining the party. The Steelhawks had just finished the hockey season, narrowly missing a playoff spot, and were ready to tear it up. So, she'd found herself on a banquette with dance music throbbing through her bones, downing shot after shot as she watched Laurent and his impossibly bulky friends drink from five-hundred-dollar champagne bottles. Surrounded by Instagram-worthy girls, naturally. One of the guys had even sprayed champagne all over and shoved a random chick's top down to lick the droplets from her breasts, right there in front of everyone.

Whatever. To each their own. But she'd hardly managed two words with Laurent all evening. He hadn't blown her off exactly, but it was clear the entire team was just there to party hard. It had left a bitter taste in her mouth. Weirdly appropriate that she'd ended the night bent over the toilet bowl after one too many Jägerbombs.

She squared her shoulders and continued up the lane. This would be different. Sure, there would be girls, booze, and other substances—she had even brought her own supply of weed, in case the quality was lacking—but this wasn't some club. This was Laurent's house. Laurent's birthday. Surely, he'd make time for an old friend, especially one bearing a gift.

Besides, unless he'd sustained a massive concussion in the past few months, his playlist was sure to be way better than your average club tripe.

The trees lining the lane ended abruptly, opening onto an already full parking area, and behind it, what she could only describe as a huge, angular slab of glass and steel. She stopped and stared for a moment. It took a massive pair to design that and called it a house.

She made her way between rows of even more shiny, obscenely expensive cars. An incredulous laugh bubbled up her throat. You didn't become a starting goaltender in the pros without a huge salary to go with it, and all of this was probably par for the course in the league, but still. Seeing it face-to-face was jarring. She and Laurent had spent the better part of high school hanging out at her house, smoking out of a homemade bong—as long as he didn't have a game or practice. But this... It was simply surreal, the dream of every young boy starting out on his first pair of skates. Few made it this far, but Laurent had.

At the front door, she paused, running a hand through her curls and giving her clothes a quick check. Music blared from somewhere inside the house. Probably useless to knock.

She pushed on the handle, and the door opened onto a sprawling high-ceilinged space, with stairs running to a mezzanine. Her gaze immediately latched on to the tall, colorful painting of a crouching goalie over the mantle. Holy shit.

"The Dominator!" she exclaimed out loud, almost giddily.

When Laurent had signed his extension three years before with the Hawks, he'd bought this house. *A pretty big place*, he'd told Lorelei. And now that she had finally gotten the chance to make it all the way to Port Carling, she could see for herself how damn big it was. Still, she'd painted Dominik Hasek on a large canvas for him, as a housewarming gift, because there was truly nothing worse than bare, white walls. Laurent had talked her ear off about the Dominator all through high school, and she'd had fun working on that red and white mask. But she'd expected the painting to end up in a bedroom or a home office, not right above the mantle where everyone could see it.

"Nice legs and she knows who Hasek is. Where have you been all my life?"

Several guys sprawled on a large couch. The one who had addressed her, his words weighed under a heavy Russian accent, pulled on a joint, and two of his friends stopped scrolling on their phones to look her over. A fourth remained bent over to finish rolling a blunt, wavy tawny blond hair shielding his face.

Still impossibly bulky. Still giving off the vibe that they'd nail pretty much anyone with tits. But their size and their swagger didn't impress her. Their brains would probably short-circuit once they realized she didn't give a shit about mingling with pro hockey players.

Well, except one.

"I'm looking for Laurent—I mean, Gilly."

That was what his teammates called him. *Much easier to pronounce in English*, Laurent had once told her. Plus from what she understood, hockey players went by nicknames. She supposed it was better than Larry or something.

"What do you need him for when I'm right here, baby?" the Russian replied.

She tilted her head. "It's his birthday, isn't it?"

The guy grinned. "Maybe it's my birthday, too. You got a little present for me?"

"Imagine so." She smiled and flipped him off. "Here you go."

To his credit, he simply burst out laughing, along with his friends.

The blond guy finally looked up and blinked at her. "You'll have to excuse Kovy," he said. "Weed doesn't help his conversational skills."

"Blow me, Presto."

"Maybe later. You're not my type," Presto replied evenly. "Gilly's out back on the patio."

She dropped her backpack by the door. "Thanks."

She crossed the living space past an open kitchen. French doors opened onto a stone patio. A pair of speakers blasted AC/DC. Good choice. With a grin, she stepped outside.

Tall and lanky, with close-cropped dark hair, Laurent manned a grill on the far side of the patio, his back toward the window. Narrow hips swayed to the rhythm of "The Jack" as he waved his spatula.

"Luc, get your ass over here and get me a shot!" he called. "Grouille ton cul. Plus vite, tabarnak!"

Oh, the sound of him cursing in French still rolled over her same as always. She plucked a clean shot glass off the table strewn with bottles and half-empty drinks and poured a measure of vodka.

She tiptoed up to him and laid a hand on his arm. "Quick enough for ya?"

He turned, and his blue-green eyes widened in shock for a moment before his mouth stretched into a wide grin. "Lorelei! Tabarnak!"

He gave a loud whoop, and she handed him the shot. "Happy birthday. Miss me?"

―――

Holy fucking shit.

Laurent never knew what to expect at his annual lake house party. Booze, girls, weed, those were a given. But beyond that, there was no telling where the night would end. Or rather the weekend. No telling how many puck bunnies a guy might rotate over forty-eight hours, or what sort of happy pills popped up, or who passed out buck naked on a deck chair at some point. Well, the answer to that last one was probably Rocky, if the previous years were anything to go by. Still, the night would bring its share of surprises.

Only he'd never imagined one of those surprises to be Lorelei. Here, in the flesh. God, he hadn't seen her in over two years.

It was almost hard to believe that she was really standing there, grinning up at him, rust-colored hair framing her face in wild curls and dark eyes twinkling, as if she'd just pulled off the most elaborate prank. She wasn't wrong. Christ, when he'd sent that invite, he'd been sure she was still in Australia.

He took the shot glass and tossed it back before pulling her into a hug so tight that her feet left the ground.

"Oh my God, Laurent!" she yelled. "Put me down!"

"Not a chance, Wescott. It's been too long. You get the full bear hug."

She pretended to struggle against him, but laughter burst from her lips. Raspy and deeper than most women. He'd forgotten how much he liked her voice. It just wasn't the same on the rare occasions that they Facetimed.

"Hey Lorelei, what's up? I didn't know you'd be coming!" Laurent's little brother stepped onto the patio, and he reluctantly set her on the ground, so Luc could greet her properly, with a kiss on both cheeks.

"I didn't know I'd be coming either," she admitted. "Figured it out kinda last minute."

No surprise there. Laurent raised an eyebrow. "What, you just hopped on a plane from Australia on a whim?"

She swatted his shoulder. "Shut up. I'd already planned on coming back to Canada. I'm not like you guys, I don't just jet off first class halfway across the world whenever I feel like it."

Luc shook his head and shot his brother a look. "Calisse. What the hell have you been telling her?"

"Only the best parts, obviously. Lore, you know Luc plays for Los Angeles now, right?"

"Yeah." She said that in her funny Nova Scotia way that sounded like she was sucking in a breath more than speaking. When he'd played there in juniors, it had taken him forever to figure out what that meant. "You told me. Who knew one of the Gill brothers would make it all the way to Hollywood? So what's life in California like?"

As his brother chattered on, Laurent turned his attention back to the grill. The burgers were done to perfection, and just when the guys would be getting hungry too, after spending the afternoon swimming in the lake or trying to score. Or both.

He glanced toward the beach at his teammates. Jayden and Colby had both set their sights on clear targets, and Max had just gotten back together with his girlfriend. Three vets, all of them major players, out of the running. Which in the normal order of things left Rocky and himself in a friendly but ruthless competition for the hottest chicks, who would soon be arriving by the carload.

But Lorelei had just sent the normal order of things spinning on its head. Despite the time they'd spent apart, she was still his oldest friend. His best friend. And he couldn't imagine ditching her to spend the night with a random bunny.

Unless she ditched him first. As far as he knew she was single, and she'd certainly picked the right place if she wanted a casual hook-up.

"Since it's your birthday, I'll spare you the lecture on eating red meat." Lorelei turned back to him, and his gaze flicked over her body. She was wearing gladiator sandals, cut-offs and a white crop top. Simple and understated, but more than enough to show off her generous curves. Fuck, she looked good.

He snaked an arm around her waist and pulled her against him as he flipped the patties. "You know, if you told me you were coming, I'd have cooked up something special for you."

"I landed in Toronto two days ago, and I was supposed

to go straight to Cape Breton to see my stepsisters, but I wasn't up to another flight right away."

"Aw, so you came to see me?"

Her head sank onto his shoulder. "Well... Yeah. I mean, you invite me every year. Figured I'd show up at least once. Plus, I wanted to see how the Dominator was doing."

He grinned. "Living his best life above the mantel, where everyone can see him."

"I may have brought another surprise. A smaller one, this time. Though you'll have to take your apron off first." She read the print in front and snorted. *"Tails I get head, heads I get tail.* Classy."

The guys started to filter onto the patio, asking for burgers. Laurent managed to serve them with one hand, keeping Lorelei close to him with the other. As if she'd simply fly off again if he let go. Which made no damn sense, but it comforted him nonetheless to feel her there, tucked in his arm, her warm body relaxed against his.

She's leaving tomorrow. You know her. Never too long in the same place. Yeah, that was Lorelei, and he'd learned a long time ago that it was no use trying to change her. No, that only got you burned.

But she was here now. One night only. So he had better make it one to remember.

Chapter Two

@ParlezQuebecois Remember, kids, tabarnak is a bad word in French, so never, ever use it.

"So now that everyone is fed, do I get my present before all hell breaks loose?" Laurent blew out a puff of smoke and handed the joint to Lorelei.

She inhaled and passed it back. They were lolling on a bench on his deck while the sunset turned the gentle waves to shades of grayish blue and soft pink. The easy lap of water on the shoreline nearly overcame the buzz of conversation coming from the house. With most of the other guests inside, it was easy to feel as if they were hanging out—just like old times.

She smiled and sipped at her drink. The mix of rum and curaçao slid down her throat, spicy and smooth. "I left it in my bag next to the front door. Be right back."

Before she could push herself off the bench, Laurent's

warm palm met her bare thigh, just above her tattoo, a swirling design of red roses done in an old school style. "No rush. Let's just chill a while. What do you think of the view?"

It was a friendly gesture. Natural. Casual. The type of interaction they'd always had. An easy touch, but then for as long as she'd known him, Laurent had never hesitated to express himself with his body. Just watching him move, she could tell he had none of the reserve or hang-ups or hesitations a lot of other guys had. Laurent simply *flowed*.

So why did her stomach flip at the contact? Bollocks, half a joint, two drinks, and she was already a little loopy. She'd grabbed a few chips and a couple of burger buns—*sans* the burger—to avoid drinking on an empty stomach, but that would hardly last an entire evening.

"It's right beautiful," she replied. "Australia's got its share of jaw-dropping sights, but lakes, you know? It makes me feel... at peace. Serene. Like I could just look at the water for hours."

"You sure that's not the weed?"

She elbowed him. "Shut up. Way to ruin my point."

He nudged her back with his shoulder. "I *do* know. That's why I bought a house here."

She snorted. "You call that a *house*? More like a goddamn fucking mansion. Seriously, why do you even need all that space?"

"Helps me clear my head." He shrugged and passed her the joint again. "Oh, and host awesome parties."

"Yeah, that too. Glad I'm finally seeing one in the making. When you say all hell breaks loose, what do you mean, exactly?"

But Laurent didn't answer. His blue-green eyes were fixed on her upper arm. "You got a new tattoo, didn't you?"

His finger grazed her skin at the edge of her sleeve. A shiver ran down her spine. Jesus, she was *definitely* loopy.

"That? I've had it for 'bout a year."

He lifted the hem to reveal a seascape of tropical fish done in bold lines and bright blue, orange and pink hues. "Holy shit, that must have hurt like hell. Gorgeous, though."

His finger traced the shape of an inked starfish, and it took her a moment to find her words. *Get a hold of yourself, Wescott.* "Um, thanks. How about you? Still no ink?"

Laurent dropped his hand. "Nope. But I'm open to suggestions. What do you think I should get?" He grinned. "And more importantly, *where?*"

Damn, was he actually flirting with her? No, this was just Laurent being Laurent. Taking the piss and expecting her to reply in kind. Right?

She raised an eyebrow. "Well, that all depends..."

"*Gilly!* There you are!" Heels clicked on the patio. A brunette with long, silky curls bouncing on her shoulders headed toward them, decked out in a dress so tight and skimpy a single sneeze would make her breasts pop out. Far be it for Lorelei to wag her finger at someone wearing revealing clothes, but there was sexy, and then there was my-skirt-is-so-short-I-can't-sit-down.

"Oh, hey... Peyton, right?" Laurent said. "Nice of you to drop by."

She came to a stop in front him, hands on her hips. From that angle, Laurent could probably see up her skirt if he bent his neck a little. "Wouldn't miss it. We had so much fun last year. Leena's here, too."

Something in the girl's tone told Lorelei that the fun she was talking about wasn't busting out a game of Clue. Twister, more like.

"The more the merrier," Laurent simply said, and took a

drag of the joint. "Only two rules in this house. No public posts on social media and no music released after 2010."

Lorelei smirked. "I'd take an earlier cut-off point, but that's just me."

Two other girls strolled onto the patio, dressed in similar attire, followed closely by Luc and Kovy, beers in hand.

"How about introducing us, bro?" Luc said. "These lovely ladies said they're friends of yours."

"Yeah, then maybe we can play some three on three," Kovy added.

Lorelei got up. "Right, I'll leave you to it."

Laurent grasped her wrist. "Hey, where are you off to?"

"I need to go get your present." And get away, because an uncomfortable feeling stirred in the pit of her stomach. This seemed to be gearing up to be a repeat of that time at the club, though no one had brought out the champagne yet. "Where I can stow my bag?"

"Put it in my study. Ground floor, third door on the right."

Good God, how many rooms did this place even have? She'd have to ask Laurent for a tour. If he wasn't too busy with Peyton and Leena and whoever else wanted to blow his candles.

What the hell did you expect?

She shook her head as she made her way back inside and across the living space, where Laurent's bulky friends, polo shirts tight on their muscular chests, were sizing up the handful of girls who'd arrived while RnB pumped from the sound system. She was here now, and it was no use feeling sorry for herself if she didn't quite fit in. She couldn't just show up unannounced at Laurent's doorstep and think he'd cancel his own birthday party. He'd taken the time to catch up with her, asked her a ton of questions about her trip while he was manning the barbecue. What more could she ask of him, with his teammates all there to let loose and girls looking to score?

She found the study and tossed her bag behind his desk between a shelf full of vintage goalie masks and a framed red, black, and silver Steelhawks jersey bearing the number 1. Back in the great room, the girls seemed to have multiplied, and the music blared twice as loud. She scanned the crowd for Laurent, gift in hand, and headed back toward the patio.

He was still outside, but Presto had joined him now, and Luc and Kovy were nowhere to be seen.

"Lore, have you met Presto?" he called out to her.

"He witnessed your buddy Kovy trying to hit on me, so yeah, we've met."

Laurent rolled his eyes. "Calisse. The idiot only puts his brain cells to good use when he's making saves."

"He's a goalie?"

"Gilly's backup," Presto said. "Could have stayed in the KHL with his save percentage, but the money is better over here. Still, surprisingly high in goals saved above expected when he doesn't play as often."

"Did he now?" She hadn't understood a word of that, but no matter. She turned back to Laurent. "So did you get a birthday cake before you open your presents or just flaming shots?"

Laurent and Presto shared a look, and Laurent smiled. "Actually, I do have a birthday cake. Sort of. Baked it myself."

He took a plate of brownies from the table strewn with half-empty bottles and red plastic cups.

Lorelei let out a squeal. "Oh my God, is that what I think it is?"

"You ought to know since you helped develop the recipe. The infamous Gill super-duper extra fudgy space cakes. Come on, let's go down by the fire. This is for connoisseurs only."

He wrapped his arm around her waist to lead her down to a bunch of Adirondack chairs placed around a fire pit. Presto got to work starting up the fire, and Laurent sat down with a satisfied sigh.

"Okay, before we dig in..." She handed him his gift. "Happy birthday. You better be careful and not get chocolate all over it, though."

He tore it open. "Yesterday's edition of the *Globe and Mail*. Wouldn't really be you if you used normal wrapping paper, Lore."

"Better than actually reading that rag. Besides, it's what's inside that matters, right?"

He unfolded the heather grey tee-shirt and held it in front of him. "Holy fuck, this is so cool."

She grinned. "You like it? My own design."

"Hey, Presto, check this out. Tabarnak!"

Laurent turned it around for his teammate to see. His favorite curse word was printed in bold red block letters, but the T had been stylized into a goalie stick, the legs of the N into goalie pads, and the final A into a Steelhawks helmet.

Presto smiled and nodded. "Fucking A. That's you, all right."

"I gotta put this on."

He shouldered out of his Hawaiian shirt. Lorelei's gaze flitted over his chest. Damn. The last time she'd seen him shirtless, he was still a gangly, pimply eighteen-year-old. Athletic, sure, but all lanky limbs.

Now, though... He'd filled out. Grown into his body, because solid muscle rippled beneath taut skin. His shoulders bulged, and a line of hair arrowed down the center of his six-pack.

Stop staring, you idiot. She forced her gaze toward the fire just as Laurent was slipping on his new tee-shirt.

"It's perfect." He smoothed the hem past the waistband of his shorts. Still, the sleeves strained around his biceps. "Come here, you."

He opened his arms, and she went in for a hug. Laurent squeezed her tight, giving her an up-close-and-personal encounter with his bulk, and her head settled onto his shoulder. Such a familiar feeling, one that filled her with a bubbly warmth that remained as they settled in front of the fire, chatting with Presto, then another teammate of theirs who wanted to cozy up in a chair with his girlfriend instead of taking part in whatever was going on inside.

So they weren't all just there to get hammered and hit on everything that moved. Relief loosened the knot in her chest. Laurent was here now, chilling with her and his buddies, yammering on about the best poutine in Montreal, rather than getting a lap dance on his couch. She wasn't going to judge anyone who went in for a little casual sex. She sure as hell understood not being relationship person. A wide gap existed, however, between settling down with someone for life and sleeping with someone you barely knew, and she found herself in the middle somewhere. She needed some sort of connection beyond the raw physical, some measure of trust.

Friends with benefits, or at least acquaintances with benefits, but not a lot of guys were down for that. That was the main reason she hadn't gotten laid in months. And now it was coming back to bite her in the ass, because Laurent had slid onto the ground beside her to rest his head on her thigh, and God, she was getting... fidgety.

You trust him. He's your friend. Would it be so wrong?

Shit, that was a slippery slope. Still... *would* it be wrong? After all, they'd gone there before in high school. An on-and-off thing they'd never really named, but in the end, it hadn't changed anything between them. They were still best friends.

They were older now, more mature. And she would be leaving tomorrow. No risk of either of them getting hurt.

That is, if Laurent was into it, too. And if the competition waiting back at the house didn't swoop in first. As long as they stayed here...

A grimy beat overlain by warbly vocals blasted over the sound system. Talk about a brutal reminder of the wild party.

Laurent sat up. "Oh fuck, no. Who the hell put on Soundcloud rap? Everyone knows that's off limits unless I'm fully incapacitated."

He sprang to his feet. Bollocks, just when she felt perfectly relaxed... But he took her hand and dragged her along. "Come on, let's go put on some real music before this garbage makes me lose my high."

She followed him toward the house. "Give them some Nine Inch Nails. They're probably all ready to fuck like animals anyway."

"Why, Miss Wescott," he teased. "I'm shocked you'd think so poorly of the upstanding young men on my team."

"What was it your buddy Kovy suggested? Three on three?"

He glanced over his shoulder, a wicked glint in his eyes. "No idea what he was referring to. Probably a Russian thing that doesn't translate."

She tossed him the side-eye, but he only laughed.

Inside, Laurent left her at the kitchen island to pour

them drinks while he switched playlists. A few seconds later, the slow, smooth chords of "Patience" by Guns N' Roses filled the air, and Laurent reappeared by her side.

Lorelei handed him a shot of Midori. No shark piss at this party, only the good stuff. "You trying to kill everyone's mood or something?"

He clinked the glass with hers and downed it in one gulp. "Jayden has been trying to score with Cait all fucking afternoon. I had to help the poor guy out."

Ah yes. The couple who'd joined them by the fire. Didn't look like either of them needed any help, but two shots and another Guns N' Roses song later, Cait stalked up to Laurent to ask directions to the bathroom. Alone, and looking pissed.

"Tabarnak," Laurent growled, "I don't know how my idiot friends manage to mess up this bad when it comes to girls."

Lorelei glanced around. Everywhere she looked, couples were making out like they were about three minutes away from getting a room. Or not. "You're saying one thing, and I'm seeing another."

Laurent poured another round of Midori. "I meant with a girl they like, not some puck bunny. It's different when you really want it."

She downed the shot. It left a sweet, burning trail down her throat to her chest, her belly. Laurent drank his and swayed toward her, eyes closed, gripping her waist as if to find balance.

Her senses awakened along with her body. Laurent's touch seemed magnified, buzzing on her skin, echoing in a low pulse between her thighs. His hand grazed her waist, his palm warm on the bare skin under her shirt, and her eyes fluttered shut.

"Wow, those space cakes are something," she said, her breath catching.

His lips stretched into a slow smile. "What can I say? I still got it."

She nodded, and locked her gaze with his. "Yeah. Yeah, you do."

He didn't look away. His hand inched farther to settle on the small of her back. A flurry of sensation bloomed in her midsection.

"Is this okay?" he asked.

His tone was still friendly and casual. But his voice carried an edge now, an undertone that mirrored the desire taking hold of her. She nodded wordlessly. He leaned closer, and his hand slid down the curve of her ass.

"How about this?"

Oh God. She bit her lower lip. If anything, she wanted him to keep going. To clutch at her. To pull her against him so she could feel if he was as turned on as she was.

"You never asked permission before."

"I didn't have to." A definite bite had worked his way into his tone. "So, is it okay?"

"More than okay," she managed.

He touched his forehead to his, and she tilted her chin up...

"*Fight!*"

Laurent startled, and his hand fell away. "What the fuck?"

"Fight! Upstairs!" someone yelled.

He rolled his eyes. "I'd better go see who got caught with his dick out in front of the wrong chick. Fucking hockey players, eh?"

"I know how the joke goes," she replied. "A hockey game broke out in the middle of brawl..."

"Pretty much, yeah." He tucked a curl behind her ear. "Don't move, I'll be right back."

"What, and miss the show?"

"Trust me when I say you're better off watching the boys drop the gloves during a game when they're not piss drunk. Far more entertaining." He took a step back. "I won't be long."

She forced her expression into something she hoped was pleasant, though her thoughts were spinning and her nerves on edge. They'd been so close, so very close to bridging a gap they hadn't bridged since they were teenagers. Yeah, she wanted it. Badly. But now that Laurent had made it clear he was down for it too, the implications hit her square in the face.

Eleven years ago, neither of them had much experience. Now, she had no idea how their sex lives compared. No idea if they'd be compatible. What if she slept with him, and it was really bad? They'd been smoking and drinking, and if it ended with three pumps before he rolled over and started to snore... Shit, that would definitely make things awkward.

She poured herself a glass of water from the sink. Too late to clear her head entirely, but this might help settle her stomach at least.

"Ugh, I told you we should have gotten here earlier. All the good ones are taken."

"Jesus, Tricia, will you stop bitching? More guys will show up, guaranteed. You think this kind of bash ends at midnight?"

Two girls were chatting behind her as they poured themselves drinks. She sipped her water and listened. Might as well keep herself entertained while waiting for Laurent.

"Besides," the second girl went on, "I didn't see Gilly making out with anyone, so he might still be looking for a hook-up."

"I mean... He's kind of, I don't know... Not as buff as the other guys, right? I need someone who can toss me around in bed. Like a big bruiser, you know?"

"Oh my God, you haven't heard the gossip? Holy crap, it's *insane*." They both giggled. "You know Leena? Last year, she had a threesome with him and some other girl. She told me it lasted all night and then some. He wore them both out."

Lorelei nearly spit out a mouthful of water. What the hell?

"You're shitting me."

"I'm not. He may not look like a bruiser but I swear to God, that guy is a freak. His goody drawer is legendary. Any girl who gets an invite back to his place knows she's in for a wild ride."

Laurent, a freak? When they were together, he'd been... sweet. Attentive. *Cuddly*.

This wasn't reassuring, though. Or soothing. No, now her curiosity had awoken, and it was ravenous. The need to discover just how good Laurent was made her heart pound faster and gripped her core. Whatever it took, she had to find out for herself. And quickly, before anyone else moved in on him.

"Having a good time, ladies?"

She whipped around. Laurent had returned, and the two girls who'd just been discussing his exploits were now batting their eyelash extensions at him.

Lorelei set her water glass down and walked toward him. "Everything okay?"

"Yeah, except I'm going to have kick my little brother's

ass for inviting a bunch of his dickhead teammates to crash the party."

She placed both hands on his chest. "Think that can wait?"

The corner of his mouth quirked up, a low flame lighting his blue-green eyes. "Depends. You have something better in mind?"

"Maybe." Now or never. You only lived once. "I'd love a tour of the house. Wanna show me your master bedroom?"

Riverview High School, Sydney, Nova Scotia, twelve years earlier

"Bonjour, la classe!"

Lorelei slumped in her seat as Madame Campbell swanned her way to the front of the classroom. Still, she replied in the same monotone as the rest of the grade ten students.

Madame put a hand to her ear. "Je n'ai pas entendu."

"Bon*jour*, Madame Campbell."

"Bien!"

God, this much enthusiasm ought to be illegal at eight-twenty AM. Hell, at three PM it would be too much.

Lorelei pulled out a notebook—new and pristine for the start of the school year—and began to draw little circles in one corner. By June, it might be totally covered in doodles if it didn't escape its spiral binding first. As she moved her pen, she pushed aside the memories of comments made by her primary school teachers. *Lorelei is a bright student, and she could do much better, but all too often she has her head in the clouds.*

Thank God for her mum who always replied that some people were just wired that way—at least while she was still living with her and Dad.

In any case, Lorelei didn't need to listen for now. The classroom rules were the same every year, their gist easily summed up by the posters dotted about the school: *Be kind, work hard.* Or in Madame Campbell's class, *Soyez gentils, travaillez fort.*

No doubt the rest of the first period would be just as predictable.

"Trouvez un partenaire!"

Yep. Pair off. It was time for the dreaded interview, where you'd have to quiz a classmate before introducing him or her to everyone else. They'd been doing it every year since grade six—or was it five? Either way, there wasn't anything new to report by now. Everyone knew everyone else and had for years.

They all knew Lorelei for sure. The kid with the weird hippie mum who insisted everyone call her Tanya, and God help you if you had the misfortune to say Mrs. Westcott in her hearing. Flighty Tanya who had run out on the family when Lorelei was still in grade three, leaving her for her dad to raise and her nana to watch after school.

Anyway, she'd already chosen her seat strategically—in the corner by the door, where she stood the best chance of being the odd one out. That way, she'd only have to introduce herself.

Five minutes into the exercise, the room buzzed with grade tens pretending they could actually hold conversations in French, at least when they weren't exchanging summer gossip in English until Madame Campbell drifted by. Lorelei concentrated on her doodles, relying on her placement at the back of the class to make her look busy.

And the ruse might have worked, too, if not for the latecomer. He straggled in then, hovering by her desk. From this angle, all she could see were arms and legs topped by a mass of dark hair that stuck out in all directions.

The hum of conversation faded, as everyone looked up. A few rows away, a couple of the popular girls traded glances. One of them shifted in her seat, hiking her skirt higher.

Madame Campbell eyed him. "Est-ce je peux vous aider?"

Whatever he replied, it made the teacher raise her brows. "Vous êtes en retard."

"'Scuse."

"Pardon?"

The boy straightened and held out a folded slip of paper. "Excusez-moi."

Was it Lorelei's imagination, or had that slipped out with a note of sarcasm? Before she could decide, he launched into a barrage of rapid-fire French that sounded nothing like their teacher.

Madame Campbell stared back, her eyes widening behind her glasses, and Lorelei could almost see her brain struggling to catch up. Then she blinked at the note. "Bien, Monsieur Gill. Asseyez-vous."

He dropped into the nearest available seat—right next to Lorelei. A wash of heat ran up the back of her neck. Shit. She was going to have to introduce him to the rest of the class, and he'd obviously taken the advanced course.

"Bonjour," she said cautiously.

"Salut." And then he went off again, his mouth forming the words too rapidly for her brain to keep up. Not to mention pronounced in a way she wasn't used to—but she suspected was the *right* way to say things. Or at least wherever Monsieur Gill came from.

Somewhere in Quebec, without a doubt.

Yeah, this was going well. She sneaked a glance in the teacher's direction before leaning closer and whispering, "English?"

"Uh, sorry..." His reply was halting. "What... what are we doing?"

"En français, s'il vous plaît," came the reprimand from two rows away.

"Comment t'appelles-tu?" Because she wasn't about to keep calling him Monsieur Gill.

She'd hoped to get it more or less right, but his smirk told her otherwise. Hell, she probably had as bad an accent as their teacher. "Laurent. C'est quoi ton nom?"

"What?"

"C'est quoi ton nom?" He repeated it more slowly and carefully, but this wasn't the way she'd learned it. Maybe her class had been wrong the entire time. "Comment tu t'appelles?"

"Lorelei Wescott... Um..." His eyes were a strange yet striking combination of blue and green, almost like the ocean in the Caribbean. They somehow had the power to pin her to her spot. "Qu'est-ce que... non. Pourquoi..." Fuck it. She lowered her tone. "What are you doing here?"

"Hockey."

Oh shit, she should have guessed. In fact, her neighbors down the street often billeted players—but she hadn't seen anyone new lately.

"Um..."

Any semblance of a reply failed in either language. Maybe it was the way he was watching her. His gaze no longer focused on her face, though, but somewhere above. Oh God, he was staring at her hair, which was better than her ass, because he'd probably call it fat like everyone else. Her hair, though. Even on the best of days it looked like she'd just rolled out of bed. She resisted the impulse to raise a hand and press her curls into compliance—as if such a simple gesture could tame their wildness.

Dirty Puck Buddies

He reached across her desk for her notebook and pen.

She snuck a glance at Madame Campbell. Busy, thank God, with another group, although the popular girls were tossing dirty looks in her direction. And wouldn't they like to be in her shoes, getting the tea on the new guy? They actually cared about this shit. Well, too fucking bad if they had to wait their turn.

At a nudge, she turned her attention back to her partner. He'd written everything down for her in a heavy, spiky script. *Laurent Gill. Mon surnom est Gilly. Je viens de la banlieue de Montréal. Je joue au hockey pour les Cape Breton Screaming Eagles. Je suis gardien de but.*

Right. She could make most of it out. Laurent Gill from somewhere around Montreal, the latest import for the local junior team. And a goalie.

She picked up the pen and wrote underneath. *Lorelei Wescott. Je viens de Sydney.* Then she sank her teeth into her lower lip. She had no idea how to say the next part in French, so she wrote it in English. *I can't wait to get out of here.*

An admission, perhaps, but he seemed safe enough. He didn't know anyone to gossip to—yet. And it wasn't as if she'd just revealed anything a normal person couldn't already figure out. She was saving her money. The second she turned eighteen, she was going to Halifax and getting a tattoo. Maybe go live with her mum for a bit. After that, she'd figure it out.

"Tabarnak."

She had no clue what that meant, but the way Madame Campbell stiffened, it might be good to commit that one to memory.

She raised her brows at him.

With a grin, he nabbed the pen out of her hand, his fingers brushing hers, and wrote it down.

Tabarnak. Then he added an arrow. *C'est un sacre.*

"Un sacre?"

It's a bad word, he added.

She grabbed the pen back. *Like fuck?*

Maybe.

After that day, the school put Laurent in study hall during French class.

Chapter Three

@TIMMYTANK WHAT DID I TELL YOU ABOUT GILLY SUCKING? THAT GOAL HE LET IN, MAN.
@LILYGILLY TOUCH GRASS FOR ONCE
@TIMMYTANK IT'S THE MIDDLE OF WINTER, DIPSHIT

Winnipeg, Manitoba, eight months after the lake house party

Laurent took a swig of beer and settled back on the sofa, though nervous energy buzzed through him. Like most of Rocky's ideas, this had been a bad one. So why the hell had he gone along with it?

Come on, G-man, don't bail on me like those other morons. True, Max and Jayden were currently holed up in their hotel rooms, probably Facetiming with their girls, and Colby had disappeared in a flash after the game, like he had all season. Only last year, they'd all hit the clubs together, but no longer. That left Laurent to act as Rocky's wingman. Letting him wander this godforsaken town by himself felt like cruel and unusual punishment, especially when a freak ice storm in Hamilton had grounded their plane until the next day.

He sure as fuck hoped it wouldn't be longer than that.

For now, he was stuck sipping a tepid Coors Light in some random girl's apartment.

"Hey, relax," a feminine voice purred close to his ear. A moment later, a hand slid up his thigh.

He caught the hand in his and gently lifted it. "I'm not in the mood, Steph. Sorry."

Stephanie only giggled and curled closer, her honey-colored curls tumbling over his chest. "Really? Why'd you text me, then?"

A moment of weakness after a defeat. Nothing like losing a game when you were fighting for a playoff spot to mess with your head. Hearing that damned goal horn go off four times didn't help. If only he hadn't let in that last one in OT, but fuck, Hammersmith, Winnipeg's huge power forward, had fooled him with a lethal slapshot. Going out for a few drinks seemed like a good idea, but then Rocky had insisted Laurent call up one of the girls he knew in town, and she'd invited them both to hang out at her friend's place.

A girl in every town. Or several. Stephanie just happened to be the first one to reply. Their last hook-up had been fun, possibly because he'd had a lot more to drink.

Never again. Too risky. You never knew what crazy shit you'd do under the influence.

"I think I'd better just head back to the hotel," he said. "I'm beat."

"Aw, come on, Gilly. The night's only starting. Why don't you have some of this?"

She reached over to the coffee table to grasp a half-empty bottle of peach vodka and lost her balance for a moment, nearly spilling the drink, which only elicited more giggles.

Yeah, definitely a bad idea. Laurent glared at Rocky. Of course, the idiot was having the time of his life, regaling Stephanie's friend with one of his classic hockey stories. Not that he particularly needed to impress his target—the blonde was practically sitting on his lap already—but Rocky got a kick out of it, anyway.

"So the ref whistles, and out of nowhere, that fucking idiot shoves me into the boards... What else could I do but smoke him?"

"Oh wow," the blonde cooed, running her hand over his biceps. "You must work out a ton to be so strong."

Laurent rolled his eyes. Talk about a captive audience. He—along with the rest of the team—had heard the story of how Rocky dropped the gloves with Jacob Trouba about five hundred times. Now Laurent was stuck in Winnipeg after a loss, listening to the five hundred first rendition. Could this road trip get any shittier?

Rocky grinned. "I can play the full sixty and never hit the bench, baby."

Laurent had to laugh. "Tabarnak, I used that line back in juniors."

Except in his case, it was actually true.

The blonde stood and pulled on Rocky's hand. "Why don't we find out how long you can go?"

Rocky's grin widened, and he followed her toward the corridor, shooting Laurent a knowing look, one that screamed, *Check me out, bro. I'm about to hit that.* A moment later, the bedroom door slammed shut.

Laurent drained what was left of his beer before rising to his feet. That was his cue to leave.

Stephanie followed him into the front hall, bottle still in hand, teetering on her heels. "Hey, where are you going?"

"I told you. I'm beat."

"That's strange." She slid her arm around his waist and gave him what she probably thought was a seductive smile, though alcohol clouded her gaze, and her mouth wavered. "Last time I remember you gave me a full sixty plus overtime."

He untangled himself. "Look, no offense, but I was just trying to keep Rocky company." Muffled, high-pitched cries drifted down the corridor. "And he's got company now."

Stephanie pouted. "So you're just going to leave me here all alone? Maybe I'd like some company."

The cries got louder. Damn it, he couldn't simply head off while her friend was getting noisily and thoroughly nailed, though Rocky certainly wouldn't say no if Stephanie offered to join in. Plus, she'd had so much to drink she'd probably pass out in the Uber.

"I'll get you home safe. But then I'm going straight back to the hotel."

She raised an eyebrow. "Right. By the time we get to my place, I bet you'll have changed your mind."

He didn't. Twenty minutes later, Stephanie slammed the door to her apartment in his face. Not the most pleasant of goodbyes, but at least he was finally free to get some shut-eye.

As the Uber took him back to the Delta, he scrolled through his phone. A few messages in the Steelhawks group chat, a voice message from his maman... God, what now? Probably something to do with Luc.

He waited until he was in his room and lying on his bed to listen to it, putting his phone on loudspeaker. Maman's voice filled the room, cheerful in her greetings, before worry colored her message.

"Salut fiston, je sais que tu es occupé mais il faudrait que tu parles à ton frère..."

Laurent rubbed his face and sighed. Luc had bought a flashy sports car, and Maman was already imagining him speeding down California freeways like something out of a movie chase. No doubt she had tried to reason with him, and Luc had told her off. So now it was up to Laurent to call him and knock some sense into him.

As usual.

Tabarnak, why did it always fall to him to fix things? Luc might be his younger brother, and Maman might still see him as her precious baby playing all the way across the continent, but it wasn't like he was sixteen and heading off to live with a billet family for the first time. Luc was twenty-two, for fuck's sake. Old enough to drink anywhere in North America and to buy a fancy car if he felt like blowing his entry-level salary.

It had been that way ever since Papa's death. It had been hard on all of them, but especially for Luc who was only ten back then. Maman had been overprotective of him ever since.

Whatever. He'd call Luc tomorrow when he finally got back to Hamilton. He and his brother hadn't spoken in a while, and it couldn't hurt anyway.

His phone pinged. What now? Hopefully not Rocky sending the group chat a disheveled post-performance selfie. The last one had been bad enough, with his curly hair standing on end, beads of sweat still on his forehead, and his gap-toothed grin smugly filling the frame.

Tabarnak!

He sat up and stared at the text message that popped up on his lock screen. The password they'd used over a decade ago. For the first time that evening, the Winnipeg gloom lifted. Warmth spread through his chest and loosened his limbs, like dipping into a hot bath after a trek through the snow.

Lorelei.

> Where are you?

A smile stretched his lips. Holy hell, he hadn't heard from her in weeks. And hadn't seen her since... Yeah. His birthday party. The warmth kicked up a notch, ready to course through his body and rush south. Nope, not going there. Lorelei hadn't mentioned anything about that night in their more recent exchanges, and neither had he. Why risk making things awkward?

But damn, if hearing from her didn't cheer him up. He plopped back down on the bed and typed a reply.

> Manitoba. You?

LORELEI SET her phone down and stared at the ceiling, only to pick it right back up when it pinged. She grinned as she read Laurent's reply. Her night had just gotten a whole lot more interesting.

True, she was currently lying on an ancient sleeper sofa in her dad's friends' basement, so the bar was low. It was terribly sweet of them to let her crash, but shit, the mattress springs creaked like crazy. After tossing and turning for an hour, she'd messaged Laurent out of sheer boredom and frustration. Yeah, and also because she was planning on contacting him anyway. But she hadn't actually expected a reply, not at two AM.

> You got a game?

> Did. Lost. Don't watch the highlights, it was bad.

> I won't, promise. But, hey, you're still up.

She tapped the side of her phone. Maybe she shouldn't have asked. Maybe he'd think she was prying. If he was out partying, or about to take a girl back to his hotel room...

No. She wouldn't go there. It was none of her business, not even after...

That night with the champagne. She might have called it Laurent's birthday party. Or that night at the lake house. But her mind zeroed in on the champagne, because she'd never, *ever* done something like that with anyone else. For Laurent, though, it might not even break the top ten of the freakiest shit he'd done with a girl.

And she wasn't about to ask him.

The phone pinged again.

> Went out with Rocky but not in the mood to party. You?

> Staying at some friend of my dad's in Toronto.

> Fuck. You taking a plane somewhere?

Her stomach gave a funny little lurch. Oh, she couldn't wait to get his reaction.

> Nope. Got to Toronto yesterday and I was supposed to grab a bus to Hamilton this afternoon but the highways are closed.

Three dots danced on the screen, then stopped. She frowned. Maybe she shouldn't have waited until the last minute to tell him she was coming, but for some reason, she hadn't wanted to give him too much of a heads-up. Easier that way. More comfortable. He wouldn't feel obligated to bend over backward and help her settle in or something. But Laurent had his entire life in Hamilton, and the hockey season was intense. He probably wouldn't have much time to see her, maybe grab a coffee here or there at most.

The opening cords of AC/DC's "The Jack" rang out in the room. She yelped and dived under the covers, swiping up to answer.

Laurent's bearded face popped up on the screen. He was lying on pristine white sheets, wearing a Steelhawks shirt. "What the hell, Lore? Are you in a cave?"

"I'm in bed," she whispered. "I don't want to wake the whole house."

"Well, too fucking bad, because you're going to have to explain why you decided to show up in Hamilton. You just passing through?"

"No. I'm staying a bit. I don't know how long." As long as it would take to get some of her artwork up in the coffee shop that had just hired her, maybe start selling a few pieces. She bit her lip. "Going back home wasn't really doing it for me. It was nice to be closer to my dad and stepsisters and all but... you know."

After a while, her family made her feel claustrophobic. It always had. Not to mention how badly she'd always wanted out of that place when she'd lived there. She wasn't about to run off to Australia again, but she needed a change of scenery.

"So Hamilton, huh?" Laurent smiled. "You picked the right spot, especially if you like hockey."

"I like anything if someone gives me free tickets."

He stuck out his lip and gave her sad puppy eyes. Even in the soft muted glow of the hotel lighting, their blue-green color seemed to hit her in the midsection. The way they always had. Even during his gangly stage in high school, you couldn't help but notice their incredible color. "You say that, but you didn't come see us play in Vancouver."

"You still going to hold that over my head? It's been four years." She stuck out her tongue, and his mouth relaxed into a cheeky grin. She'd wandered out west to experience real mountains. Only Vancouver was way over her budget, when she worked in an organic grocery shop. A rented room out in Abbotsford had been the most she could afford. "I finished my shift at six on the dot, there's no way I could have made it in time for the game. Besides you had that rookie thing afterwards."

"The rookie dinner, yes. The new guys almost cried when they saw the bill." Laurent sighed.

She bit her lip. It didn't seem fair to make them pay for dinner when the veterans earned so much more. Still, as initiations went, it wasn't anything like the shit Laurent had witnessed in juniors.

"Anyway," he added, "if you're in town, no more excuses."

"I promise I'll come watch you play, and we can grab a drink whenever. Just call me when you're free."

"Yeah. Tomorrow. Team has a day off and then we're in town for a week—if we can get out of this place. I mean, just let me know when you get in."

Her heart thumped against her ribs. Sweet of Laurent to want to see her the moment she got there. Sweet and weird and slightly terrifying after what had happened.

Chill. He probably won't bring it up, and if he does, we can just laugh it off.

She should count herself lucky to have a friend in Hamilton. And not just any friend. He could introduce her to a bunch of people, tell her where the best restaurants and bars were, show her around. Hell, he might even hook her up with a funky art gallery or two—if such things existed in Hamilton.

Laurent would help out any way he could. That's just the way he was. Nothing to read into it.

She smiled. "I will. But I have to get some sleep now." She yawned for emphasis.

"Sure. Me too." He paused for a moment, but she couldn't read the expression in his gaze. "Chat soon."

"Bye. Be talkin'."

She hung up, switched off her phone and closed her eyes. But her mind was still buzzing, and she knew sleep wouldn't come for a long time.

Chapter Four

@lilygilly A DREAM COME TRUE TODAY!
@SHSlut is that what I think it is? Our all-star goalie?
@lilygilly YES!
@timmytank guess you've hit your summit. It's all downhill from here.
@lilygilly you are SO MEAN
@Eddie4prez cool it, you two, before I come over there and hose you down.

Hamilton, three days later

Laurent pressed the side button of his phone, and the screen lit up. Four fifteen. No word from Lorelei. Was she having trouble finding the place? Did she get his text telling her he had taken a seat on the second floor?

He'd chosen this coffee shop specifically because it was low-key and understated, nestled at the end of a narrow street. A place that wouldn't be too crowded in the middle of the afternoon, even though the pastries here were several notches above typical coffee shop fare and drew their share of connoisseurs.

He leaned back on the padded bench and exhaled deeply before taking a sip of his matcha latte. Fifteen minutes wasn't that bad. He'd known Lorelei to be an hour late on occasion, though they had been far less busy back then. Shit, how was this the only afternoon they could actually meet up before their respective schedules took over?

He picked up his phone again and scrolled through his unread messages. Mostly media inquiries, from journalists or head of Hawks' PR Shawntelle Alexander. With the All-Star Game just around the corner, they were ramping up. He'd have to make nice for the cameras walking the red carpet and plastering on his best smile, as if he was stoked to be all alone in Dallas while his buddies jetted off to tropical destinations for a little R&R.

Though he'd happily stay behind in Hamilton if Lorelei wanted company.

He set his phone back down. *Stop. That's not what she's here for.* Yeah, that night they'd spent together at the lake house had been mind-blowing, but it was just one night. Nothing more. He had no reason to believe this was any different from the arrangement they'd had back in the day. Scratching an itch and moving on.

Hell, that was some itch. One he wasn't sure Lorelei wanted to admit to after the fact. Yeah, and he'd probably taken it further than he should have, so he'd better zip it when she showed. The last thing he wanted was to make things uncomfortable between them, especially now that she'd be living nearby.

"Excuse me..."

He set looked up. A young woman with a shy smile shuffled over to him, clutching a paper napkin. Ah, yes. She'd been sitting two tables away with her boyfriend, and he'd felt them stealing a few glances his way when they'd first arrived.

"Hi, um, I don't mean to intrude, but I was wondering if maybe... I mean, I'm big, big Hawks fan, and..."

Laurent smiled. "No problem. Do you have a pen?"

He didn't mind signing a coffee shop napkin, even taking a picture or two. Seventh player and all. The team wouldn't even exist if fans didn't come to cheer them on at games.

Just as the woman was whipping out her cell phone for a selfie, he spotted a riot of loose, rusty curls. Lorelei appeared at the top of the stairs, holding a colorful coffee mug and a small plate bearing a blueberry muffin. She froze in place, as if unsure whether to interrupt or not.

Crap. Talk about shitty timing. The women snapped the picture and turned to him with watery eyes. "Thank you so much, really, this means the world to me."

"Yeah, my pleasure. Have a nice day."

She thanked him again and nearly skipped back to her seat. Lorelei made her way over to the table. Her lips curled in a teasing grin.

"You know, I'd have you sign a paper cup, but I always bring a reusable one."

"Shut up, you. Come here."

He stood to kiss her cheeks before pulling her into a hug.

A memory ignited in the back of his brain. Sometime in high school. For him, the two-cheek kiss was something he did without a thought. Not so much for these Nova Scotia kids. Lorelei had ducked away for a moment, and embarrassment had crept along his spine in a series of hot, uncomfortable prickles, another reminder, yet again, that he wasn't like these English kids. Different language, different customs. Just a hug—and only if you were really good friends. That was the way. But somewhere over the course of a few months, familiarity had taken over. They'd become closer. They'd developed their own rituals.

Now it was *their* thing to take the best of both cultures.

He closed his eyes for a moment and breathed in deep. Something in the shampoo she used, her perfume... A fruity fragrance with hints of coconut that seemed to seep into him and make his entire body relax against hers.

Dial it back. It's just a friendly hug. He let her go and settled back onto the bench, though the feeling of her stayed on his skin, a gentle tingle. Just the way it had after she'd left that morning last July.

Except she was here now, sitting right down next to him. And this time, she wouldn't be flying off again for a while. "How have you been? You look good."

She did. She was wearing some sort of fuzzy sweater with large bright flowers that looked both retro and modern somehow, and it made the rosy color in her cheeks stand out. "Really? I didn't even have time to brush my hair properly this morning."

Laurent clenched his hand before he could reach out and tweak a curl. That tousled morning hair looked just fine spread across his white pillowcases. Phantom sensations tingled across his palms as he recalled plunging his hands into those soft curls, wrapping rebellious strands around his fingers...

He pushed the thought away from his mind. "Were you late for the bus?"

Her smile widened. "Yeah, well, I better start setting

five different alarms if I don't want to be late for work. I got a job at a coffee shop downtown." Her eyes darted around to take in the high ceiling, potted plants and pale wood paneling. "The Daily Grind. Don't know if it's as nice a place as this one."

"I have to admit the pastries here are unbeatable." He nodded toward her muffin. "You should eat that before I nab it."

She nudged his shoulder with hers. "It's a hundred percent plant based."

"Like I care."

"Then go buy your own."

"Can't do the empty calories." He patted his stomach. "I have to watch what I eat during the season."

Was his mind playing tricks on him, or did that rosy tinge on her cheeks deepen just a little? But she simply rolled her eyes. "So I guess going for a few drinks is out of the question?"

"I'm reasonable, not a monk. If you want to go out tonight..."

"Can't," she replied with a sigh. "I have to be at work at six tomorrow for training. And then in the afternoon I'm meeting my potential landlords."

Laurent raised an eyebrow. "Landlords? You found a place then?"

"Maybe. It's a married couple renting out a room in their house. David and Mason. We already talked on Zoom but they want to meet me face-to-face. Fingers crossed, because in the meantime I'm staying at a youth hostel, and call me crazy, but I think I'm getting too old for that."

"Yeah, no shit." He shook his head. "Lore, you know you can stay my place, right?"

Okay, this time, she was definitely blushing.

"I mean, not necessarily with me in it," he added quickly. Shit, and he didn't want to make things uncomfortable? "I could go crash with one of the guys, and you could have the place to yourself. Just until you land on your feet."

"That's... really sweet of you." Her smile faltered, but then she mock-punched his shoulder. "Not going to suggest *I* crash with a buddy of yours?"

No. Fucking. Way. Lorelei had more than enough moxie to tell off any one of his teammates if they started acting like douchebags, but still, the idea of her staying with one of the guys didn't sit well with him. At all.

Might as well grunt like a caveman if he admitted to that, though. He simply laughed and took a sip of his latte. "Believe me when I tell you, it would be far worse than a youth hostel."

Hamilton, ten days later

"What are you cooking?" David, her new landlord—or was it house-mate?—leaned over the frying pan and inhaled. "Smells delicious."

Lorelei looked over her shoulder and smiled. "Vegan taco meat. Walnut, mushrooms and tofu. I swear by it."

David sat at the island and inhaled deeply, eyes closed under his thick-rimmed glasses. "You're going to convert Mason to soy, I just know it. I tried when we first started dating, but my efforts in the kitchen made him run the other way."

"It's all good as long as you enjoy eating together, even if it's not the same thing. And if it's made with love." She stirred the sizzling mixture and added a sprinkle of cumin.

"Thought this would be nice for sports night. With nachos and cheese and avocado dip, of course."

David slapped his hands together. "Yay! Your first sports night with us! That's something to celebrate. I got the nice kombucha from the store."

"What, you don't crack open a couple of cold ones?"

"Please, I'm not *that* big a basketball fan. Blech." He crinkled his nose and stuck out his tongue. "I might not have convinced Mason to give up meat, but at least he stopped drinking horse piss."

Lorelei tipped the taco filling onto a platter before assembling the rest of the meal on a large tray that she set down on the coffee table. David trailed behind her, glasses in hand. Mason was already sitting on the couch, his bulky frame nearly folded in half, typing away on his phone.

"Baby, I hope you're messaging your mother there. She called me twice today—*twice*—because she absolutely needs to know what time you can come pick her up in Toronto before she books her plane ticket."

"Okay," Mason grunted.

"I'm *serious*."

Another grunt. "I'll do it tomorrow."

"God, just get it over with. Do it during one of the commercial breaks, it'll take three freaking minutes."

Lorelei curled up in a large leather recliner and eyed the bickering couple. She'd never been one for opposites attract, but you couldn't get more opposite than this. Dark-haired and fine-boned, David taught grade three, and would happily chat your ear off about any subject under the sun. Mason was an electrician and as quiet and reserved as his husband was loquacious. Somehow, they'd met playing World of Warcraft online and had bonded, or so David said, over their love of collecting plushies. And yeah, the lower floor of the townhouse house was pretty much crammed with baby animals and Pokemon.

Well, she supposed her parents were an odd couple, too. Rich the strait-laced corporate guy and Tanya the bohemian artist with dried clay caked on her forearms... Only they'd never bickered in front of the TV. At best, they fought—but at least they were communicating then. It was better than the times they ignored each other for days on end. She'd only been nine when Tanya finally left, but she still remembered the tension overlaying the house, like a deep blanket of snow and just as cold.

Lorelei switched her attention to the game. She found basketball about as interesting as watching paint dry, but thankfully David provided more than enough entertainment. In between commenting on the players' looks and scrolling on his phone for advanced stats, he'd chatter away about the latest sports-related gossip, before switching to historical tidbits about the teams.

"You should do the color commentary," she told him. "You're a million times more interesting that the guys on TV."

"For basketball, maybe," Mason said. "For hockey, forget it. He doesn't know a cross-check from a forecheck."

David gave him a sharp elbow nudge. "Well, excuse me, some of us didn't grow up in the backwoods of Michigan skating on ponds all winter."

Mason snorted. "You're Canadian, and you live in a hockey town."

"So? Lorelei's Canadian, too, and she's not a hockey fan." He glanced at her sideways. "Are you?"

She laughed. "No, I'm not, but..."

Heat rose to her cheeks. Crap. What was the big deal? Maybe because she hadn't told David and Mason that she had a close friend in Hamilton, and not just any friend. It was as if she was keeping Laurent a secret or something.

Your dirty little secret.

She shook the thought away. Nothing dirty about it. At least not anymore. Sure, seeing him again face-to-face... Her body remembered all too clearly the earth-shattering pleasure it had experienced at Laurent's hands—literally—and was not above demanding more. Thank goodness for self-restraint, or at least busy schedules. Lord knew when she'd get a chance to catch up with him again.

"Okay, here's the thing," she said. "You know the Steelhawks?"

David rolled his eyes. "Girl. Does a bear shit in the woods? You can't live here and *not* know the Steelhawks."

"I might know someone on the team. Laurent Gill?"

Mason tore his eyes from the screen to gape at her, and David's jaw dropped. "Oh my God. What position does he play?"

"Goalie," Mason supplied. "And a damn good one. Candidate for the Vezina."

"He's an old friend of mine," Lorelei continued. "A buddy from high school." *Let's leave it at that.*

David stared at her wide-eyed. "Shut up. Like... how well do you know him? Christmas card friend? Coffee once a year friend? Help-you-bury-the-body friend?"

Lorelei hesitated. "More like the last one, but we haven't seen each other much these past few years. I was traveling, and obviously he's super busy."

Mason nodded slowly. "That's dope."

"So you haven't met any of his teammates?" David asked.

"Actually, I have. Sort of."

David had now turned his whole body toward her and

was clutching the back of the chesterfield. "Max Ducharme?"

Lorelei frowned, and flipped through the list of Laurent's teammates, the ones she'd met last summer. Kovy, Presto, Jayden... "No, that doesn't ring a bell. Sorry. Why him, specifically? I thought you didn't follow hockey."

"I don't, but I sure as hell know who Max Ducharme is."

He took his phone from the table and swiped through it, then handed it over to Lorelei. A social media post showed a handsome guy with high cheekbones and blue eyes, holding a picture-perfect dark-haired woman in his arms. Her hand was resting on his chest and a diamond ring glittered on her finger.

"Right. Who's that?"

"Addison Holtz," David said, as if Lorelei had failed to recognize the prime minister. "Only one of the greatest pairs skater this country has ever seen. I was such a huge fan growing up, and she had such amazing chemistry with her partner, but then she had this tragic accident..." He paused to contain himself. "She and Ducharme just got engaged."

"And David nearly cried when he heard the news," Mason added with a smirk.

"For *joy*," David said pointedly. "I was just so happy for her, after the way things ended with her partner. Anyway, Lorelei, if you ever get the chance, you know..."

She couldn't say no. After all, Laurent had insisted on inviting her to a game before the end of the season. But mingling with the wives and girlfriends...

Come on. It's nothing. A good action for a good cause. "Sure thing." She smiled and reached for a bottle of kombucha. "I'll see what I can do."

Lorelei's bedroom, Sidney, Nova Scotia, twelve years earlier

The moment Robert Plant's voice began to bounce from one headphone to the other, like a tennis match playing itself out in Lorelei's ears, realization struck. This was music made to listen to while high.

Too bad she didn't have any weed. In any case, nearly midnight on a Sunday when Dad was home wasn't the best time to light up.

She leaned back against the pillows propped against her headboard and let herself get lost in a song that encouraged her to pull up stakes and ramble on. Though she might not be looking for the queen of her dreams, she was definitely searching for something beyond the walls and sloping roof of her tiny bedroom.

Her gaze landed on her on-going art project, a mural on the low wall under the eaves, an empty spot where she couldn't even fit a table. She'd had to crouch to paint the details of the sun lowering behind mountains that faded into mist. She'd only started to add a meadow with wildflowers in the foreground. Cliché, maybe, but it served as a reminder of what she wanted.

Two years left. Two more years of scraping together what money she could put aside from part-time jobs and get the fuck out of here. After that? Time to ramble on and broaden her horizons, to find new inspiration for her creations... Just like Tanya had.

A movement at the window snagged her attention. A face. On the second floor. Her pulse accelerated, and she stiffened before recognition set in.

Laurent.

She tossed her headphones aside, pushed off the mattress, and heaved at the sash, until he could shove his lanky body through the opening. Winter air rushed into the space, and she slammed the window shut. "Holy shit, you scared me."

He unfolded himself but stooped under the low ceiling. "I texted the password."

Tabarnak. It was his calling card ever since that single French class, months ago now. Because, yeah, it turned out he was, in fact, billeting with the neighbors down the street, and he'd discovered he could access the shed dormer that led to her bedroom via a tree in the yard.

One day last fall, he'd simply shown up and knocked on the glass. Then asked if she'd help him with his English homework. From there, they'd developed a warning system. Except, usually, he waited for her to reply before coming over.

She eyed her cell, lying neglected on her desk. "I guess I didn't hear my phone."

"What are you listening to? You must have been really into it."

"Just a playlist I made of my dad's music. It's old." She reached for the headphones. "But you can listen if you want."

Normally, he would have made himself at home on her bed, stretching his long legs until his feet hung over the end. Tonight, he just stood there, his gaze pinning her in place until she shifted her weight from one foot to the other. An uncomfortable awareness of her outfit—ratty tee-shirt, sweats, no bra—worked its way up her spine.

God, why should she care? He ought to have realized she was about to climb into bed.

"Or not," she said to fill the silence as much as anything. "Sometimes I feel like I was born in the wrong era, you know?"

The admission slipped out unconsciously, but now she'd have to trust him with it. But she could do that.

Right?

In all the months they'd been hanging out when his hockey games and her after-school jobs hadn't intervened, he'd given her no indication that he'd let something like that come back to bite her in the ass. And it would if certain people got hold of that information. Some of the kids at school had always taken cruel delight in reminding her she didn't fit in with the rest.

He flopped onto the bed and stared up at the ceiling.

"Is everything all right?"

He sighed. "We just got in."

"From the road trip?" She'd never been someone who paid attention to hockey before, but hanging out with Laurent had forced her to follow the Cape Breton Screaming Eagles. Two games over the course of a weekend, plus all the travel, made for a rough schedule that found the boys making up for sleep on the team bus—when they weren't trying to catch up on homework to the light of their cell phones.

"Yeah. Roads got bad."

"So how'd it go?"

His expression told her everything she needed to know. "Got lit up Friday in St. John. Coach started me again today in Halifax. I was supposed to bounce back. Instead, I got pulled."

"Oh, shit." She sat on the edge of the mattress, nudging him over with one hip. "What did your coach have to say?"

"Same old crap. It's a team effort and all that, but... Calisse. I'm supposed to focus on the positive when these things happen. But I can't. I let in some bad goals, and we've been stuck on the bus for hours, and I can't think about anything else. All I see is that fucking puck going past my glove every time."

She poked at his foot with her toe. "Is this where I'm supposed to tell you happy thoughts like it's a Disney movie? Whistle while you work? The sun'll come up tomorrow?"

His lips stretched at the corners, though they stopped short of a smile. "That's why I like you. You don't deal in bullshit."

"Good to know. I'll check that off my list of potential careers. No bullshit dealing."

"No, but you're real. You keep it real." Still, something in the way he held himself was off. Tension floated around the lines of his shoulders and jaw. It was like he'd been carrying a burden, one he couldn't shrug off, for far longer than the past four or five hours or even since Friday night.

"You didn't come over here at midnight to tell me about your weekend, did you?"

His mouth opened, and he took a breath, before closing it again.

"Come on. What's up?"

"It's just..." The full weight of his stare fell on her, and she noticed the first signs of facial hair shadowing his upper lip. "Do you know why I showed up to school late the first day?"

She'd heard rumors, but then that was the currency the kids at their high school dealt in. Making up crap about other people they knew nothing about. More bullshit—with maybe a side of wishful thinking in some cases. She'd overheard a couple of girls with their heads together saying Laurent got kicked off some team in Quebec because he got caught in bed with the coach's daughter... Being sent to Sydney at the butt-end of the league was a form of exile.

"No."

"Good, because you weren't supposed to. My coaches know and my billet family and the teachers, but that's all."

The raw emotion lacing his tone had her pressing closer. "You don't have to tell me if you don't want."

"No... No, I should. So my dad, he got sick last year."

"Oh no."

"He died at the end of August. It happened very fast."

"I'm sorry." Everyone said that when a person lost someone, but she hoped he understood that she really meant it.

"He had cancer." His accent deformed that last word, but her brain untangled it. Same awfulness in French as English, only the way he said it, it sounded like a curse.

"That's... that's a lot to deal with."

"Yeah, well. I thought maybe I should stay home. My maman needed me, maybe. She's just got me and my little brother now, and Luc is a handful."

"Can't be easy to be separated from them like this." She didn't know much about his life wherever he came from, but the suburbs with a big city close by sounded a lot more exciting than Sydney. And since her mum and dad had broken up, she knew what separation was. Having it be as permanent as death only made everything worse.

"I almost didn't come out there. But then my uncle talked to me. He thought I shouldn't pass up the chance to play junior hockey. It could be a chance to something bigger. And I listened. I *listened*."

"You think you shouldn't have?"

"After the weekend I just had? Hell, no."

She turned to face him, stretching out fully beside him. Her arms circled his shoulders, and she laid her head against his chest, where she could hear the steady thump of his heart. "Pack up and go home if you want, but why would you want to waste this chance?"

"You sound like my uncle. Doesn't that make me selfish when maman is dealing with everything by herself?"

"She's not alone, though, is she?" She planted her hands and leveraged herself to meet his gaze. "She has your brother. She must have other family."

"Yes, but..."

"What do you think she'd rather have you do? Come home or do your best here?"

He ducked his head. "She told me she wanted me to play hockey."

"Did she now? Then I don't see where you have a choice. You're just going to have to show your uncle and your mum they were right."

His hands slipped to her back. "I don't know if I can."

"I know you can. And I believe in you." She wasn't sure where this was coming from, but in a way, he was living what she *wanted* to live eventually. Striking out on his own and making a success of himself. Doing what he loved. She couldn't tell him as much, but she needed him to do it to prove she could—when the time came.

The creak of floorboards sounded in the hallway, and Lorelei sucked in her breath. Neither of them moved until the footsteps faded and the door to her dad's bedroom closed with a soft thud.

Laurent pulled away. "I better go."
"Depends on what you mean by that," she whispered.
"Back to my billet, I mean. I'll see you at school."

Chapter Five

@HamiltonSteelhawks Check out the boys' pre-game fits. Look good, feel good, play good.
@timmytank Dream on. LA gonna light you up.
@lilygilly I could never be Hawksmin. I'd block so many trolls.

The Steelhawks barn, late March

Electronic music booming in her ears, Lorelei took a swig from her beer can, and settled her shoulders against the plastic-backed seat. Overhead spots came up, and the players hit the ice for warmups, corralling pucks, gathering speed. Shooting at the gaping cage that was pretty much at eye level.

Finally, Laurent skated out and circled the Hawks' end of the rink, loose and easy, before gliding toward the net—toward *her*, since she was sitting directly behind it.

"Best seat in the house," he'd said on the phone. "You can watch me make epic saves up close for two whole periods."

She'd smiled and run her finger over the e-ticket he'd sent to her cell. "Cocky much?"

"Just getting into the zone. Gotta to have rock-hard confidence when you get out there."

His gear alone ought to do that for him. She'd been to a couple of his junior games back in Sydney, and she'd caught him on TV a time or two. Without fail, a funny jolt rippled through her stomach when he strode out big and bulky, like he was wearing armor, his blue-green eyes glittering behind the cage of his mask.

His face turned in her direction, and she waved, though he probably couldn't see her in the crowd. Should she go down to the glass? Maybe not with all the kids holding up signs and vying for a puck. Anyway, he needed to focus on the game ahead.

Laurent skated to the boards near center ice, squirted water into his mouth, and dropped to the ice, pelvis low, legs bent at the knees, lower legs sweeping the frozen surface. Left, then right, and again. He rose, and eased into a side lunge. Left, right, the movement almost hypnotic...

Oh God. Despite the chill this close to the ice, her cheeks heated. *Don't you dare let your mind stray.* But it was impossible not imagine a different kind of rhythmic sway. Pelvic thrusts deep, deep inside her, and each one tearing a hoarse cry from her throat.

Is that good for you? Do you want more? Ask like a good girl.

She closed her eyes. Okay, no big deal. A memory like that could pop up every so often. Perfectly natural. Especially when she had gone months without getting laid. Way too long. And the last time had been lackluster, compared to what had gone down with Laurent. Almost as if he'd rewired her brain to crave something other guys couldn't give her.

Two things I can do with a silk sash. Blindfold you, or bind your hands. Which one you up for?

Right, save that for later. After the game when she might need to... take the edge off.

With a deep breath, she opened her eyes and focused on the jumbotron. Much better. The camera briefly panned over to the opposing team in their white and black jerseys. LA. She tried to pick out the name Gill from the mass of players. The whole reason Laurent had invited her to this particular game—he was facing his brother's team. Damn it, if only she'd asked what number Luc wore.

She glanced back toward the net where Laurent had taken up his position. The red-and-black-jerseyed Hawks players shot at him, but he turned every puck aside. Lorelei drained her can and sat back, rolling her shoulders and neck. Damn it, why couldn't she relax and enjoy this? Sure, she wanted the Steelhawks to win, but it wasn't like she was down on the ice. It wasn't like she would have to stand down there for sixty minutes and stop hard little bits of frozen rubber.

Maybe it was just the electricity filling the arena. The warm-ups had given way to multicolored lasers darting and flashing in time to a relentless beat, and the surrounding spectators were cheering, yelling. All fans of the team in their jerseys bearing unfamiliar names like SHELTON, EDWARDS, and KELLY on their backs—but she was just a fan of the guy in net. She'd even dug out her own jersey tonight, the number 1 tracing her spine, topped with GILL. Laurent had given it to her years ago.

The scoreboard flashed, and the arena announcer ran through the Hawks' starting lineup. At each successive name, the cheers built until "...and in goal, Laurent GILL!"

The crowd responded with a chant of "Gil-LEE, Gil-LEE, Gil-LEE!"

Well, this could be a learning experience, at least. Though when the game actually started, it moved so fast she could barely keep up. Players pursuing the puck carrier up, down, left, right, banging into each other. This close, she could actually hear the scrape-swish of their lethally sharp blades and the clack of their sticks on the ice as they battled.

BOOM.

One player smashed another one against the boards. The shudder of the glass rattled through her bones. The crowd's roar lifted Lorelei to her feet. Holy crap, a fight. They held each other by the jerseys, and a fist crushed its opponent's nose. The other guy returned the favor with a loud crunch. Around them, the other players closed in, grappling, red jerseys holding back white. Among them, she spotted Luc, grabbing a Steelhawk by the collar, getting up in his face, mouthing off.

"No friends on the ice," Laurent had told her. "No brothers, either. If I'm in net, Luc will try to put one past me."

Striped-shirted linesmen intervened, separating the combatants. The whole thing couldn't have lasted more than thirty seconds, but shit, a wild energy buzzed through the entire arena. Hostile yet somehow joyful. She'd never felt anything like it before.

A ref skated to center ice and turned on his mic. "Hamilton number 13, Los Angeles number 42, five minutes each for fighting. Hamilton number 17, two minutes roughing."

As two Hawks skated toward the box, the guy next to her raised his hands like a megaphone. "Fuck you, refs!"

The rest of the crowd took up the chant. "Ref, you suck! Ref, you suck!"

The game resumed. A face-off in the Hawks' zone, followed by the LA players fanning out. The puck streaked across the ice from one to the other while the Hawks closed ranks around the net, sticks changing position with each pass.

Lorelei leaned forward and kept her gaze fixed on Laurent. "Come on, come on."

A shot. Laurent stretched into a split and the puck ricocheted off his toe.

Another white jersey retrieved it, shot. Laurent's arm whipped out like a windmill, and his glove snapped shut, slamming into the blue of his crease.

Thunderous cheers broke out, and the crowd took up the chant of "Gil-LEE, Gil-LEE, Gil-LEE" once more. Lorelei grinned. If only his teenage self could see this.

Laurent handed the puck back to the ref, before reaching for the water bottle on top of his net. Then he flipped his mask up and squeezed a jet of water into his mouth. With a second jet, he doused his sweaty face and the back of his neck.

Oh. Lorelei bit her lip. Deep in her belly something twinged. Again. Yeah, she would definitely have to take care of that later, or she'd never get to sleep.

And the rest of the game didn't get any better. By the start of the third, the Steelhawks were up by two goals, but LA kept pushing. After every whistle, players congregated, getting into each other's faces, shoving each other. A few cross-checks. A couple of sneaky punches before the refs could intervene.

And then one of them broke away. Just him and twenty feet of clear ice before he hit the crease. Both teams skated in pursuit, heads down, legs churning in their effort. The LA player shot, and Laurent bent over double as if he was sucking the puck into his body. A second later, a huge, white-jerseyed teammate crashed straight into the Hawks' net.

Sticks and gloves hit the ice. Everyone paired off, grabbing jerseys. Fists started to fly. Laurent reached for the player who'd seized him, but another red jersey flew between them and pulled the LA guy away.

Boneheads. They were all massive, fucking boneheads. With shit for brains.

You didn't see basketball players or football players haul off and punch each other like that. At least that was what her cool, rational mind thought. Her body, on the other hand... Seeing Laurent all red-faced, his teeth clenched, his fists tight, ready for mayhem ...

Bollocks, what the hell was wrong with her? Thank goodness there were only ten minutes left. That had to be enough time to pull it together before meeting Laurent. Had to or else she might give in and ask him point blank to take her home.

The thought lingered until the final buzzer. Possibilities danced in the back of her mind while she made her way through the crowd to the spot where Laurent had told her to meet him. They'd done the whole friends-with-benefits thing before. Would it be any different if they tried again?

Hands over your head. Tell me if I'm pulling too hard... unless you like it that way.

Okay, aside from *that*, Laurent hadn't changed, and neither had she—or not much. He was still the same sweet, down-to-earth guy. Well, not much on the ice. Or in bed.

But just the two of them hanging out? They could chill and talk about anything, the same way they had in school—like they had last summer. He was still her oldest, most trusted friend. He wouldn't make her feel weird or awkward if she suggested a little messing around. They could at least discuss it, right?

On the lower level, a burly security guard stood right in front of a AUTHORIZED PERSONNEL ONLY sign on a double door. Lorelei stopped a few feet away and gave him a polite smile, but the man stared blankly ahead. No use negotiating with security. Laurent would come get her when he was ready.

Feminine voices behind her made her glance over her shoulder. A group of women descended from the upper level, taking the stairs with practiced ease in their high heels. Their blonde hair, skinny jeans, and cropped puffer jackets seemed to be a uniform, one that made Lorelei extra aware of the polyester that comprised her oversized red jersey.

"I told Raphaël to have a word with the coach," one willowy blonde with tan skin said to her companion. Her accent sounded a lot like Laurent's. "Calisse, he has to stand up for himself!"

Behind her, a pretty brunette held the hands of two adorable kids in jerseys, followed by a dark-haired woman typing away on her phone.

Lorelei smiled. She'd seen this last woman before. Addison Holtz. Easy enough to recognize from the countless pictures and videos David had shown her. But before she could think of an excuse to approach her, the security guard opened the door and the group filed through. Yeah, they'd be authorized. The door slammed shut with a metallic clang.

Lorelei took out her phone. No message from Laurent. How long did it take to shower and dress? Another ten minutes? Twenty? Thirty?

"Ma'am," the guard said, "this is a restricted area."

Lorelei rolled her lips between her teeth. She hadn't taken a step toward his precious door. "I know. I'm waiting for someone."

He advanced, like he was planning on herding her back up the staircase. "If you want an autograph, wait outside the parking lot with the other fangirls."

"No, you don't understand. Laurent Gill told me to wait here for him."

"Sure, he did." His jaw ticked. "I'm going to have to ask you to leave."

Fucking hell, this guy was starting to get on her nerves. "Look, I can show you his text messages. Or call him. I'm not a fangirl, I'm his friend."

"Ma'am—"

But before he could go on, the door opened. Face still red from exertion, eyes shining, Laurent stepped over the threshold.

His mouth stretched into a grin. "There you are! So, what did you think?"

———

LAURENT BUTTONED his shirt and adjusted the collar. All around him, his teammates—some in their arrival suits, others in nothing but towels—were winding down from the game, taking their time to savor their victory and share the best moments. Whenever they played against LA, fights were a sure bet, especially since a few LA guys crashed his birthday party last summer.

"Holy fuck, Killer, that punch you landed on that fucking moron was a beauty," Max called from his stall. "Two fighting majors in one game. Is that a record for you, or what?"

Jayden shrugged his massive shoulders, but a smile crept over his lips. "I'd have gone for a third, easy."

"Yeah, so you can brag about it to Cait," Laurent said.

Jayden's smile turned into a grin. "Oh, she watched this one, believe me."

Laurent frowned. "Calisse, isn't it like four AM in Paris?"

Jayden had been doing the transatlantic thing with his girlfriend since September when she'd taken a job as an au pair. Once the season was over and they could finally reunite, he'd feel better than after scoring a hat trick.

"Love doesn't care about time zones." Max let out an exaggerated sigh. "Neither does Facetime sex."

Something Laurent had never tried himself. He probably could have asked Lorelei. She might have been down for it. Hell, she might be down for a lot of things he'd never suspected.

Do it. Bind my hands. And don't worry about being gentle. I want you to take charge.

Fuck. He didn't need this along with the adrenaline from the game still pumping through his veins. He'd better keep it under wraps. She was waiting outside for him. Usually, he was the last one out of the showers, but here he was, already dressed and ready—in more ways than one.

He slipped on his coat and pocketed his phone. "See you tomorrow, les boys."

"Hey, you going out with Luc tonight?" Rocky called after him.

"Yeah, we're going to Big Smoke for dinner. We need to catch up."

"Hit me up if you go to the club after that."

Laurent shook his head. "Jesus, we're leaving for Florida in the morning."

Rocky sniggered. "I'll nap on the flight. What else are planes for?"

Easy for a defenseman to say, but Laurent couldn't risk it. He needed his full focus for the next stretch of games. They were in a playoff position—all the more reason not to slack off. If they'd worked harder last year, they would have made it further than the first round. The team was counting on him.

Still, when he entered the public area of the arena and spotted Lorelei, arms crossed over a Steelhawks jersey—*his* jersey—all thoughts of playoff pressure fled his mind. Thirty saves out of thirty-one, a .968 save percentage, a gorgeous woman waiting for him... If only he hadn't let in that one goal. This evening might have been perfect.

"There you are! So, what did you think?"

Lorelei's mouth curled into a bright smile. "Hey, you. Congrats on the dub."

She stretched out her arms, and he pulled her into a quick hug. But her fingers crept into the short hair at his nape and tightened. He breathed in a deep lungful of her fruity scent before she pulled away.

"You were amazing," she said.

A laugh escaped him. "Not like you've never seen me play."

"Yeah, but... wow. That was really something."

"Nice to watch from behind the net, right? Plus, we always have fun when we play LA."

Lorelei raised an eyebrow. "What's fun? Stopping a

bunch of high-speed pucks, or getting into the other guys' faces?"

He offered her his arm, and they set off toward the parking garage. "I know you don't approve of fighting, but it only pumps us up."

She dipped her head and eyed him through her lashes. "Yeah." She sucked the word in on a breath. "I can tell."

"Besides, if there's anyone who deserves the rough stuff, it's Dalton Nash and Brock Lee. Remember those motherfuckers?"

"Oh, were they the ones who crashed your party?"

He nodded. "Not only that, they have a history with Jayden and Max."

Lorelei's eyes widened. "Max Ducharme? Didn't he go to the box for fighting?"

"Yeah, number 13. Why do you ask?"

She giggled. "Okay, so the thing is, my roommate David is a huge fan of his fiancée, Addison Holtz."

"Addie. Yeah, of course. She's great."

"So when he found out I knew you and that I was going to get the VIP treatment at a Steelhawks game, he asked me to try and get a selfie with her. And... well, I did see her come down with all the wives and girlfriends, but I didn't want to run up to her like some crazy person or anything."

He stopped in his tracks. "You want to go to the family lounge? Addie's really nice. She won't think you're crazy if you want a picture with her."

A tinge of pink crept up her cheeks. "That's really sweet, but I'd feel weird about it. I mean, she probably just wants to meet up with Max, right?"

Lorelei, feeling awkward? Last summer, she hadn't given a shit about waltzing into his party. Not to mention traveled the world by herself. How could the Steelhawks family lounge be more intimidating? Somehow, even after knowing her for more than a decade, parts of her remained a complete mystery.

"Another time, then."

She nodded. "Right."

"Besides, I'm meeting Luc." He checked his watch. "He should be out any second. We're getting dinner, and I would definitely ask you to come along, only he insisted on this fancy steakhouse."

Lorelei wrinkled her nose. "Imagine. Thanks, anyway. I wouldn't want to get in the way of brotherly bonding."

More like tough love. Maman had called again last week and asked him to pump his brother for info. What he was up to in LA? Laurent already knew the answer—hockey, girls, and parties. Still, he better make sure Brock and Nash weren't pushing the partying angle too hard.

"But, um…" She sidled closer to him. "Maybe we could meet up later?"

He almost froze in his tracks again. A hot ripple of energy careened through his chest, as if he'd just made an epic save.

Tabarnak, was she suggesting they hook up again?

He considered her. Her dark gaze burned with a low fire. He knew that look. It had been imprinted in his mind since they were horny teenagers. He'd seen it again at his birthday party, when they were doing shots, in his kitchen just before she'd let him slide his hand over her ass.

There's a lot of sex going on in this house.

She'd murmured those words right into his ear when they'd gone upstairs, her breath a warm rush against his skin. His throat had gone dry, he could only nod.

Do you want there to be more?

Fuck. *Fuck*. It was almost eleven PM. Dinner would

take another two hours at least, and then he needed to get some serious shut-eye before the trip to Florida. If Lorelei came over...

He'd work that luscious body all night. He wouldn't stop until exhaustion took over. Last time, the champagne on top of shots and weed had sapped some of his energy, and they'd still fucked on repeat until she told him she needed to rest.

But he was on fire now. Fresh out of a win, nothing but Gatorade and protein in his system. Shit, he was tempted to call off dinner and take her home right now, pedal to the metal.

You keep a chilled bottle of champagne in your room?
For when I'm in the mood to celebrate. You want a taste?
Are you going to untie me first?
No. Open your mouth.

He needed to focus. Road trip tomorrow. Playoffs. And Luc was flying back to LA.

He exhaled. "Look, I'd really, really love to hang out, but we might finish late. And I need to get up early, so..."

She nodded. "No problem. I get it. Your schedule is crazy. We can hang out when you come back or after the season's over or whatever."

Right. That would be far more reasonable. With the playoff race heating up, starting something was a bad idea. Especially something that might take his mind off his game.

Chapter Six

@HamiltonSteelhawks Another win in the books. The boys were buzzing!
@FreshHockeyStats That's a season high in fights for Killer Kelly. No Lady Byng for him this year.
@Eddie4prez Things you love to see.

Big Smoke, two hours later

"Hey, can I have another scotch here?" Ice cubes clinked as Luc waved his empty glass at a passing waiter.

Laurent lifted a forkful of wagyu steak to his mouth. The full, fatty flavor of simply seasoned beef melted on his tongue, and he pushed aside the mental image of a certain lovely redhead scowling. At these prices, he had no room for guilt trips.

He swallowed. "Easy there, frerot," he said in French. "That's your third."

Luc snorted and sawed away at his T-bone. "Fuck off. I need it after that game."

"I wouldn't even bother with this, but we're done playing you for the season. You guys need to work on your power play. You almost gave up a shorty."

"Shit, if your buddy Max hadn't jammed his elbow in my teeth, I wouldn't have whiffed on my pass. Can't believe the ref missed that."

"What's the point in whining now? Man up and ask Max to go next time. He has no problem dropping the gloves."

His brother's blue-green eyes narrowed. Chirps usually flew between them, especially after a game, but obviously Laurent had hit a nerve. "I don't know what I hate more—when you act like my coach or Maman."

The waiter placed another scotch on the rocks in front of Luc, and he tossed it back, downing half of it in one go. Good thing he was taking an Uber back to the hotel. No point in trying to keep up with him. Laurent didn't want to end the evening in a holding cell.

"Speaking of Maman, you should call her more often."

Luc rolled his eyes. "Did she put you up to this?"

Laurent glared at him. "No, but it would be nice of you to get in touch more regularly. You know how she worries with you on the other side of the continent."

"She has nothing to worry about." Luc drained his glass. "Calisse, I'm old enough to take care of myself."

Laurent tamped down a flare of annoyance. Snipping at his brother would only make things worse. "Look, she just wants to be sure you're all right. Hear it from *you*, not me, because when she can't get hold of you, she sends *me* a bunch of texts."

Luc bit back a laugh. "All right. I promise to call and tell her I've been doing my laundry and eating my greens like a good boy."

"You do that. And while we're on the subject, I don't give a shit if you eat your greens, but don't fuck around with Dalton Nash and Brock Lee."

His brother shrugged and attacked his steak again. "They're my teammates. If we didn't hang out sometimes, it would look funny."

"You remember what they did at my party last year, right? That son of a bitch Brock all but attacked Jayden's girl."

Luc dropped his cutlery with a clatter. "What am I supposed to do? Call him out in front of everyone for something that happened months ago? He already got his ass kicked over it. You know I can't start trouble in the room over that kind of shit."

Yeah. He did know. Calling out the vets' shitty behavior got you nothing but a shitload of grief, something he'd learned the hard way in juniors.

"I'm not asking you to take it that far," Laurent replied in an even tone. "But the less you hang out with them off the ice, the better."

"Stay out of trouble, yeah. Like you and your teammates are a bunch of saints," Luc muttered. "I've seen the crazy shit you pull. And I heard all about that time you went to Chez Parée. Remember that?"

Christ, he would have to bring that up. "I couldn't forget if I tried. No need to remind me, especially not in public."

The Steelhawks vets had made it a tradition to visit the legendary gentleman's club when they played in Montreal and encourage the rookies to consume as many high-end drinks as possible. Unlike the rookie dinner, at least, the vets footed the bill. Yeah, the memory of one act in particular would be seared into his brain until he was ninety. Leather and handcuffs, things he'd never expected to resonate so deeply inside him. Luc had no way of knowing about that part, only the epic amounts of Grey Goose he'd consumed to try and erase the feelings.

He turned his attention to his steak, sneaking glances across the table. Hopefully he'd driven his point through Luc's thick skull. Though Luc might be onto something about the Steelhawks not being saints. Far from it. But there was trouble and there was *trouble*. One got you into hot water, and the other just got you hot. And bothered. He knew which kind he preferred.

Maybe we could meet up later?

Damn it, he was going to have to take care of that, if nothing else. Usually, he could work off the extra tension through yoga and meditation, but this was different. Darkness and a deep, raw sort of hunger ran beneath the surface. It had nothing to do with stress or competition or the desire to win. An hour of trying to clear his head wouldn't get his mind off Lorelei's eyes locking with his and that enticing smile.

Luc put down his fork and patted his belly. "Crisse, that was good. So, you off to bed after this, old man?"

"I told you. We're leaving for Florida in the morning. You have a flight home, too."

His brother checked his phone and started scrolling. "You tell me not to hang with Dalton and Brock, but you're the one leaving me in the woods here. I'm not going to go to a club solo."

Laurent chuckled and pulled his wallet from his pocket. "You want a wingman? I'll give you Rocky's number. If you're lucky, he might still be on the prowl somewhere."

"*Lucky.*" Luc grinned. "That's my nickname, isn't it?"

A text or two proved Rocky was still out with some of the rookies. Luc hopped into an Uber, leaving Laurent to make his way back to his car. He unlocked the door, folded himself into the driver's seat, and leaned against the headrest.

Breathe. In. Out. In. Out.

No good.

He took out his phone. Looked at it blankly for a moment. Set it on the dashboard, face down, then picked it up again, unlocked it and swiped until he reached Lorelei's number in his contacts.

Fucking shit, it was after midnight. Maybe not too late to contact Lorelei, but... Something stopped him from pressing his thumb on her name. He couldn't tell her to come over now, no matter how much he wanted it. Especially not after blowing her off. Sure, she'd given him an opening, but that didn't mean she was at his beck and call.

You didn't treat your best friend like some puck bunny.

His thumb hovered over the screen. He should simply put his phone down and drive home. But he couldn't shake off the pull Lorelei had on him. Maybe if he just asked for a pic... How would she react? Given the late hour, she'd have to know what kind of pic he meant.

You're playing with fire, dumbass. Even a dirty pic would be too much of a test for his resolve. Besides, he had an entire stock of memories to get himself off without needing a refresher.

He turned the ignition and drove to his waterfront rental. The other guys may have invested in property in Hamilton, but he'd never bothered. His lake house up north—that was home. Even at his parents' place in Montarville was more of a haven. The apartment served its purpose during the season, though. A place to eat, rest, watch TV...

And hook up.

Most of his teammates preferred taking a girl back to a hotel, even when they weren't on the road. Not him. Here, at least, he had decent matcha for his morning drink.

He dropped his coat in the closet and headed straight to his room. His gaze landed on his nightstand—pale beech wood, sleek and minimalist, like the rest of his furnishings. An innocent enough piece of furniture until he opened his goody drawer. Which was full of things he couldn't exactly tote around in his pockets.

You know, I heard some girls talking. Is it true what they said? Are you that wild in bed?

He stripped down and stretched out on his mattress, closing his eyes to picture Lorelei straddling him, wearing nothing but bright red panties and a matching bra. Simple cotton, no frills—something comfortable to travel in, but the way her breasts overflowed the cups of her bra... Shit. His palms itched to explore their fullness, to run all over them, to feel her nipples harden.

Define wild.

I think the exact term they used is freak.

Yeah, he knew what kind of rep he had. Threesomes, battery operated devices, something rougher if a girl was up for it. That relentless hunger that built and took hold, not letting go until he gave in. And it wouldn't be satisfied with plain vanilla. He needed more to feel satiated, though he stepped cautiously. Scaring someone off wouldn't get anyone where they needed to go. He'd become good at gauging expressions. When he opened his bag of tricks and showed what was available, he always let his partner pick first.

Control was key. Whoever he was with had the power to choose just how far they took things.

Those girls might call him a freak because he busted out a vibrator and a blindfold. But what the hell would they say if they knew what he really fantasized about?

Lorelei wasn't like them. His defenses crumbled around her, especially after a few shots and a few joints.

They're not wrong. You want to take a look at my drawer?

She had. And then she'd taken out a black sash. He'd looked at her, and then at the length of silk, and back at her.

Two things I can do with a silk sash. Blindfold you, or bind your hands. Which one you up for?

Shit, the memory made his cock hard as stone. He took himself in hand and stroked slowly. Picturing the silky material straining against Lorelei's wrists, her curls splayed on his pillow, her face flushed, and her mouth parted to let out breathy little pants.

I want you to take charge.

He'd gone about it all wrong. They hadn't discussed anything—boundaries, safe words, all of the things that you were supposed to make clear beforehand. But he'd wanted her too much, and she'd been so fucking turned on. Squirming, thighs rubbing together to alleviate some of the pressure. More and more as he let the hunger overtake him.

Open your mouth.

He stroked his cock faster. That thing with the champagne... He hadn't planned it either. He always kept a chilled bottle handy on his birthday. But as soon as he'd seen Lorelei spread out on his mattress, wrists bound, her gorgeous body open and willing to receive any pleasure he could give her, he knew.

He'd poured some between her plush lips for her to swallow. Some of it had trickled down her chin.

You want more? Ask like a good girl.

Please, Laurent.

He'd sent more cascading down her breasts, her belly, lapping it up ravenously, then back to her mouth. Then back down again as she whimpered and cried out and still asked *more*. By the time his tongue had found the sweet spot between her legs, only a few strokes had sent her to a screaming, shivering peak.

Fuck, now *he* was going to come. His eyes squeezed shut, and he tightened his grip. The way she'd clenched around his tongue, his fingers...

Oh God, Laurent, it's so good... Oh God, go deeper...

His lust spiraled and snapped, sending hot spurts of cum onto his abdomen. For a few moments, he kept his eyes closed, holding onto the image of her, and let his breathing slow. Then he reached for a tissue.

When he was done cleaning up, Laurent stared at the ceiling. That ought to take the edge off—at least for now. Help him sleep. Help him focus. He'd have the channel the rest into his game.

At least until after the playoffs. After the Cup final with any luck.

Once that was over, he'd be free to explore... whatever this was. As long as she was still around. With Lorelei, he never knew what to expect. And there was no telling what might happen when they saw each other again.

Sydney, Nova Scotia, twelve years earlier

Laurent pulled up to the employee entrance behind the Canadian Tire store and cut the engine. Without the rattle of the motor, nothing but music filled his car.

He needed something to drown out the permanent loop in his head that told him he was going to let in a few soft ones tonight. Mick Jagger singing about rape, murder, and impending doom did the trick. Clearly, Lorelei's taste was rubbing off on him.

Maybe he should do something about that. War might be a shot away, but love was just a kiss away. Or so the Rolling Stones would have him believe.

The steel door next to the loading dock opened, and Lorelei stormed out. Her coat was unzipped to reveal a red polo shirt and black uniform pants, and her hair floated about her head in a riot of orange curls.

He tightened his grip on the steering wheel. One of these days, he was going to give into the impulse to straighten one of those springy locks of hair to watch it bounce back. Or wrap it around his finger…

She flopped into the passenger seat, slamming the door, and cranked the volume higher. "Ugh."

"Rough shift?" He raised his voice to make it heard over the next tune. She'd burned a CD of her dad's stuff and given it to him for Christmas, because the radio in his clunker had long since stopped working.

"The usual idiots, wanting to know where that thing"—she bent her fingers into air quotes—"they need to fix something in the washroom"—more air quotes—"might be. And I'm supposed to figure out what they mean based on that. Out of however many tens of thousands of products we carry. Add in half the school having nothing better to do than come in and annoy me at work, and I guess that makes it your typical Saturday."

He put the car in gear and pulled back out onto the main strip, headed toward town, while Robbie Robertson sang about taking a load off. Maybe Laurent could help with that. "Listen—"

"We need to talk," she said.

"What's up?"

"Oh, just the cherry on the shit sundae that today is." To emphasize the point, her breath came out in a huff. "You're going to have to stop sneaking into my room."

"What? Why?"

"My dad caught on. Did you know you've worn a path through the back yards?"

"Tabarnak."

"Exactly. But that's what happens when you walk through snow."

God, how could he have been so stupid? Even if he wasn't doing anything beyond getting help with his homework, listening to music, shooting the shit, and taking hits off her bong when one of them could score a little weed, he should have known it would look bad to an outside observer.

"So how much trouble are you in?" He asked the question carefully, because he was pretty sure he was going to hate the answer. Crisse, he already hated that he was going to hate the answer.

"Jesus Christ." She rolled her eyes. "You're not going to

believe this. Dad thinks there's something *up* with us. Like... boyfriend stuff."

He clamped his lips shut before he could say something really dumb. Something like *Do you want there to be?*

"I couldn't convince him you're a friend who's a boy, and not, you know, a *boyfriend*." Again with her eyes rolled toward the ceiling.

He was starting to loathe that facial expression even more than her non-answer. Because she still hadn't said whether or not she was in trouble. Given what she was saying, though, it almost didn't matter.

"I can't get it through his head that I totally don't want a boyfriend."

Laurent closed his fingers around the wheel. "Is that because you want a girlfriend?"

Her mouth opened and closed, and then she pressed her lips together—like she was thinking about it. God help him if she replied in the affirmative, because he'd just have to accept it.

"Who do you see me going after?" she replied. "Taylor Langille or Kat Clancy?"

Right, the popular girls who liked to hang around Centre 200 after hockey games and flirt with the guys. The same girls who treated Lorelei like crap because she didn't fit into the mold the same way as the others. Which happened to be exactly why he found her way more interesting.

Because hockey aside, he didn't fit in here, either.

"Point taken."

"The point is," she shot back, "why the fuck would I tie myself down to someone? I don't need anyone holding me back, not when there's a whole world out there to see. And Dad, at least, ought to get it. It's not like I didn't have a front-row seat to watching everything blow up between him and Tanya."

Her mum, who for some reason, felt better if Lorelei called her by her first name.

Laurent focused on the road and fought to keep his tone neutral. "So you're telling me I can't come around anymore?"

"Oh. No. No, of course not." She tugged at her seatbelt as if it was too tight. "He wants you to come to supper."

"To check me out?"

"To meet you. And yeah." One side of her mouth quirked up. "And also maybe he figures he'll get a meat-and-potatoes meal out of it."

Laurent bit back a laugh. She'd been experimenting with vegetarian foods all year, and her dad was probably tired of variations on tofu. "Just don't make anything like that fried bologna."

"Gross." She pretended to gag. "I'll see if Nana is up for making her chicken the way Dad likes."

"That sounds good." His billet family tried, but their cooking wasn't anything like his Maman's.

"Anyway, just make sure you come in through the front door from now on. And leave the same way."

Like a normal person. When, somewhere deep inside, he suspected he was anything but.

Chapter Seven

@TheDailyGrind While you're picking up your fave coffee and treats, don't forget to check out our revolving exhibits. All local artists. Give them some love.

Hamilton, early June

Lorelei nodded her head to the ever-changing beat blasting in her headphones. The synths, the bass, the rattle of drum fills, off-set by Geddy Lee's soaring vocals… So what if the song had come out before she was born? Classic was classic like the rest of the stuff she listened to, a legacy of her dad.

She swept the peach watercolor marker over the length of the canvas before swiping it again in the other direction, all in time to the music.

The song ended, and she sat back to scrutinize her work. She'd been messing around for a while with no set image in mind, but it sort of looked like a sunset. A sunset over water, maybe, with those swirls of blue and green clashing with the warmer colors. She let out a deep sigh and put the cap back on the marker. Nothing better to erase a long shift at the coffee shop than to empty your head with good music, a blank canvas, and lovely colors.

She stretched her neck, and her stomach growled. Crap, what time was it? She glanced at her laptop. Oh shit, almost seven. Time to head downstairs and see if she could lend a hand with dinner.

David and Mason were both in the kitchen, preparing what looked like potato salad. David smiled at her while he chopped celery. "You busy creating another masterpiece?"

She sat at the island. "Just having fun with the watercolor markers I bought last week."

"You know you could paint in the garage if you want," David added. "We're fine with it, right, baby?"

Mason grunted in a way that Lorelei had learned meant *yeah, sure.*

"That's very sweet of you," she said, "but I need to save up for supplies. I left all my painting stuff at my mum's place before I left for Australia."

"And where does she live?"

"She's in New Brunswick—or at least she was, because she moves around. Not traveling all the way up there any time soon."

And not just because it was hours away, even by plane, but she and Tanya hadn't exactly parted on great terms the last time they'd seen each other. Who knew, maybe she'd dumped all of Lorelei's painting supplies into the trash.

"Can I help with anything?" she asked. "Want me to whip up something for dessert?"

Before they could answer, a faint buzzing sound

reached her ears. She jumped in her seat. "Bollocks, is that my phone? Did I leave it down here?"

"Yeah, on the coffee table," Mason said. "Not the first time it's gone off."

"But we didn't want to bother you," David called after her as she skipped over to grab it.

Laurent. *Oh fuck.* Her heart gave a painful thud. They hadn't talked since the game, almost two months ago. Road trips, days at the gym, and the general grind of the season had eaten all of Laurent's time. Work had kept Lorelei busy, as well, with long shifts at the coffee shop, finding time for creative endeavors, and pursuing opportunities to get her art in front of eyes that might buy or commission. All they'd managed were a few sporadic texts. Why was he calling now? *Just answer it, you idiot.*

She swiped up. "Hey, you. What are ya sayin'?"

"Hey, you." She heard him smile on the other end. "You got a minute?"

"Yeah, sure. We're just making dinner." She paused and pressed her lips together. "How've you been? I'm right sorry you guys didn't win."

Laurent sighed. "At least we didn't go out in the first round this time. And we took it to double overtime before New Jersey managed to beat us in game five."

"I saw that. First time I was some nervous in front of a game."

Actually, she'd watched all the Steelhawks playoff games. Mason wouldn't miss a single one, and David followed along, phone in hand, scrolling on social media and commenting on this season's WAG jackets. Because they apparently needed custom ones for each round.

"Aw, that's so sweet of you," Laurent said.

"We even went to a bar for game one, and I busted out the jersey. Can I say I'm a bonafide Steelhawks fan now?"

"Went to a live game, watched the playoffs at a bar, wore a jersey. Yup, you check all the boxes."

She laughed. "I'll learn to live with it. Now Mason is rooting for Vancouver to win the Cup, but I haven't been following as closely."

"Actually, that's why I'm calling. I'm having people over to watch game three on Saturday. You wanna come?"

Oh. Her heart gave another lurch. And this time she felt it all the way down to her stomach. "So... is this like a party?"

"No, just a few of the guys and their girlfriends, beers, finger food, you know. Hey, you can meet Addie properly this time. She and Max will be there for sure."

She bit her lip. Shit. She wanted to see Laurent—in fact, now that she had him on the phone, the want was fast turning into a need. She hadn't taken it personally last time he'd turned her down. He wasn't the type to invent bullshit excuses, and an athlete of his caliber needed to prioritize rest to face such a high level of competition on a regular basis.

That didn't make her any less desperate to shoot her shot again. Hell, just hearing his deep voice... But drunken teammates and girls gone wild was one thing. Meeting his group of friends in a more intimate setting, on the other hand... Back in high school, she'd avoided Laurent's teammates with good reason. She most definitely didn't fit the mold of the type of girls they preferred. She didn't fit in, period. And she'd long accepted that.

Get over it. This isn't high school anymore. And it wasn't like her to back down when time came to step out of her comfort zone. Besides, some of the people she'd met at Laurent's birthday party were nice. Presto, that big guy Jayden, his girlfriend Cait. Sure, Cait looked the part of the gorgeous blonde WAG, but she was really friendly. Maybe they'd be there as well.

"Great," she finally said. "Yeah, I'd love to come. Thanks for the invite."

"Game starts at eight, but if you get here a little later, that's fine." He paused for a second and cleared his throat. "Offseason for me now, so... I can sleep in the next morning."

Holy crap. If this wasn't another type of invite, she'd lose her mind. She breathed in through her nose. "Noted. Text me your address, okay?"

"Sure thing. See you on Saturday."

She hung up and put her phone back on the coffee table. Jesus, how was her head spinning from a two-minute phone call?

"Everything good?" David called from the kitchen.

She returned to the island. "That was Laurent. He's having a get-together at his place on Saturday so... Guess I'm going."

David's jaw dropped. "Oh my God, you're going to hang with the Steelhawks? What are you going to wear?"

She shook her head. "No idea. Should I wear something special? It's not a party, just... chilling."

Chilling that would hopefully end with another private tour of Laurent's bedroom. Damn, perhaps she *should* wear something special. Maybe she could distract him from the game.

Lorelei stopped in front of Laurent's building and craned her neck to gaze at the ten or so levels of steel and perfectly polished glass. Despite the warm evening, a shiver ran down her spine. In the lobby, the wooden soles of her wedge sandals clacked on the marble floor, as she marched past a row of mailboxes to the intercom. She pressed the button next to his apartment number.

After a few seconds, Laurent's voice crackled from the loudspeaker. "Yeah?"

"It's me. Lorelei."

"Come on up."

The second door buzzed open. In the elevator, she quickly checked her appearance. She'd gone with her denim cut-offs to stay casual but matched them with a black halter top printed with bright red cherries that bared her shoulders and her back. And also pushed up her boobs. If she was being completely honest, that was why she'd picked it out of her closet. She was competing for attention with the playoffs, after all.

"Nice top," David had commented as she was about to leave. He'd raised an eyebrow and grinned. "Very nice for meeting *a friend*."

For once, Mason had intervened. "Babe, I've told you this before. Mind your own damn business."

"It's okay," Lorelei had replied. "I decided I wanted one of those fancy playoff jackets, but to do that, I need to become a WAG, and for that I need a hockey player. Gotta get his attention somehow."

She'd been joking, of course, but not as much as her roommates might think. She had no intention to nab anyone, just... reconnect with a trusted friend who had also happened to give her the most mind-blowing orgasms of her life.

The elevator came to a stop. She fluffed her hair before exiting.

Laurent was waiting in front of his door at the end of the corridor. "Over here!"

She grinned. "You're wearing the tee-shirt I made for you."

Laurent glanced down at his chest. "Tabarnak. Yeah, I wear it all the time."

He pulled her into a hug, and his lips descended, lingering on one cheek before moving to the other, brushing the skin at the corner of her mouth. Oh God, she wanted to pounce on him there and then, press her lips to his, feel his hands all over her, and she hadn't even crossed the threshold yet.

He stepped back, and his full attention landed on her cleavage. Just as she had hoped. He wrenched his gaze away and let out a shaky breath. "Crisse, you look amazing."

Her cheeks flushed. "Thanks. I didn't know what to bring, so..." She fished in her bag for a Tupperware container. "I made sweet potato fries."

"Yummy." He took the container and placed his hand on the small of her back, ushering her inside. "I made plenty of veggie-friendly finger food too. Come on, the third period's just about to start."

"What's the score?"

"Vancouver's up four to three."

At first glimpse, Laurent's apartment was similar to his lake house—white walls emphasizing the space, sleek minimalist furniture, a sprawling bay window that led to a balcony overlooking Lake Ontario. Yet it also lacked any personal touch that would stamp his mark on the place, like the painting of Hasek or a framed jersey.

Perhaps Laurent kept more personal items in his

bedroom? If everything went well, she'd find out soon enough. In the living room, at least, the only thing hanging on the wall was a gigantic screen blaring a commercial. A bunch of his teammates watched from an equally oversized U-shaped chesterfield. She spotted Presto and Jayden, beers in hand, but didn't recognize anyone else.

"Let me get a plate for your fries," Laurent said, his hand still on her back. "In the meantime..."

He nudged Lorelei toward the balcony. Addison Holtz leaned against the railing with a tall, bulky guy who had his arm wrapped around her waist. The warmth of Laurent's palm vanished, and Lorelei's eyes widened.

"What are you doing?" she whispered.

"Let me introduce you. Hey, Addie!"

Addie and her fiancé both turned. So this was Max Ducharme, then. Curly brown hair, striking blue eyes and chiseled features that looked like it came straight from a magazine spread. And Addie was exactly how Lorelei imagined a competitive figure skater—petite, with a pixie-like face, her graceful limbs emphasized by skinny jeans and a tight black top.

Lorelei's stomach clenched, but she shook it off. *You belong here. You know Laurent as well as any of them.*

"This is my friend Lorelei," Laurent said. "Addie, she's a big fan of yours."

Lorelei elbowed him. "Shut up, will you?" Then she turned to Addie with smile. "Sorry about that. My roommate David is actually the big fan, but he did show me a lot of videos of your performances and wow. Really impressive."

Addie smiled back. "Thanks. That's very nice of you. Usually, it's Max who gets all the attention."

"Well, it would make David's day, possibly his year, if I could take a selfie with you."

"Can I be in it too?" Max chimed in, though his tone was more teasing than serious.

"Sorry, Addison's fiancé, you're going to have to sit this one out," Laurent said. "The third just started."

Max drained his beer. "Fine, let's go watch Vancouver kick Jersey's ass. Nice to meet you, Lorelei."

"Likewise."

The guys filed back inside, and Lorelei took her phone from her crossbody bag. "If this is too weird, just say the word. I don't usually go up to people I don't know asking for selfies."

Addie laughed. "No problem. It's been ages since anyone asked me for a picture. It's actually sort of flattering that I still have some fans."

Lorelei sidled up to her, grinned and took three quick pictures. "Thank you so much. I'll make David promise not to post anything on social media. I don't like having my face on there either."

"You and me both. And it's not easy when you're with a pro hockey player, especially one who loves the limelight like Max. Or Gilly." She paused for a moment. "How do you two—"

"Addie, you need to see this!"

Lorelei's jaw dropped. Hell, she was probably doing a pretty good impression of a goldfish.

The willowy blonde with the French accent from the game last winter barged onto the balcony, phone in hand. "Okay, so Tori just sent me the color scheme she planned for Viv's baby shower, and she thinks it's better if everyone picks a dress that matches, so we need to tell her if we're okay with the colors or not. Blush pink and pearl, how adorable is that?"

She said all of this in a rapid staccato, barely pausing to catch her breath.

A line formed between Addie's brows. "When is that again? I don't think I've gotten an invite."

"September. And everyone's invited. All the girls, I mean."

"Right." She turned back to Lorelei. "This is Véronique. Véronique, Lorelei."

The blonde barely glanced up from her phone. "Hey."

Addie waited a beat, then continued. "You see that hockey takes up a lot of our social calendar, even in the offseason."

Lorelei smiled. "Guess that makes sense. Laurent's teammates were always having parties back in high school."

"High school? So you guys are old friends then?"

She nodded. "Twelve years and counting. We met when he was playing for Cape Breton."

Véronique finally stopped scrolling on her phone. "That's funny. I don't think he ever mentioned any friends he made there when he came back home in the summer."

Lorelei raised an eyebrow. "You knew Laurent back then too?"

"Of course. My husband and I are both from the same town as him." She pointed inside to one of the guys sprawled on the chesterfield. "Raphaël plays on the third line."

"Um... That's great."

What else could she say? Véronique returned to her scrolling. "By the way, Addie, do you have Cait's contact? I need to put her in the Whatsapp group."

"Sure, um... Hang on a second."

As she pulled her phone from her pocket, Addie slid a pained look in Lorelei's direction. With a bob of her head, Lorelei headed back inside. Nothing left now but to actually watch the game. And pray it didn't go into overtime.

Chapter Eight

@FreshHockeyStats With tonight's victory, New Jersey locks in a 2-1 lead over Vancouver. But advanced stats suggest things aren't over yet. Check out my article.

"I can't believe you're not throwing a party for your birthday. Offseason isn't the same without a lake house bash."

Laurent took a sip of beer and relaxed against the couch. "Not this year, man," he told Presto. "Not with everything else going on. The wild party will have to wait."

Not that he wanted one at the moment, when this felt so much better. Pink Floyd on the speakers, a nice cold IPA in his hand, and Lorelei sitting close enough that their sides brushed. His arm stretched along the top of the couch behind her, and he itched to drop it to her shoulders, to pull her closer still, but he didn't want to give the impression he was staking a claim in front of the guys or anything.

But fuck, he'd been waiting the whole evening to touch her. *Really* touch her, kiss her, pull her to him and give his hands free rein to roam over her body. And from the moment she'd emerged from the elevator in those cut-off shorts and that mouth-watering top, her gaze locking with his and a flush blooming over her cheeks, he knew she wanted the same thing.

Dirty, hot sex.

Tabarnak, he'd been tempted to tell everyone to get the fuck out and go watch the third somewhere else. Now, two hours after the final buzzer, with Presto and Jayden happy to chat and chill on his couch, his patience was running out. Sure, they'd come without a plus-one. Kicking them out would be a dick move, but he sure as hell hoped they wouldn't ask for any more beer.

"Never thought I'd hear you say that," Presto said. "Are you going to ask the arena DJ to change your music?"

"Oh, do they always break out 'I Am a Wild Party' when you hit the ice?" Lorelei asked with a grin.

"It's turned into my walk-on music, yeah," he admitted. "But Maman wants us to do a family thing for my birthday this year, so I'll be in Quebec. I think she's looking for an excuse to get Luc back home."

"Between Max's bachelor party and the wedding," Jayden added, "we'll get it out of our system."

Presto let out a bark of laughter. "Tell that to Rocky."

"Well, it's not Gilly's fault you're spending most of the summer in Europe."

"Oh wow, where are you going?" Lorelei asked.

"Italy. My cousin's getting married in Tuscany, same

day as Max. Switzerland too, the Alps, mostly hiking. Then Yes-Man invited me to his place in Finland."

Lorelei leaned into Laurent. "Yes-Man?"

Her low murmur sent a shiver down his spine. "Yeah, Jesse Makinen, Max and Colby's linemate."

"You and your crazy nicknames."

"You got something against Gilly?"

Lorelei shrugged, and a teasing glint sparked in her eyes. "I like Laurent better. And, well... It would feel weird to call you Gilly when... you know."

Fucking shit, he *did* know. The way she'd cried out his name last summer echoed on permanent loop in his mind whenever the thought of her urged him to take himself in hand. That and a vivid image of her red hair spread over his pillow and her pale wrists bound in black silk. He wanted to hear it again. And again. And again.

His cock stirred in his pants. Yeah, he needed the guys gone right fucking now.

He drained the rest of his beer and stood. "All right, les boys, let's call it a night. It's almost one AM, and I need to work out in the morning."

Technically, he wasn't lying. He just wasn't specifying what type of workout it would be. Because there was no way he was letting Lorelei out of his bed before noon.

Jayden glanced at his watch. "Fuck, you're right. I told Cait we'd Facetime before she went to work. Gotta get home."

Presto sighed. "Might as well."

They both rose and said good night to Lorelei before Laurent walked them to the door. As it closed behind them, he took a moment and inhaled deeply. One, two, three, four... God, he'd been waiting far too long for this. *Pace yourself. Don't pounce on her like some animal.*

Besides, they still had things to discuss. At the very least, they needed to set some proper boundaries before they went completely nuts.

"So, about my nickname—"

He turned to find Lorelei standing right behind him. Her gaze sharp and heated. Before he could say anything else, she grabbed a fistful of his shirt and pulled his mouth to hers.

Holy fuck, *yes*. He wrapped his arms around her waist, pressing her soft, lush curves closer, nudging her lips open with a flick of his tongue. Lorelei moaned, and her fingers slipped into his hair, her pelvis grinding against his.

Shit, if they kept this up, they weren't going to discuss anything. He'd skip the preliminaries and fuck her up against the door.

He pulled back. "Lore... Hang on a moment..."

She stared up at him, face flushed. Such raw lust burned in her eyes, it knocked the air from his lungs. "Are you serious? I'm going fucking crazy here."

"I know. I know. Me too, believe me." He exhaled, trying to calm his breathing, to gather his thoughts, but it was goddamn near impossible with those luscious breasts pushed up against his chest, and her hips still rocking against his. "Let's go back to the couch."

She slunk back, and he took her hand. Once they were seated, the fog of lust in his mind dissipated to an extent, though the slightest move from her would no doubt snap his self-control.

"All right, I just want things to be clear between us."

She raised an eyebrow. "What do we need to make clear? We're just... making each other feel good, right? Scratching an itch. Like we did in high school."

He wasn't going to go down that particular road.

Because that would shed light on a whole mess of... feelings, if he was honest. Feelings he had no desire to dig up, especially not when his body thrummed with the need for release. "It's not about that. I need to know if we're on the same page. If you want the same things I do."

Lorelei ran a hand up his thigh. "If you mean sex, I think the answer's pretty obvious."

He wrapped his fingers around her wrist, then circled his thumb over the delicate skin. "The stuff we did at the lake house went beyond plain sex. Were you into that?"

A half-laugh, half-moan floated from her cherry-red lips. "Don't you remember how hard you made me come? Shit, I thought that was obvious, too." She dropped her tone to a throaty murmur. "I *loved* it."

His cock throbbed with a fresh wave of arousal. "What did it for you? Tell me."

"All of it." She turned to face him, shifting her knees until one settled on each side of his hips. "When you tied me up so you could do whatever you wanted with me. When you poured champagne down my body and licked me all over." She leaned in to kiss him, and her hips started their maddening rhythm again. "When you made me beg. When you slapped my thigh while you were fucking me. God, you made me crave more, you have no idea."

He dug his fingers into the curve of her ass. "I think I do."

Their mouths met again, the kisses growing hungrier, more desperate. He pulled back again, panting. "We can try... other things. If you want. I'm up for anything as long as you are. But I need to make sure I don't cross any lines." He pushed her hair back. "We're going to need a safe word."

She bit down on her bottom lip. "A safe word, huh?"

"Yeah. The moment either of us says it, we stop whatever we're doing. No questions asked. It's over. That's it. A random word like... cannoli or doorknob."

"What about Madame Campbell?"

He laughed. "Your old French teacher? Well, if you want to make me lose my boner, that'll do it."

"Good. That's settled then." Her lips curled into a wicked grin, and her hands slipped beneath his shirt to tease at his waistband. "But what if my mouth is otherwise occupied?"

She popped open a first button, then a second. He threw his head back on the cushion as her hand slid over the thin material of his boxer briefs to cup his erection.

"Fuck," he rasped. "Right, well... Just punch me really, really hard in the stomach if I do something you don't like."

She nudged his knees apart and slid down between them. "Noted."

A moment later, she worked his pants and boxer briefs over his hips. Her tongue circled the head of his cock, and then her lips parted and she took him in. A groan tore from his throat. Shit, the feeling of her hot, wet mouth around him, sucking softly, pulling back to let her tongue slide over him... She'd barely begun and already sizzling jolts of arousal rippled up his body before gathering in the pit of his belly.

He glanced down. The sight of her red lips moving up and down his length like that... God, she was fucking killing him. He plunged his fingers into her silky curls, stroking softly, then tightening his grip just a little. She increased her rhythm. He tightened again. This time, she gave a low moan and the vibration traveled all the way up his spine.

Fuck, she liked this. Liked it when he pulled her hair.

He tangled his fingers in her curly mane and jerked his hips up.

"This is so fucking good," he panted. "Keep going. Take me deeper."

She hollowed out her cheeks to increase the friction, taking every thrust of his cock into the wet heat of her mouth. Her fingers tightened around the base of his shaft, and the head grazed the back of her throat. Holy hell, he wasn't going to last much longer.

"I'm going to come," he groaned.

Somehow, she took him even deeper. Fuck, *fuck*, was this really happening? He twisted his hand in her hair.

"You want this, then? You want me to come in your mouth?"

Her fingers dug into his thigh, and her tongue swirled over the glistening head. White-hot sensation pulsed and throbbed deep within, and his arousal finally reached breaking point, overflowing in powerful spurts. He cursed loudly and held her head in place, lost in the force of his orgasm.

For a few moments, his world shrank to nothing but ragged breathing while his mind reeled. *Crisse*, he'd never come so hard from head alone. Lorelei had turned him inside out, and they hadn't even left the couch yet.

She pulled away. Breathless as he was, her lips parted. The flush on her cheeks had spread to her neck, the top of her breasts.

She was turned on. Really fucking turned on. All that from sucking him off while he pulled her hair and came in her mouth.

She licked her lips and smiled. "So what now?"

Dirty Puck Buddies

Lorelei pulled in a shaky breath. A bitter, salty taste lingered on her tongue. *First time for everything.* But then most of her firsts were with Laurent. First time she'd had sex, first blowjob, first heartache as well—though he wasn't aware of that one.

Her gaze collided with his, and he blinked lazily, hiding for a moment his lust-darkened blue-green irises. What was it about him that provoked her, that pushed her out of her comfort zone, and overcame her inhibitions? She'd never let a guy come in her mouth before. The idea had always turned her off... until now. Was it simple trust or something more? Something undefinable?

It didn't matter. At this point, she was ready for anything. *More* than ready. As long as it alleviated the throbbing ache between her thighs.

"Get up." The sharp command in his tone made the hair on her arms stand on end. Last summer, he'd done this. Taken over. Taken control. "Strip."

He tucked himself back into his briefs as she rose and unbuttoned her cut-offs.

"Not too fast. Take your time."

She slowed her fingers, splaying them over the curve of her belly, then with a swing of her hips, edged the denim down her thighs until it pooled around her ankles. His gaze followed the movement hungrily, lingering on the dark satin of her panties before sweeping up to her top. At his nod to continue, she tugged at the knot at the base of her neck and eased the dark cotton down her breasts.

Laurent sucked in a breath. One by one, she undid the hooks in the back until the scrap of fabric fell to the floor. God, her skin was so heated, so sensitive that even the air of the room felt like a physical touch. The ache between her legs twisted tighter.

Her thumbs grazed the edge of her panties.

Laurent stood and curled his fingers around her wrist. "No. Keep them on. Bedroom. Now."

She nodded shakily. God, finally. She'd been waiting for this moment ever since she'd gotten out of the elevator. "Lead the way."

A half-smile tugged at the corner of his mouth. "When I just had you strip? You go first. Down the hallway, second door on the right."

She turned and swayed toward the hallway, letting her hips swing with every step, and damn if she couldn't feel Laurent's gaze on her rear like a physical touch. To think at one time in her life she would have died before parading half naked in front of a guy. Even Laurent. Somewhere in the back of her mind, *lard-ass* comments still echoed. It didn't matter how many times Laurent reassured her there was nothing wrong with her body.

"You know what I want to do when I see you like that?" he asked in a low voice.

She slowed her pace and fresh wave of arousal blazed to life in her stomach. "What?"

"I want to rip those panties off and fuck you from behind, right up against that wall. Nice and hard." She could already feel his heat at her back. "Do you want that?"

She bit back a moan. "Yeah, I do."

"Later, then." He traced a single finger down the length of her back. "If you're a good girl."

The throb grew more intense, and her knees quivered. How was she still standing? Thank God they were nearly at the door. Laurent turned a dimmer switch and a soft, yellow glow filled the room. The lamp in the corner reached in an ornate spiral toward the ceiling, but the bed and the nightstands were styled in spare, low lines like his living room.

Her gaze darted over the pale gray comforter. A stainless-steel spindle headboard, of course. A shiver ran up her spine.

"Get on the bed." The deep, raspy need in his voice sent a tremor between her legs.

She inhaled sharply. The mattress dipped under her weight as she extended herself over the comforter, then looked back over her shoulder. Laurent stood, thumbs hooked in the pockets of his jeans, gauging her every move.

"That night after the game," he said. "You wanted to hook up, didn't you?"

A smile stretching her cheeks, she rolled onto her back. "Of course, I did. I almost sent you a dirty pic to change your mind, but I didn't want to mess with your head right before the playoffs."

"I would've been down for that." The fire in his gaze roared higher. "I got myself off thinking of you the second I got home. I came so fucking hard picturing you all spread out on my bed, begging for my cock."

This time, she couldn't hold back the moan that emerged from her throat, and she pressed her thighs together. God, what was he waiting for?

He crossed his arms in front of his chest. "What about you? Did you touch yourself thinking of all the things I did to you?"

"Yes," she murmured. "So many times... I've lost count."

"Show me. But don't take your panties off."

She slid her hand down her stomach, letting her eyelids drift shut. Her fingers slipped easily between her wet folds, but she kept her strokes light and slow. No point in getting there too fast. She was already on the brink. She wouldn't let herself come this way—not unless he demanded it. But if he wanted a show, she would damn well give him one. She spread her legs wider and raised her hips, back arched, then pinched her nipple with the other hand, parting her mouth in a sigh. Her fingers quickened, almost of their own accord. Holy shit. So close. So, so close. She couldn't slow down if she tried.

"Fuck, you're so beautiful when you're about to come." He sat on the edge of the bed next to her and grabbed her wrist.

Her eyes shot open.

"Let's see if I can help you."

"Please," she sighed. "Please, I'm almost there."

"I know. I can tell. Your panties are soaked through, and that pretty blush of yours is spreading all the way across your tits." He lifted her hand and licked the tips of her fingers. "But first, I want to do something for you."

He dropped her hand and opened a drawer of the nightstand. Her breath hitched. Would he tie her up again? But Laurent took out what looked like an elongated egg, purple and smooth and slightly curved at the tip.

"Wait, is that…?"

"Do you trust me?"

She nodded. "Always."

"Grab the headboard and don't move." He pressed a button, and the barest hum tickled her ears. "If you let go, I stop. Now legs apart."

Lorelei sank her teeth into her lower lip. The low command in his voice, the way he loomed over her, still fully dressed…

He pressed the device to her skin—not where she wanted it. It buzzed against her lower belly. "How's that?"

She jerked her hips. "What do you think?"

He didn't move, damn him. "Does it feel good?"

"I know where it will feel better."

Finally, he traced down her body until the vibrations hit where she needed them—against the drenched material of her panties.

Pure sensation sizzled through her body. She threw her head back and cried out.

"Oh God, that's..." Too much. Not enough. *"Oh my God."*

He pulled back. "I'll go slow, don't worry."

"What?" This was way too slow as it was. "No... No, I need more..."

Her thighs clenched, drawing together, but he swatted the inside of her leg. "Keep them open for me."

He pressed the vibrator against her again. The rapid pulsations settled deep inside her and radiated through her body, sending her soaring toward her peak. Then stopped.

She tightened her grip on the metal bars and whimpered.

"Good girl."

Again, and again, and again. Start, stop. Like a crank turning so, so slowly. And each time, he wrenched a cry from her. The hollow feeling inside grew until it gnawed at her relentlessly, but still he wouldn't let her come. And fuck, his control over her was driving her even crazier.

"Take my panties off." The words emerged on a sob. "*Anything*. This is too much."

"If I do that, you'll get there too fast. I want to savor this." He increased the pressure, and the vibrations circled over her entrance. "Don't you?"

"I can't... I need... *Please...*"

She grasped at words, at coherent thoughts, and came up empty. A red haze took her over, blinding her to everything but the need for release. Tremors raced through her limbs, and her breath came in short pants.

Laurent reached for a stray curl on her forehead and pushed it back, stroking her cheek. "You've been so good, letting me push your gorgeous body to the edge. Do you want to come with this?" Maddeningly, he pulled the device away to show her. "Or do you want my cock?"

"Your cock. *Now*. I can't take anymore. Please, Laurent, *please* fuck me until I come."

He switched the vibrator off and set it aside before rising and stepping back. *Finally*. Shit, she'd been craving the sight of him naked, and now she drank it in as he reached for the hem of his shirt. He pulled it over his head, revealing a lean but perfectly toned chest, chiseled muscles taut under smooth skin. A light dusting of hair trailed all the way down to his waistband.

Strong fingers worked the buttons of his jeans, and then he pushed them down, too, along with his briefs. His cock sprung free, straining toward her. Her mouth watered, and she tightened her grip on the spindles. She wanted her hand on that. Her mouth. Except she was too desperate to have him inside her.

He reached inside the drawer again and pulled out a condom, then rolled it down his length.

Fuck it. She released the headboard and lifted her hips to take off her panties.

He settled himself between her legs and slid the head of his shaft over her folds before thrusting into her in one swift stroke. Oh God, she was going to die from the agonizing pleasure him filling her so completely. The thrill shivered up and down every single one of her nerve endings, wave after wave in cadence with the motion of his hips.

"Yes, please, this is so good," she moaned and dug her fingers into his back. "*Harder.*"

"You want harder?" he grated. "You'll do what I told you."

She gritted her teeth and reached for the headboard again.

As if rewarding her, he lifted her knees and hit a spot so deep stars burst in front of her eyes. Almost there, just out of reach... He smacked the side her thigh, and a hoarse cry burst from her throat. Another crack. Pleasure swirled together with the sting, and sent her spiraling to impossible heights. Her fingers squeezed cold metal, cries torn from her throat, and still, he plunged inside of her, stretching her, hitting that spot again.

Oh God... Finally...

Lord only knew how long it lasted. A second, a minute, longer. But when her muscles finally relaxed, and she came back to herself, Laurent's eyes squeezed shut and his jaw clenched. Still straining. He let out a string of French curses and with one final thrust, slumped over her, his weight pinning her to the mattress. Covering her. Grounding her.

For a moment, the only sound in the room was the rasp of their breathing returning to normal. She pushed her hands into his hair, the short strands prickly against her palms. How she remembered this. Playing at wrestling, though she could never overpower him, all innocence, and her fingers threading into his hair. Pulling at it until it stood in a spiky mess.

The recollection brought a smile to her lips.

With a contented sigh, Laurent settled his head on her chest. "That's nice." He sounded drowsy. "Don't stop."

What a strange contrast in this man. Yeah, he got off on

domination, but he was still up for a cuddle in the afterglow.

"You're not going to fall asleep, are you?"

Laurent laughed against her skin, and the vibration sent delicious curls of warmth through her body. "Not a chance. I believed I promised you a reward earlier."

"If I was a good girl."

"You were very, very good."

Sydney, Nova Scotia, eleven years earlier

Ligament, tendon, muscle. Each bit of his anatomy made its presence known as Laurent eased himself into a split. Or at least what passed for one, when his butt didn't quite hit the scratched hardwood floor of Lorelei's bedroom. Ignoring the pleas for mercy from his lower body, he pushed it another inch.

Held.

To a count of four, he inhaled, then released a stream of air. One, two, three...

From her spot sitting cross-legged in the corner, Lorelei swiped at her sketch pad. "You ever think of trying yoga?"

Laurent waited until he'd reached eight before replying. "Yoga? What's that going to do for me?"

"Make you more flexible."

He started another count. Inhale on four, exhale on eight. He was supposed to keep this up for two whole minutes, though his hips and thighs protested that time must be up already. "This is supposed to make me flexible."

She pressed her lips into a line and scribbled something on her pad. "Is it working?"

From the speaker, Roger Daltrey let out an anguished scream. Laurent could commiserate. Or his legs could. "It *has* to."

His goalie coach had challenged him with this over the

offseason. *Your legs are long enough. You ought to be able to cover more of the crease.* Right.

He leaned forward until his elbows supported him and bent his knees, right then left, to shake off the worst of it. "If I get this, maybe I'll let in fewer goals next year. Or at least avoid embarrassing sweeps in the playoffs."

"Didn't the other goalie get lit up too?"

"If I'd done my job, it wouldn't have been close." He pushed to his feet. "What are you drawing?"

She hugged her pad to her chest. "None of your business."

Was it his imagination, or had her cheeks gone pinker? "Well, put it down. I need you to help me with the next part."

She eyed him. "Do I look like I can do a split?"

Right. She was sensitive about her weight, but what did that have to do with anything? Sure, she was a little round, but he didn't even notice until someone else called attention to it. "You don't have to. Just... here... Get on the floor."

She pulled her ankles closer to her body like she wasn't planning on budging. "I already am."

"Just come over here."

He coaxed her out of her corner and got her to sit facing him in the space between the bed and her window, where they both fit under the low ceiling, as long as they remained on the floor, anyway.

He stretched his legs apart. "Now take my hands and pull until I say to stop."

Their fingers entwined, and he pushed aside a burst of heat in his lower belly. Now was a bad, bad time.

"How long do we do this for?" she asked.

"Until it works. I have to be better next year."

She ducked her head until she captured his gaze. "Maybe you should give yourself a break. Just for this year."

He swallowed. Made himself focus on the discomfort. She had this ability to reach inside him at times that was, frankly, scary. "No one gets breaks in hockey. No days off."

"It's not every year you lose someone close to you. You've been dealing with a lot."

He looked away, unable to face the way she saw through him. "It needs to go away. Tabarnak. By next season, it better be gone."

Her grip tightened on his hands. "I don't know if it ever goes away. It just fades."

She was talking about her mum, probably, though her mum might not be dead, she was still gone, not present, and as long as she didn't communicate, it was much the same.

He relaxed out of the stretch, but their hands still made contact. Christ, he was supposed to do four more reps of this, but something was raging up inside him. Something that wanted out. Now. And soon it would unleash itself.

Sure, they were alone. Her dad was gone for the day. Part of him wanted to give in. Another part wanted to run the fuck back to his billet family.

He bolted up, nearly bumping his head on the low ceiling. Her sketch pad lay in the corner.

She lunged for it. "Don't even think it."

Calisse, now he *had* to know what was in there.

"Come on." He made a grab for her, and she shrank against the wall. "What can you possibly be hiding?"

"It's private."

"Then why were you doing it in front of me?"

Her lowered lashes caused a thread of suspicion to unspool inside him. No, she wouldn't dare... Would she?

Curiosity goaded him to poke the beast. "You're not drawing something dirty, are you?"

"No." She chirped the denial like a baby bird, setting off a flare of triumph, mingled with something else. Something deeper.

He pinned her with his arms, her generous curves soft and pliant against his chest. "Now you have to show me."

Her eyes widened, but something blazed to life in their dark depths. Heat. An awful lot like whatever was seething inside him. "What do you want me to show you, exactly?"

His throat went dry, and a million thoughts fought their way toward release. Words in French, in English, curses and blessings and everything in between. Awareness vibrated through him. The realization that they were in her bedroom. That her bed was just behind him. That they'd be alone for hours yet. But mostly her body pressed to his. Open. Willing.

At least, if he wasn't misreading her. Because this felt like an invitation to cross a line. One he wanted to accept. Badly.

He swallowed. "Do you ever wonder what it's like?"

Her smile told him she was on the same page. "Wanna find out?"

Chapter Nine

@HamiltonSheelhawks: A video montage, on and off the ice, of our favorite tendy in honor of his birthday.
@Lilygilly What is that tee-shirt, and more importantly where can I get one?
@timmytank You should just put on his gear and get into the nets. You could do just as good a job.

Montarville, Quebec, June 25th

The mouth-watering smell of meat on the barbecue hit Laurent's nostrils the moment as he stepped onto the back deck. He closed his eyes and inhaled deeply. No, it was more than just the meat. The scent of mowed grass, the earthy hints of the freshly watered flowerbeds... All of it blended into the familiar scent of summer at home.

"Here you go, fiston. Made it the way you like it." Maman handed him a glass of homemade iced tea, her smile accentuating the crinkles near her eyes. She'd always been a handsome woman, with her dark hair, blue-green eyes and long, thin nose, but his father's illness had aged her before her time. More than a decade later, the worry lines had never melted from her face.

Or the worry itself, for that matter. Because after Papa's passing, she'd transferred all her anxiety to her sons. To Laurent and Luc. It wasn't as bad now that they were older, but the set of her shoulders and her easy smiles told him she was relieved to have them both by her side. His gaze flitted toward Luc, who was manning the grill with one hand and scrolling on his phone with the other. Tabarnak, the idiot was going to ruin perfectly good strip steaks if he wasn't careful.

"Merci, Maman." He took a sip. "Yeah, that's perfect. No one does it quite like you."

"For once, you're home for your birthday, so you deserve a little pampering."

He bent to kiss her on the cheek as she passed, heading back in the kitchen. A pang of guilt hit him in the chest. It *had* been years since he'd celebrated his birthday at home. Was it only because of the epic lake house party that had somehow become a tradition with the guys? Or had he stayed away because family gatherings made his father's absence even more glaring?

He stared at the river, visible in the distance. The setting sun glinted off water gently lapping at the shore of an island midstream. No matter the season, the water was some shade or other of gray, depending on the lighting and the weather. Some days it tended toward steel blue, but today?

He took his phone out to snap a picture, then opened his conversation with Lorelei.

Dirty Puck Buddies

> Help a guy out. What color is the St-Laurent?

He sent her the picture. A string of moving dots popped up. Seven thirty. She must be off work at this hour.

> Harbor gray. There's a hint of very light green in it. Nice view 😊

> Thought you'd like it 😊

> Glad you made it home safe

Safe travels. That's what she'd said when she kissed his cheek, the last time they'd seen each other, just before leaving. Only four days ago, but already it felt like an eternity. In fact, any stretch of time between hook-ups was just too damn long. She could walk out the door at noon, and by early evening he'd already be craving more of her.

You need to slow the fuck down. And he'd tried, he really had. Maybe she was trying, too. Their respective schedules only allowed them to see each other once or twice a week, and from the vagueness of her words or the hesitation in her voice, Laurent got the impression she sometimes turned him down on principle more than anything else. As for him, he'd made a conscious effort to suggest they go out somewhere so she didn't assume he was only after sex. Because that's what friends did, right? They hung out and did stuff, like taking a walk in the park to catch up or going to an art exhibit. But his good intentions had backfired spectacularly when they ended up making out on a park bench then taking an Uber back to his place to spend three hours fucking instead of going to that exhibit.

It wasn't entirely his fault. How was he supposed to

resist her when she wore a light, flowery romper suit that rode up far enough to show her rose tattoo? The buttons down the front were begging him to pop them open. But yeah, spending a solid week at home would do him good.

Ease his addiction a bit.

At least until he got back.

His phone pinged.

> When did you say you were coming back?

He couldn't help but smile. It was as if they were thinking the exact same thing at the same time.

> July 3rd

He hesitated, then kept on typing.

> In the meantime you could send me a picture with a nice view.

He couldn't expect to go completely cold turkey, after all. He needed a little something to get him through.

> I'm on the bus... Later 😉

A meaty hand slapped down on his shoulder. "Hé, ça va? Ça fait un boutte!"

Laurent pocketed his phone and whipped around. His uncle Jean-Paul shook his hand before pulling him into a hug.

"Salut, mononcle," Laurent said. "Great to see you."

Jean-Paul grinned. No one could tell the front teeth were fake, but he'd lost both of them playing in the minors, though he liked to tell anyone who would listen that Chris

Nilan had knocked them out during a scrum. "Likewise. So Jersey gave you a hell of a time, huh?"

Laurent lifted his chin. "We gave them hell right back. At least until game five."

"But they needed overtime." Jean-Paul nodded. "Next year. Just keep at it."

He would have to, if he wanted to keep his starter's spot. No matter how big your contract was, you were always a couple of bad games away from being benched. Or worse, traded. Kovy would only be too happy to step in, and the Eagles, their minor league affiliate, had a talented young prospect between the pipes. The kid was fresh out of college and hungry for a chance at the show.

"Enough of that," his uncle said, as if reading his thoughts. "It's good you're home. You and Luc both. You know there's nothing that makes Chantal happier."

Laurent nodded, and the guilt he'd managed to push back surfaced again. "I know. If it helps, I think my days of throwing a huge bash for my birthday are over."

After all, his best buddies on the team were more or less settling. Max was about to get married, Jayden was at the very least thinking of proposing to Cait, and Colby had been conspicuously averse to partying this season. That only left Rocky, but he was a freak of nature in more ways than one, and he'd probably end up busting out of the nursing home to go to strip clubs.

"Sooner or later, you start to realize what's truly important." Jean-Paul looked over to Luc and shook his head. "Your brother's still young, but tabarnak, he's been throwing money around like it's candy."

"I'll keep an eye on him, promise. But first we'd better go rescue those steaks."

As they approached, Luc glanced at them over his

shoulder. "Salut, mononcle. What'll it be? Rare? Medium rare?"

Laurent pressed a finger into one of the steaks and snorted. "I think it's a bit too late for anything other than burnt to a crisp. Calisse, what's the first rule of cooking? You let go of your fucking phone."

Luc rolled his eyes. "Like you're never on your phone? Besides, this is important."

"Oh yeah? DMing girls on social media can't wait?"

"Crisse de cave."

"Here, let me handle this." Jean-Paul took the tongs from Luc and moved the steaks off of direct heat. "You boneheads go argue somewhere else."

Luc stepped away from the grill and finally put his phone back into his pocket. "If you really want to know, frerot, I was making plans for our evening."

"*Our* evening?" Laurent repeated. "I just got here. My only plan was to chill at home with Maman and Jean-Paul."

"Well, I got here two days ago, so I'm not just going to hang around on the deck then go to bed at nine. You know who messaged me today? Sandrine."

The gulp of ice tea in Laurent's mouth got stuck halfway down his throat. "Sandrine Ouellet?"

Stupid question. Of course, Luc was talking about Laurent's ex. The only proper girlfriend he'd ever had—back in high school. And the question had always lingered in his mind. If he hadn't gotten together with her, would things have worked out differently with Lorelei?

No matter. It was all in the past now. But spending time with his ex was not on his bingo card this summer.

"She wants to see us," Luc insisted. "I mean, not just us. It would be the whole gang. Véro and Raphaël are in town too."

Fantastic. Just what he needed. Raphaël Bisson—Biz to his teammates—was an okay guy, but Véronique was shallow as a puddle, and as far as Laurent could tell, the only thing she was interested in was building a lifestyle brand off her husband's career.

"Come on, you can't hide at home for a week. At least come hang out with me."

Laurent sighed. He couldn't say no to that. And he could understand why Luc was restless. Left alone in Montarville with their grieving mother, his brother had gone through some rough shit right after their father's death. His memories of home had to be far less rosy than Laurent's.

"Not tonight. I got up at five AM, and I need to rest. But starting tomorrow, we'll hang."

Luc mocked-punched his shoulder. "You got it, old man."

"Boys! Come set the table," his mother called from the house. Some things just never changed.

Laurent's phone buzzed in his pocket. He glanced at the screen and slowed his steps. A message from Lorelei, with a picture attached.

Holy shit, he probably better not open that where his family might catch a glimpse. His uncle would just laugh and slap him on the back, but his mother would be appalled and assume Lorelei was nothing but a shameless puck bunny. As for Luc, he actually *knew* Lorelei, which somehow made it even worse. Laurent quickly locked his screen again, though temptation made his fingers tingle.

No, he wouldn't give in before he'd retreated to his room for the night. Whatever it was, chances were, he'd need to relieve the pressure right then and there. And hope it would be enough to get him through the week.

Hamilton, The Happy Badger Pub, June 30th

"And our last question tonight... Name this lead guitarist featured on Michael Jackson's 'Beat It.'"

David's elbow dug into Lorelei's side and he bounced on his barstool. "Oh, you must know that! Please, *please* tell me you know that!"

Mason patted his arm gently. "Babe, calm down. You're going to spill our beers."

Lorelei frowned. "Wait... what was the question again?"

David flapped his hands around. "Something about a guitarist who guested for Michael Jackson."

Right. Shit, she did know that. She closed her eyes. It was right on the tip of her tongue...

"Eddie Van Halen!" someone cried out from the table next to them.

David let out a sound halfway between a wail and a growl. "Damn it!"

"And that is..." The host made a show of whipping his mic around. "Correct! Three points to Quiz in My Pants. Final tally, please."

Someone else at the bar scratched some numbers on a sheet of paper and gave them to the announcer.

"And the winners of tonight's epic trivia showdown are... Quiz in My Pants, with a hundred twelve points!"

The bar broke out in applause. David scowled and tapped the tip of his fingers together.

"Followed by the Jane Eyreheads, with a hundred eight points!"

More applause. Mason cheered and clinked his beer bottle with Lorelei's. David barely cracked a smile.

"Oh, come on, sour puss," Mason said. "Second place isn't bad. It's the best we've done in a long time."

"I know, but I truly thought Lorelei was the missing piece of the puzzle, and that we would finally beat those guys. You know how long their winning streak has lasted? Four games. *Four*."

"Enough to win you a playoff round," Lorelei remarked, then paused. Had she just made a hockey joke? Good God, the heat must be getting to her.

Luckily David focused his attention on Mason. "I told you, babe. I told you months ago, we needed someone on the team who knew about art and music. Those are our weak links."

She raised an eyebrow. "Oh, is that why let me rent your spare room?"

David paused before answering. "I admit, seeing how artsy you are, the thought did cross my mind. But I saw it more as a bonus."

She gave him a side hug and put her head on his shoulder. "I'm sorry. I'll try to do better next time, I promise. Please don't kick me out."

David rested his cheek on top of her head. "There, there. I forgive you. We all have our off days."

It was more than just an off day, though. It was an off week. She was distracted, irritable, and when she got home from work, she was so tired she didn't even want to paint or draw. Maybe it was just because her boss was being a tremendous pain in the ass—constantly looking over her shoulder, snapping at her when she did the slightest thing wrong, giving her the worst shifts. And she had to play nice because he'd promised to display some of her art at the shop in August. Maybe it was this sweltering muggy weather.

And maybe you just need to get laid.

She straightened and shoved the thought away, chasing it down with a swig of beer. No, she wasn't going to act like a desperate, infatuated airhead pining after her lover. True, Laurent had taken her higher than anyone else in her life. With him six hundred fifty kilometers away in Quebec she'd been feeling restless, tossing and turning in bed before finding sleep, body buzzing with tension despite her exhaustion.

Almost restless enough to cave in and ask for Facetime sex. Which she hadn't done. Because she needed to prove she could go without it, at least for a few days.

David had taken out his phone and was scrolling through social media. Right, they'd had to put their phones on airplane mode during the trivia quiz. She opened the settings on her cell and switched it to normal. A message popped up. Laurent.

> thanks, you 😊

She opened the conversation. Just above was her own message.

> Happy birthday, you

Sent five hours earlier. *Stop it. Don't go down that path.* What did she care that Laurent had taken so long to reply? It was his birthday, and he was surrounded by family and friends. And fuck if she was going to become some crazy person starting at her screen at a message marked read and left unanswered.

Besides, he hadn't been too busy to reply to her last message. She resisted the temptation to scroll up. Better not risk David catching a glance of the picture she'd sent

Laurent, a shot of her backside taken in the bathroom mirror, wearing only a lacy thong.

> About to take a shower.

> Hope you'll be thinking of what we did last time I was in there with you. I sure will be later tonight with my hand around my cock.

She locked her screen. Trivia night at the Happy Badger with Mason and David was not the place to get turned on. These barstools were already uncomfortable enough.

"Hey, have you seen this?"

David handed her his phone. She frowned. "The Steelhawks social media feed? You follow them in the offseason too?"

"Duh, it's where you get all the news of engagements and stuff. But look, they made a video for your friend. You didn't tell me it was his birthday."

"Why would I? He's not even in town. He's back home in Quebec with his family."

Lorelei pressed play. It was just a short clip of Laurent during the season—making great saves, pulling up his mask to wave at the crowd, talking to the press with a smile on his face. Then goofier stuff, like antics with teammates in the locker room, and a montage of him saying "tabarnak," though they bleeped him every time which added a comic effect. The video ended with Laurent stopping outside the arena to greet fans and sign jerseys for adorable, overexcited tots.

Wait a minute... Her eyes widened. "Oh my God. That's my shirt."

David leaned in. "Your shirt?"

"I mean, the shirt I made for Laurent for his birthday last year. He's wearing it in the video."

David grabbed his phone back, and this time, even Mason leaned it to watch. "Um, have you looked at the comments under that video? There are a bunch of people asking where they can buy it."

"You're shitting me."

"See for yourself."

She scanned through the comments. Holy crap, David was right.

"Well, you know what that means, don't you?"

"No, I don't. They can't buy it anywhere. That's an exclusive, custom job."

"Lore, do you have any idea how much exposure this could give you? You gotta get your ass on social media."

She shook her head. "Uh uh. No way. I'm not posting my design on the Internet where someone can steal it."

"I hate to break it you, but they already can. Anyone can get a good shot of that shirt and copy it. And if word gets out who did this, or the Steelhawks ask Laurent, they're going to look you up online."

Mason took a sip of beer, a pensive expression on his face. "He's right. If you want to make a living off your art at some point, you're going to need to do it anyway."

Damn it. No way to argue with that. Fucked up as it was, you couldn't showcase your work without being on social media these days.

Well, you could. You could try to talk your boss into displaying a few things in exchange for kissing his ass. Only the traffic through their coffee shop and the amount of traffic you could generate online if you worked at it didn't compare.

But it wasn't just the idea of posting her art online that

made her queasy. Social media made it way too easy to see things she'd rather not see. Or look up people she'd rather not know anything about.

"Fine," she muttered. "You can help me set it up if you want."

David gave a little shimmy. "Oooh, fun! Let's go home right now and do it!"

"First, I'm getting us another round. Gonna have to get closer to paralyzed before I take this on."

Chapter Ten

@LORELEIWESCOTTART: LOVED WORKING ON THIS PIECE. I DIDN'T SET OFF TO PAINT A SUNSET OVER WATER BUT THAT'S JUST HOW IT TURNED OUT. DÜRER WATERCOLOR MARKERS ARE A MUST.

Montarville, July 2nd
"Who wants another shot? Aweille donc!"

Laurent raised his head from his lounge chair and glanced over his sunglasses. On the opposite side of the pool, two bikini-clad girls dangled their feet in the water. They waved empty shot glasses, and Luc swaggered over, holding a clear tequila bottle by the neck. Izo Cristalino Extra Anejo, the most expensive brand available at the SAQ, had set him back three hundred bucks.

But they couldn't arrive empty-handed, and the high-end tequila went with their surroundings. Paved terraces, manicured lawn, huge stone house in a newly developed sector of town where properties started in the millions... Biz —or more likely Véro—had expensive taste.

Just like his little brother.

Whatever. The kid could have his fun, as long as he wasn't driving later. After all, he himself had made girls and tequila a birthday tradition for several years. Yeah, he'd told his uncle that he'd keep an eye on Luc, but he could hardly blame him for wanting to have some fun.

"Your little bro sure knows how to party," Biz said from an adjoining chair. "Learned from the best, eh?"

Laurent snorted. "Trust me, he didn't need lessons."

"Funny, he wasn't like that when he was younger. I remember him being all quiet and reserved. Guess you never know."

Yeah, Biz's father had coached Luc, back when his brother was a shy, skinny kid. The type that might make himself a target for bullies. But as far as Laurent knew, things had never gone that far.

Though he could never be a hundred percent sure. Those years he'd played junior hockey in Nova Scotia had separated them. Luc hadn't confided everything that had gone down during that time, and Laurent didn't want to push, especially not more than a decade after the fact.

He glanced at his brother again. Luc had settled between the two girls, wrapping both arms around their waists while they snuggled closer, hands on his bare pecs. Clearly, he was doing fine now, so why dwell on the past?

With a sigh, Laurent rolled his shoulders. Being home was relaxing yet somehow unsettling. His roots lay here. He would always fit effortlessly back in with people who had known him for so long. To them, he wasn't Gilly, professional starting goalie for a team that regularly made the playoffs. Here, he was Laurent, Chantal's kid who had made it to the show. And there was something comforting about knowing he could always go back.

On the other hand, that also meant coming face-to-face with certain parts of his past. Something he hadn't thought of as a problem until now. After all, he didn't have any dark secrets buried, or any unfinished business. Why then was his stay stirring up some uncomfortable feelings in a way it never had before?

Two pairs of high-heeled sandals clicked on the paving stones surrounding the pool deck. Laurent turned his head to the side. Arm in arm, Véronique and Sandrine came to a halt beside Biz, both in dressed in cover-ups whose netting showed off their skimpy swimsuits.

"Raph, are we going to Club Chasse et Pêche tonight?" Véro asked. "I've been dying to try that place out."

Sandrine gave an excited squeal. "Yes, that would be so amazing!"

She hadn't changed much. Barely at all, in fact. Same shiny light brown waves of hair, glowing golden skin, bright smile. As if she'd been floating through life in a bubble of perfection.

"I'll do what I can, chérie," Biz said. "Though I told you, it's one of those places you have to book weeks in advance."

"If you'd name drop, they'd find us a table," Véro insisted.

Biz laughed. "I play for the wrong team for that to work around here. It's not like we're in Hamilton."

"Name drop Laurent too, then," Sandrine suggested. "You guys may not play for Montreal, but they won't say no to two Steelhawks players."

Laurent flipped his glasses over his forehead. "Not sure I can make it tonight. I'm leaving tomorrow so Maman wanted us to have dinner together."

Sandrine's smile didn't falter. "That's too bad. Maybe you can join us for drinks later?"

With the afternoon sun glistening off her golden skin, it wasn't hard to remember why he'd dated her for almost a year. When he came home for the summer between grade eleven and twelve, all of a sudden girls had wanted to hook up. They sent him DMs and flirted with him at parties. Had he changed that much? Maybe the hockey aura had finally overpowered his zits.

Sandrine was the type of girl he'd only dreamed of landing. And then just like that, she was his, and it was so easy, so uncomplicated. She only wanted to spend time with him and wear his jersey and post pictures together on social media. To say she was his girlfriend.

Nothing messy about that relationship, no blurry lines to keep him up at night. No wondering if they were friends one day or more than friends the next. No questioning when he went over to her house if they would just smoke up and listen to music, or if they'd end up having sex. No torturing himself over what his teammates would say, because one look at Sandrine in their tagged pictures was all it took for the guys to slap him on the back.

Sandrine was the opposite of Lorelei, and that was exactly what he'd needed. Until it wasn't.

"Yeah, we'll see," he replied at last.

She tilted her head. "Come on, we need to celebrate before you leave. Maybe there's a way to make sure you'll want to come back."

Was she hinting at something? Hard to tell. That gorgeous smile of hers didn't let anything through, and when things got ugly, the bubble of perfection turned into a hardened shell. When that shit with the rookies had gone down his senior year and he'd needed comfort, someone who would listen to him like he wasn't crazy...

You're overreacting. I'm sure it wasn't that bad. Anyway, why do you care? You won't be on that team next year. Just let it go and have fun.

Fuck it, he shouldn't hold that against her now. They simply weren't on the same wavelength and couldn't make it work long distance. Their relationship had ended in typical teenage fashion, with an awkward and abrupt breakup. So why did her presence grate on him so much? Why did it make the hollow feeling in his stomach worse?

Lorelei. He wanted Lorelei. Being here, being with his family and his brother and Sandrine, having to deal with these memories only made the craving stronger.

You don't have to pretend in front of me. What happened was fucked up, and whatever you need to let out... Your secret's safe with me. Your secrets have always been safe with me.

And it wasn't just physical. He wanted to hear her voice, talk to her, if only for a minute, to soothe the ache a little.

He took his phone from his shorts. Five-thirty. Would she still be at work, or had she gotten off earlier? He could try in any case.

He rose to his feet. "Excuse me. I gotta make a phone call."

Biz raised his eyebrows. "Everything good, man?"

Crap, did it show on his face? Perhaps this wasn't the best time to call Lorelei. After all, he'd be back in Hamilton tomorrow.

Yeah, and he needed to know when they could see each other before he lost it.

"All good. I'll only be a minute."

Dirty Puck Buddies

The Daily Grind coffee shop, Hamilton, early evening

"For goodness' sake, Lorelei, how many times have I told you to clean the sink before you wipe down the tables, not after?"

Lorelei pressed her lips together. One, two, three, four... Always best to count as high possible before replying to Theo, though usually a curse threatened to burst out by the time she reached five.

She gave the tabletop a few sprays of cleaner and swiped it with her rag. "I'm almost done here."

"That's not the problem. The problem is I have a system, and I need my employees to follow it."

She glanced over her shoulder. Sure enough, her boss was glaring at her from behind his thick-framed square glasses, a permanent scowl etched on his face. Good fucking Lord, what the hell did it matter if she did the tables then the sink, and not the reverse?

It didn't matter. It didn't save time, or make anyone more efficient. It wasn't any more hygienic. No, this was all about Theo running the coffee shop like a dictatorship because he got his rocks off treating underlings like garbage. Unfortunately, she was in no position to defect at the moment.

"Sorry," she said. "I'll remember next time. Sink first, then the tables."

Theo sighed. "It just makes more sense. I thought by now you'd see that, but apparently for some people it takes a bit longer to understand basic stuff."

One, two, three, four, fu-u-u-u-ck... She focused on her circular motion of her hand. God, how satisfying would it be when she could finally quit? She nursed a fantasy of wadding up her beige apron possibly with a mug inside—or a rock—and tossing it in his stupid face.

All in good time.

"Oh, by the way, you're closing tomorrow and opening on Saturday."

She shot up. "What? I thought Keira had taken those shifts."

Theo shrugged. "She asked me to move things around. Senior staff have priority, you know that."

Bollocks. Saturdays they were usually slammed. She'd have to come in early. Too early. And if she closed the previous evening after a grueling shift...

Laurent. He was coming back tomorrow. They hadn't made plans or anything, but assuming he wanted to see her, she thought she'd at least get to sleep in Saturday morning. And recover. In case they did something she needed to recover from.

Well, maybe they wouldn't have sex all night this time. Right?

Go ahead and keep kidding yourself. Just thinking about seeing him again made her knees shaky and the throbbing pick up between her legs right where it had left off. There was no way she wouldn't pounce on him and demand he make up for eight days of forced abstinence.

"Besides, you're off at four on Saturday and starting at eleven on Sunday, so that gives you a nice big break," Theo continued, clipboard in hand.

He paused, as if waiting for her reply. Of course.

She forced a smile. "Thanks, Theo."

"I always try to be fair. That's what makes me a good manager."

She hurried to finish the cleanup before she could blow a gasket. When she finally took off her apron, she let out a deep breath. Sweet, sweet freedom, if only until tomorrow.

She grabbed her bag and fished out her phone. Two missed calls from Laurent. A knot formed in her stomach. God only knew if it was the good sort of knot or the bad sort.

She unlocked the screen and called him back as she walked to the bus stop. No answer. Shit. He was probably having dinner or something.

Half an hour later, she was home, lying on her bed with the delicious scent of homemade frittatas wafting from downstairs. She should probably go help Mason with dinner, but she really needed to get off her feet for ten minutes.

She scrolled through her photo album, pressing on the tiny colorful thumbnails of her paintings. She needed to post something on her account tonight. True, she only had about twenty followers so far, but posting more and hoping for shares was the only way she'd make it grow. Perhaps she could make time-lapse videos of projects she did on her tablet...

The first chords of "The Jack" rang out. She dropped her phone, and it landed square the bridge of her nose before tumbling to the side of the bed.

"Ow!" She scrambled to grab it and swiped at the screen. "Fuck! Hello?"

"Straight to business, then." Laurent's voice was half-amused and half-concerned. "You all right?"

She rubbed her nose and winced. Thank goodness he couldn't see her. "Yeah, I'm fine. I just... bonked myself with my phone."

His laugh vibrated in her ear and fluttered all the way down to her stomach. "You weren't napping before you, um... bonked yourself, were you?"

She tutted. "Stop that. I got home a few minutes ago. I tried calling you when I left work. Is everything okay?"

"Sure. We're about to have dinner. Just wanted to say hi."

She raised an eyebrow. Weird reason to call twice in a row. "Okay, then. Hi."

"Oh, and I also wanted to know if you were busy tomorrow night. My flight's coming in around four, so you could come over whenever you finish work."

She covered her eyes with her hand. "I'd love to, but my asshole manager is making me close tomorrow night *and* open on Saturday."

"Oh shit. How early on Saturday?"

"Like... six-thirty?"

Laurent let out a slow breath. "Tabarnak. That sucks."

"I know, I know. I was supposed to have the morning off, but he just switched the schedule around. God, I hate that guy. Anyway, I don't have to work until eleven on Sunday, so if you're free..."

"Saturday is Max's bachelor party."

"Oh." *Don't ask, don't ask, don't...* "What do you guys have planned?"

Great. Why couldn't she keep her mouth shut? Now on top of having to work, she'd have to think about Laurent getting lap dances at some fancy strip club.

"Golfing, dinner, and dancing."

"That's it?"

"Pretty much. Colby set up the whole thing, and he told us Max didn't want anything too crazy. After dinner we're going to meet up with Addie and her friends at some posh club that just opened downtown."

She'd only met Max that one time, but she felt like

kissing him right now. As far as bachelor parties went, that sounded pretty tame.

"I have no idea how late it'll last but..."

She shook her head. "Look, it's fine. We can see each other next week or something. No sweat."

He paused. "I mean, you could come over afterward. If you want."

Her heart knocked against her chest. "After the club? Would you want that?"

He laughed. "Come on, Lore, you have to know I'm fucking dying to see you. But you let me know if you're too tired and you're going to bed or whatever. I won't take it badly. Promise."

She bit her lip. *Fucking dying to see you.* Yeah, so was she. And it made her heart rate speed up. Once again, she couldn't tell if that was good or bad, but it was nerve-wracking, either way.

"Okay. We can do that."

"Great. What about you, though? What have you been up to, beyond dealing with your asshole boss?"

"Actually, I started an account to put some of my art online."

"Really? That's awesome. Give me your handle so I can follow you."

She flipped over to her stomach and kicked up her feet. "I'm already following you. You just have to follow back."

"Oh, you mean on my official account?" He laughed. "I hardly ever check that one. I just post Steelhawks content there once in a while. You should follow my private account."

"A private account? Imagine."

"A lot of the guys have one. Lots of stuff they wouldn't

want the fans to know." Some voices echoed in the background. "I gotta go now, but I'll text you my handle."

"No problem. Have a great evening."

"Bye, ma belle."

She hung up. A moment later, a text popped up.

@domforevr39

Dom, eh? Maybe that stood for Dominik Hasek, but she'd have to ask Laurent to make sure.

A few seconds after she added him, he followed her back and a feed of images popped up. Laurent with his teammates in the locker room celebrating a win, Laurent wakeboarding, several views of the lake house. And the most recent, Laurent and Luc with a group of friends by a pool. Posted only two hours ago.

She tapped the image. Right, that girl, Véronique—she'd posted the pic and tagged Laurent. She had her arms around her husband, Laurent's teammate. Next to her, a shirtless Luc struck a goofy muscle man pose, and Laurent was standing between his brother and a young woman with wavy hair, one arm slung over her shoulder.

Lorelei frowned and zoomed in. Had she seen that girl somewhere before?

Realization washed over her like ice cold water. Oh God, no wonder she looked familiar. Sandrine, Laurent's ex. And this wasn't the first time her face had taunted Lorelei through a screen. Although that other time, Lorelei had brought it entirely on herself.

Burning shame rose to heat her cheeks. Ten years and the memories were still just as mortifying. As soon as she'd learned that Laurent had a girlfriend, she'd looked her up on social media. A little detective work, and pretty soon she was scrolling through pictures of Laurent and that little bombshell having fun over the summer.

And each one had been like stabbing a fucking pin into her skin, but still, she couldn't stop.

The pain almost helped. Convincing her that there was no way that she and Laurent could have made it work, because he was a hockey player, and Sandrine was the kind of girl hockey players dated. Perfect body, perfect smile, radiating perkiness and confidence.

And now Lorelei was back in that same place, with that flawless, glowing face on her screen, unable to tear her eyes away. Had Laurent taken advantage of his trip home to reconnect with his ex? After all, he'd reconnected with *her* as soon as she'd come back to Ontario. Or did they just hang out with the same friends?

This is what you get for using social media.

She closed the app and locked her screen. No, she wouldn't let herself fall into that same trap again. High school was over, and who the hell cared if Laurent had met up with his ex, anyway? He sure hadn't wasted any time inviting Lorelei over for a hook-up.

No, she had nothing to worry about. Laurent would let her know for sure when he was free on Saturday night.

She sat up and her gaze landed on her top drawer of her bureau. Well... Perhaps it wouldn't hurt to send him a little preview, just in case.

Chapter Eleven

@VeloursBoitedeNuit Planning an event? Let Anya show you around our private guest space. Many options available no matter what kind of experience you're into.

Velours nightclub, Hamilton, July 4th

Sex. The vibe in this place fairly throbbed with it. The heady beat of the bass pulsated through Laurent, inciting him to move. To get loose and let his hips sway. To find one of the girls in slinky dresses and high heels in the main room below and get down.

Only none of them were the one he wanted.

Max leaned an elbow against their private bar on the mezzanine. "I gotta say, Ched, you outdid yourself. If there was ever a place made for a bunch of horny motherfuckers like us, this is it. Well done, man."

Colby was typing on his phone. "I aim to please."

"Any idea when the girls will get here?"

"Gabby just texted. They're on their way. Not long now."

Laurent drained his champagne glass. Colby hadn't stopped glancing at his phone all night. Sure, he had to keep in contact with Addie's maid of honor, since they were hosting this bachelor party together, but his fingers twitched in short jerky motions.

The music must be getting to him, too. Hell, this whole place with its black marble tops and dark red velvet hangings that begged for touch. That screamed sensuality. That made you hard up for action. Max was right, Colby had chosen the closest thing to a strip club that didn't include actual strippers.

Laurent glanced at his watch. Almost midnight. Should he text Lorelei? He didn't want to wake her if she'd fallen asleep, but then waiting for her to contact him on top of this place was a special brand of torture. He'd been fine during the golf tournament and at the restaurant, chilling with the guys and enjoying a divine steak dinner, but as soon as they'd arrived at the club, that restless feeling had grabbed hold of him. And now it wouldn't let go.

Rocky held out a half-empty bottle of Dom Perignon. There was plenty more where that came from. "Come on, G-man, let me top you up."

He took a few more sips. A warm, bubbly sensation fizzed through his veins. The taste reminded him of Lorelei, and how she'd squirmed and sighed when he'd lapped champagne from her skin.

His phone buzzed in his pocket. He whipped it out so fast he almost spilled his drink.

Having fun?

Thank fuck. Lorelei wasn't asleep. The only thing that could have ruined the mood tonight was ending up in blue ball hell, waiting for her to answer a text message before crashing at three AM.

> Won the golf tournament. Got a hole in one.

> For real or is that a joke?

Feats on the golf course didn't usually impress her, but still, he got a kick out of bragging. On the team, only Jayden came close to besting him.

> For real. But that was before I was six drinks deep.

> Oh… I wanted your opinion about something, but if you've had too much to drink…

That definitely pinged his radar. Sure, she might ask him a completely innocuous question, but odds were he was about to get lucky.

> LOL. I can still type.

> I bought new lingerie this afternoon. Can you tell me if it fits?

Very lucky. That minx. She had to know he'd grab that bait, but fuck if it didn't make him want to make her work for it a little.

> Only if you ask nicely.

Hell, whenever he said that in bed, it pushed all the right buttons. She got insanely turned on when he made her beg for what she wanted. Rebellious and bold as she was, he'd never have guessed in a million years, but being held down and bent to his will ended up with her screaming his name. Guaranteed.

> Please, Laurent. It won't take long.

A smile tugged at the corner of his mouth. Oh, he planned on it lasting all fucking night.

> We got here less than an hour ago.
> Ignoring my friends would be rude.

He glanced toward the back room. The girls had just arrived, and Max had wasted no time snuggling with Addie on a red velvet couch. Jayden and Cait were at the bar, locked in a tight embrace, and even the captain and his wife had their hands all over each other. As for the rest of the guys, they were either busy trying to hit up Addie's friends or three sheets to the wind.

> Pretty please? You're the only one who can help me with this.

> All right. But you better make sure I can see your outfit from every angle.

> Whatever you say.

He pocketed his phone. He should at least pretend to get into the swing of things. This was Max's party, after all, but at this point it practically qualified as a team building event, even if everyone was trying to score some way or another. He made his way to Rocky and Colby, who were leaning over the banister of the VIP section. Probably checking out the girls on the dance floor below and discussing who they might invite upstairs.

Rocky nudged Colby. "Like shooting fish in a barrel, huh?"

"You cast your net so wide, we'd have our party overrun with chicks in five minutes," Colby replied.

Laurent settled on the other side of Rocky. "Ched is right. Can't you act like a gentleman and focus on the ladies present?"

A bit ironic, since the only girl he planned on spending the night with was still at home, hopefully snapping some dirty pics for him.

"There won't be enough to go around," Rocky complained.

Colby sipped his scotch. "You probably wouldn't be doing Addie's friends any favors, anyway."

Rocky paused to think for a moment. "No, no, he's got a point. Better consider all my options."

They started for the back room. Colby froze, his gaze lingering on Gabby, whose tight glittery dress did a very good job of showing off her flawless figure. Laurent and Rocky exchanged glances. Though Colby liked to pretend otherwise, he'd been drooling over Gabby for more than a year, and judging by the heated look she threw him over her shoulder, it was pretty damn obvious something had gone down between them.

Rocky surveyed the other girls. "That blonde chick with the pixie cut is pretty hot. Check out that ass. Must be one of Addie's figure skating friends." He waggled his eyebrows. "Super flexible, right?"

Leave it to Rocky to launch any notion of subtlety

straight into the sun. "Jesus Christ, please don't tell me you're going to cold open with that."

"Oh, aren't we acting all high and mighty? Who you got tonight?"

Laurent drained his glass, which helped to keep a straight face. "No one. I'm just here to celebrate Max."

Colby slapped his shoulder. "That's the spirit. But that doesn't mean you have to celebrate alone. Even the captain isn't going to do much sleeping tonight by the looks of it."

Another buzz in his pocket. His attention immediately tuned out everything else. "Maybe. I guess."

Wait. Go somewhere more private. Too late. The alcohol and the teasing and the ten fucking days he'd gone craving her had burned off the last of his patience. His thumb was already swiping at the screen.

A picture of Lorelei, taken from the neck down, popped up. Nothing but creamy skin, mouth-watering curves and shiny black satin that dipped low and hiked up in all the right places. She'd taken an overhead shot to emphasize her luscious cleavage, kneeling on her bed, her thighs parted. His gaze traced the rose tattoo snaking up to her hip. Damn, he could remember the feel of those thighs clenching around his waist as he pounded into her...

Rocky grabbed his phone from his hands.

Tabarnak, was he that hammered that he hadn't seen the idiot coming? Usually no one beat his reflexes, but if the shot was screened... Yeah, the lamp lit.

Rocky laughed. "Fuck me, man. Now I get it. Who's sending you dirty pics?"

Laurent snatched his phone back. "None of your business, asswipe."

"She's got a sort of pin-up thing going, too, though

usually pin-ups show their faces, am I right? Not that I'm complaining. That's some booty call."

A booty call. Technically, Rocky wasn't wrong. But somehow it felt wrong to apply the term to Lorelei. Because shit, he had a long history of booty calls in basically every city they played in, and none of those girls held a candle to her. Or made him feel the type of need that had been clawing at him for days.

"Get fucked," he growled. "Literally or figuratively, whatever you can manage. Come on, Ched, let's get another drink."

As soon as they were at the bar, his phone buzzed again. Colby was still staring at Gabby. Perfect. At least he wouldn't be trying to sneak a peek at the screen.

This time, Lorelei had taken a similar shot to one she'd sent him a few days before, over her shoulder in the bathroom mirror to give him a good view of her gorgeous ass.

> So, what do you think?

> You're a fucking knockout. Show me the front again. Show it better.

Another picture. This time she was leaning over the sink, tits pushed up and nearly spilling from the cups of her bra. She'd lined her lids with black, giving herself a cat's eye look, and she was wearing that bright red lipstick he loved so much. It never failed to conjure an image of her lips moving up and down his cock.

> Like that?

Holy fuck, he was getting hard. God, just imagining that he was the one bending her over, fucking her from behind and watching in the mirror as her breasts bounced with every thrust...

> How fast can you get to my place?

A quick look told him Colby had disappeared—and Gabby too, which checked out. Rocky was sitting on a couch with the cute blonde who yelled out something in Russian before grabbing a bottle of vodka and filling two shot glasses. Well, that would do it. Rocky could pack in more than anyone on the team, but vodka was his kryptonite.

> You're leaving now? I thought you didn't want to be rude.

The hell with that. No one would miss him at this point, and he wouldn't make good company, anyway. Not when he was about ready to snap.

> If you want my real opinion I need to touch that satin to see if it's as soft as it looks.

> Take my word for it. I'm touching myself thinking of you, but I kept my panties on so I don't come too fast.

Fuck. He stared at her text. Something stirred deep inside him, something dark and primitive and predatory. Something begging to be unleashed. Lorelei was the only one who had gotten a taste of it, but if she kept this up, he wouldn't be able to hold anything back.

> You're playing a very dangerous game.

> That's how I like it. Dangerous.

> You're a little cocktease, you know that?

> I know.

> If you come over tonight, going to give you a lesson in discipline. And I won't stop until you've learned. Thoroughly. Understand?

The three dots moved. His breath caught in his throat. Shit. Had he taken things too far?

> I'll be there in half an hour.

———

HEART HAMMERING JUST a little more with each step, Lorelei moved down the corridor to Laurent's door. She clutched the strap of her bag. Hell, why was she even nervous? It wasn't like this was their first hookup.

Somehow this time was different. She'd provoked him, and he'd risen to her challenge. Delving deeper and deeper into this game.

You're a little cocktease, you know that?

The tone he'd taken both unnerved her and thrilled her. But God, she didn't want their game to stop. No, she wanted to push it, to see just how far it would go.

She stopped at the threshold. He'd left his door ajar, just a crack. She took a deep breath, pushed it open and slipped inside.

Darkness blanketed his apartment, save for the faint light coming from the street lamps outside. Laurent stood just beyond doorway, arms crossed, wearing a suit and pale shirt with the top buttons open. Waiting for her. He met with silence, but his gaze pierced her through. A tremor of want unfurled all the way from the pit of her stomach to her throat.

She gave him her sweetest smile, closed the door behind her and dropped her bag to the floor. "Hey, you."

He raised an eyebrow. "You said half an hour. It's been forty minutes."

She sank her teeth into her lip. "I'm so sorry. I couldn't get an Uber."

"Never mind. Lose the dress and show me what you came for."

God, when his voice got all deep and commanding like that, with his accent giving it just a little bit of grit... Slick heat gathered between her legs, and her hands trembled as they reached for the hem of her flimsy summer dress to pull it over her head. She'd chosen it specifically because it was a breeze to take off.

Laurent's gaze slowly traveled up her legs to her black satin panties, the curve of her belly, her push-up bra. He sucked in a breath. The set had cost her more than she could reasonably afford, but damn if it wasn't worth it to have him look at her like he was a starving beast just about ready to go in for the kill.

"So, what do you think?" she murmured. "Worth the wait?"

He grasped her wrist, so quickly that she barely even had time to register before he whipped her around and pulled her roughly to his chest. She threw her head back against his shoulder, desperate for more contact.

"Your little plan worked," he growled next to her ear. "Happy?"

She arched her back. The solid ridge of his cock dug into her ass, and she rolled her hips against it. "Very happy."

One arm snaked across her belly and stilled her movements while the other pinned her forearms in place. She wiggled against the restraint, but it was like trying to budge solid rock.

Laurent tutted. "Always so impatient. Like you wouldn't mind if I slammed you against the wall and spread your legs to fuck you as soon as you walked through the door. Are you wet for me already?"

He didn't have to ask. He must know that she'd been ready for him the moment they'd started texting. "See for yourself."

She felt him smile against her temple and one hand cupped her mound, the palm kneading against her center while the tip of his fingers pressed against her entrance through the satin. She closed her eyes and couldn't hold back a whimper.

"Fuck, you're drenched. It wouldn't take much for you to come, would it?"

She shook her head. He drew his hand back, the other still holding her in place, and it moved against the small of her back until she heard the metallic click of his belt buckle. Oh God, was he really going to...

"Too bad. I said I was going to teach you a lesson first." He pulled his belt free, brought the ends together and snapped them with a rough jerk of his hands. "Give me your wrists."

Her knees wobbled. They'd done this before with the silk sash. With his belt, though... She obeyed. Oh God, the sight of him strapping the band of black leather around her wrists then tightening the buckle until it pinched her skin... She gasped for breath.

"That hurts."

"It's not proper discipline if it doesn't hurt. Now lean over. Hands on the wall."

His words sent a shiver though her, a small thread of apprehension twining through the anticipation. Still, she raised her arms, and her curled fists fell against the smooth, white surface. Laurent stepped back. No longer touching, but it didn't matter. The heat of his gaze contacted every part of her—thighs, ass, back, bound wrists. Her arousal cranked up another notch. And another, because she sensed the tension he was holding back.

For now.

"Tell me why you sent me those dirty pics." His voice dropped another octave, and his tone darkened. The sternness vibrated through to her core. "You knew damn well I was busy."

"You asked me to."

Crack. He slapped her ass—enough to sting, enough to make her wonder if the next time might be harder. The snap of his leather belt echoed through her mind, and her breath came out in a rush.

"You've got some nerve, putting this on me. Answer me."

"I took those pictures because I thought you'd like them."

He hissed in a breath. "I did. I got fucking hard, and I couldn't stop looking at my phone. Is that what you wanted? To torture me?"

She glanced over her shoulder. "No. I only want to please you."

"Face the wall. You don't get to bat your eyelashes at me and hope I'll ease up."

Crack. This time a moan escaped her lips.

"Now tell me the truth. Why did you do it?"

She closed her eyes. Lust raged through her with such force that she struggled to put a sentence together. "I—I knew you'd invite me over."

He stroked the spot where he'd slapped her, soothing the burn, but inflaming her more when his thumb ran under the edge of her panties. "That's better. Go on."

"I thought you might go home with someone else, and I wanted you all to myself."

As soon as the words left her mouth, she realized it was the truth. Part of her hated to think Laurent wouldn't text her because he'd picked up some other girl at the club. She wished she could smother that part, keep it quiet and out of the way, but too late.

Laurent didn't know that, though.

This was a game. Just a game she could stop at any moment with a single word. But the need overcame any misgivings.

He cupped the curve of her ass and squeezed. "Such a greedy little thing. You say you want me all to yourself, but have you been good while I was gone?"

It's just a game.

"Yes. I haven't been with anyone, I swear."

"And why is that?"

His hand slid between her legs and rubbed the silky material against her slick folds. Her eyelids squeezed shut, and she moaned again, louder. Holy shit, he hadn't even taken her panties off, and she was close to coming.

She needed to say what he wanted to hear. Now. And too fucking bad if it hit a little too close to home, if it tightened the knot in her stomach while her entire body was screaming for release.

"I can't stop thinking about all the things you do to me." Her breath came out in harsh pants. "With your tongue and your hands and your cock. It's driving me crazy because it's never enough. No one else has ever made me come the way you do." She swallowed. "Just you, Laurent."

His breath matched hers now, rapid and ragged. "Good girl. Maybe you deserve a reward."

He rolled her panties down to her knees. Something metallic crinkled. A condom wrapper? He wouldn't hold back now. They'd both pushed each other to the very edge, and if she had to wait one more second, she would shatter into a million pieces.

"Please," she whimpered. "Please hurry... *ah*."

He entered her in one forceful stroke, and the air left her lungs all at once. She couldn't breathe, couldn't speak, couldn't do anything but give in to the crushing, burning pleasure that swept over her with every thrust. He loomed over her, pinning her wrists roughly against the wall, and she could only arch her back more, angling her hips for his cock to hit deeper.

"Fucking hell, you're desperate for it, aren't you?" Laurent rasped. "I could do whatever I wanted, and you'd still be begging for more."

He pulled out.

"No," she cried. "No, I'll do anything you want, just don't stop. Don't stop."

He grasped her hip with his free hand, fingers digging into her skin, slipped back in, and pounded harder. Too good, too much, almost unbearable but she was so, so close...

"Oh God, Laurent," she moaned. "Oh God, *yes*, keep going."

A surge of dizzying sensation swelled from her center,

ebbed, swelled again, overwhelming her, and still Laurent thrust, hard, again and again, and she rode each wave further, moaning his name until she broke.

He withdrew. Though her body was limp and satiated, it protested against the sudden emptiness. She struggled to clear the haze. What was he doing?

He whipped her around again, keeping her wrists above her head. Took the condom off. And took his cock in hand.

Oh. The last traces of her orgasm quivered back to life. She held his gaze as he stroked his shaft. Two, three, four times. Laurent cursed, and hot wetness spilled on her belly.

For a few moments, he remained still, catching his breath. Then he stepped back and studied her. In her mind, she saw what he was seeing—his belt binding her wrists, his cum glistening on her skin.

She let him do that. And she would let him again. She couldn't refuse him anything, just as long as she could feel this high again. No other high she'd ever experienced, including when she and Laurent had smoked up together, even came close.

"Woah. That got a little intense right there." He exhaled and tucked his cock back into his pants. "Are you okay?"

She nodded. "Yeah. Yeah, more than okay. That was... unreal."

A lie, that. It had been real. Very, very real. Perhaps as real as they'd ever gotten. The admissions he'd forced from her...

With gentle hands, he lowered her arms and unbuckled his belt, then leaned in to kiss her mouth. Slowly, almost tenderly. "I was afraid I'd taken things too far."

"If you had, I would have used the word. That's what it's for, isn't it?"

He smiled and kissed her again. "Come on, ma belle, let's get you cleaned up. That way I can get you dirty all over again."

She ran her hand up his chest and fingered his collar teasingly. "I'm counting on it."

Chapter Twelve

@MRS_SHELTON10 ANYONE KNOW WHEN MAX
AND ADDIE'S WEDDING IS HAPPENING?
@SHSLUT NO IDEA BUT I HOPE WE GET ALL
THE PICS
@HAMILTONWAGS SOURCES SAY IT'S GOING TO BE
A BIG GLAM DESTINATION WEDDING, STAY
TUNED!

Lorelei emerged from the bathroom wearing cut-offs and a blue tank top. She shook back her curls still damp from her shower, and a delicious aroma tickled her nose. Sugar and vanilla and butter and sin. Oh, that was simply divine. Enough to make her mouth water. She followed the scent to the living room.

Laurent stood behind the island in shorts and a white tee-shirt that stretched over his muscular shoulders. He pushed a spatula under a golden scone and set it on a large plate. Her stomach growled. God, those looked delicious, just like everything Laurent baked, and she was absolutely famished. *No kidding.* After last night, replenishing her energy had become a definite priority. Along with about a gallon of strong coffee if she wanted to get through this day.

She made her way toward the island.

Laurent eyed her over his shoulder. "Hey, you. Sleep well?"

"Yeah, all four hours." Bollocks, just saying that out loud made her dread her shift at The Daily Grind. It was already bad enough when she was rested, but it would be ten times worse with her mind and body still reeling from a night of non-stop, no-holds-barred fucking—emphasis on holds.

She couldn't bring herself to regret it, though. At least not now. Despite her exhaustion, she was still riding on that endorphin high. "You got coffee?"

He pointed toward his glossy black espresso machine with chrome fittings. A white cup was already waiting under the spout. "Locked and loaded."

With a smile, she went to press the start button. Fresh coffee poured into the cup with a soft whir, and she inhaled deeply, as if the aroma alone could revive her. Much better than anything they had at work, that was for sure. "I see you've been busy. No wonder you weren't in bed when I woke up."

"I thought homemade scones and jam would be a nice surprise." He set the last of the scones onto the plate and gave her a boyish grin. "You know, something to brighten your day before work."

Her heart fluttered in her chest, almost painfully. She stared into her coffee. Oh fuck, what was that just now? She hadn't felt that since... Well, since she was a stupid teenager with a stupid, monumental crush on her best friend. She'd mercilessly smothered that crush, and she'd do it again.

It was the sex. Nothing more. It had to be. Too many orgasms had fogged her brain, and some bullshit hormonal thing was making her mistake lust for something else. Also, what straight woman could resist the sight of a man baking delicious goodies after making her come half a dozen times? Laurent wasn't playing fair.

She took a sip of coffee. "I'm glad you still take the time to bake. I wasn't sure you'd keep at it after going pro."

Back in high school, Laurent's hobby mostly involved experiments in baking weed into various types of cake. But it went deeper than that. He'd learned cooking and baking from his dad. He'd told her about his memories of spending time in the kitchen, watching Papa throw together an elaborate dish or a fancy dessert, and it was the only time she'd caught him blinking back tears.

Laurent took a jar of jam from the cupboard. "It helps me relax and focus on the present. Same as yoga. And that's the head space I need to be in during a game."

"So does baking count as training?"

He raised an eyebrow. "A lot of stuff counts as training. Anything that gets the heart pumping…"

She pressed her lips together. That was bait. Tempting, but she couldn't take it. The digital display on the espresso machine read nine fifty-five, which meant she had about fifteen minutes to drink her coffee, eat breakfast, and haul ass if she didn't want to be late. God forbid she give Theo an excuse to be on her case all day.

"You want a scone?" Laurent asked. "Jam's made from scratch too. It's strawberry."

"My favorite."

He cut a scone in half and nodded toward the stools lining the island. "Go ahead and sit."

She hesitated, then sat, slowly and carefully, on the padded cover of the stool. She couldn't help a wince.

Laurent turned. "You okay?"

"Yeah, just... You know how it is. I'm guessing you feel it in your muscles the next day when you play hard. *Really* hard." A flush of heat rose to her cheeks. "Sitting and walking straight might be a bit of a challenge today."

He locked his gaze with hers. "I want to say I'm sorry, but..."

"It's not like I'm sorry."

Wasn't she? The state she was in this morning begged the question. Was being sore as hell worth it—to the point where she couldn't even sit without grimacing? Or having red patches on her collarbone and neck where his beard had abraded her skin? Or knowing that the small bruise on her wrist was from the belt pinching her?

Yes. Yes, it was worth it. Because the discomfort still reminded her of how fucking amazing Laurent felt deep inside her, flexing those strong muscles of his to take what he wanted and make her come, again and again, flesh slapping against flesh, her cries filling the bedroom.

Enough of that now. Coffee, scone, and then work. No matter how much she wished she could just stay here, sleep it off, then wake up again and maybe...

"I know what I'm getting you for your birthday next year," she said, eager to change the subject. "I'm designing you an apron with the lamest baking pun I can find, to match the one you have at the lake house."

He handed her a plate with a jam-filled scone. "What, something like, no loafing around?"

"Or pun in the oven?"

He laughed. "At least I could wear that one around Maman. Or you could just make one that says tabarnak."

"Oh, speaking of which... Would you mind if I said on social media that the design is mine?" After all, that was the reason she was on social media in the first place. "I think some fans like it, and I wouldn't want anyone to steal it."

"Sure. You planning on making more?"

She shook her head. "No. That's an exclusive design. Just for you. But if you could, I don't know, send me a pic of you wearing it so I could post it and tag you, that would be great. Whenever you have the time."

He smiled. "I'll make time. Count on it."

She smiled back and lifted the scone to her mouth. Her eyes closed for a moment. Oh God, that was incredible. One of the reasons, along with cheese, she could never fully commit to becoming vegan. Crumbly and buttery to perfection, with the sugary tang of the jam bringing it all together.

When she opened her eyes again, Laurent had stepped closer. "And?"

"It's delicious." She licked the jam off her lips. "You sure you don't want to open a coffee shop so you can be my new boss?"

His eyes lit with a familiar fire. Okay, maybe she was baiting him, too. Just a little bit. "That depends. Are you willing to work overtime? After hours?"

He reached out to brush his thumb against the corner of her mouth. Her breath caught in her throat.

"You missed some," he murmured, but his touch lingered at her lower lip.

Don't you dare, Lorelei. Stop this right now. But the way he was looking at her, the closeness of his body... She sucked the tip into her mouth.

"Fuck," he rasped. "I'm not even hungry anymore. I want to spread jam all over your body and lick it off."

He pulled away only to step between her legs for a kiss.

The throb of desire reawakened, urgent and demanding, tempting her to jerk her hips against his erection. She forced herself to remain still, but reining in a wild horse might be easier. Lust rose in an uncontrollable wave, sweeping away everything its path, and shit, she *hated* feeling so helpless. There was just no way, *no way* could she do this, not when she had to leave for work, not with her body aching and in desperate need of rest.

You have to go to work. You HAVE to go to work. She broke the kiss, and Laurent's mouth trailed down her throat, his hands finding their way under her tank top to slide over her waist.

"I can't," she protested weakly.

"I know, ma belle. I know." He gently bit the curve of her neck, his short beard bristling against her sensitive skin. "Crisse, the way you took my cock last night... You're way too tender for me to fuck you again. But I can make you come with my mouth, nice and slow... Just say the word and I'll drop to my knees right fucking now."

She whimpered. God, she wanted it so bad, wanted *him*, his mouth on her, licking and sucking, making her melt like warm butter then shattering as she cried out his name.

Then what? Then she'd be late. She'd feel like shit. And she'd have to come down eventually. There was only one thing left to do.

"Madame Campbell."

Laurent froze, straightened, and took a step back. Already her body was screaming in frustration, but at least she'd managed to get hold of herself.

"Damn it," he grunted. "You're going to be late for work, is that it?"

She nodded. "Yeah. It sucks, but I don't have a choice."

Laurent sighed. "Drives me crazy that you have to

spend your days doing what that asshole tells you. You know, you should quit and find a job somewhere else where the manager isn't such a fucking tool."

"Quit? Like it's so easy to find another job? I'd have to apply and do interviews and all that shit all over again."

His expression shifted, as if he'd just realized something. "No, you *could*. Seriously. Quit and take a vacation before finding a new job. To Hawaii, for example?"

She shook her head. "Laurent, what the hell are you talking about?"

"Max's wedding. You could come as my plus one. Five days in Hawaii, free of charge. I think there's still room on the jet."

Her jaw dropped. "The jet as in a *private* jet? Okay, now you're being crazy."

He held out his hands. "What's so crazy about it? If I tell Max I'm bringing someone, he'll be cool with it. There's going to be like a hundred people there."

An image flashed through her mind. Addison Holtz in a stunning wedding dress, the Steelhawks players in custom-fit tuxedos, all accompanied by girls in slinky dresses, with perfect hair and diamond earrings and tiny designer bags. Girls like Sandrine Ouellet. And then her, whose fanciest item of clothing was probably the black silk lingerie set that she'd stuffed at the bottom of her bag this morning in favor of something more comfortable.

But she couldn't tell Laurent that. He'd just say he didn't care what she wore. And she sure as hell couldn't tell him that, when she imagined what a hockey player's plus one might look like, Sandrine's face popped into her head.

"I mean, none of the guys would bring one of their buddies to a wedding," she said, forcing her tone to flatness. "Won't it be weird if you do?"

His expression closed off. He shrugged. "Yeah, you're right. Forget I mentioned it."

An awkward silence hung between them, as if both of them had retreated into a corner and didn't quite know how to get out of it. She gulped down her coffee. Crap, maybe they needed to clear the air with whatever was bothering him... but she was running out of time. She tore a paper towel from the nearby roll to wrap up her scone.

"Look, I have to go. But I'll call you this week, okay?"

"I might be at the lake house. I want to get someone to check out some repairs on the dock before I leave. But yeah, give me a call, and I'll send you that pic for your account."

Damn it, why was this conversation making her feel like shit? She was just being reasonable. She couldn't tell Theo to fuck off and just jump on a private jet to Hawaii. That was insane. Right? "If it's not too much trouble."

Laurent brushed his lips across her forehead, but his attempt at a smile didn't reach his eyes. "Whatever's good for business."

Sydney, Nova Scotia, eleven years earlier

Lorelei pulled up in front of the gray hulk of the airport's low terminal, cut the engine, and put on the hazard lights. The fastest way out of Sydney, but not for her. Not today. Someday, though. She was another year closer.

She glanced across at Laurent in the passenger's seat. "We're here," she said needlessly.

His uncanny blue-green gaze seemed to penetrate to her core. "Right."

"I guess we're going to need a cart." Again, the obvious, but she didn't know what else to say.

"Right."

She forced herself to get out of the car and track down a luggage cart, before returning to an unloaded trunk. Hockey bag, sticks taped together, a bulging suitcase. His life. No, that wasn't right. His life was waiting for him. Back on the South Shore of Montreal.

This was only the essential he'd needed to survive the school year, and he was taking it home with him. The only thing he was leaving was his car, because he didn't trust it to make the long road trip back to Quebec.

His car and her.

God, could she be any more dramatic? Did she really think he needed her to survive? He had a family back home, and she didn't blame him for wanting to go back to them over staying in Sydney.

She watched him put his things on the cart, shifting her weight from one foot to the other and resisting an urge to sink her teeth into her lower lip.

"So," he said when he was done, "text me?"

"Maybe. If I have time. I'll be slaving all summer at Crappy Tire." Because texting felt like something you did with a boyfriend. Little heart emojis and angsty I-miss-yous and maybe a racy pic here and there.

The pics she might do, though even that might be too much. It would certainly remind her of all the sweaty afternoons they'd spent whenever the house was empty. Listening to music, getting high, figuring out sex.

Maybe it was better without the reminder of what they couldn't do for the next few months. Anyway, he'd be back in September, and they could pick up where they left off.

She crossed her arms over her chest. "I guess this is goodbye then."

"No, wait." He moved away from the luggage to stand before her. His shoulders blocked the morning sun. "I need to say something first."

Oh no. This wasn't doing anything for her resolve. But she had to stand firm. He was a friend first. A friend. Who was a boy. But still a friend. And she couldn't mess things up with the one person who got her on a level no one else had.

He curled his fingers around her upper arms. "I should thank you. For everything."

"What did I do?"

"What did you do? Tabarnak. This year could have been nothing but a pile of shit. Most of it was."

She ignored the sudden uptick in her pulse. "That's Sydney for you."

"You gave me an escape from all that."

"Well, happy to oblige. I guess? If ever you need saving from shit, you know who to call."

His fingers tightened. "Have it your way, then."

And then he dipped his head. His lips brushed the side of her face. She fought off the urge to glance around in case anyone had seen that. Because small town, and everything. If word got out at school they were doing couple-y things, he, at least, would never live it down.

In any case, he still blocked her vision, because his head dipped again. Damn it, she forgot about this. It was always both cheeks. But somehow his aim was off. Their noses bumped, and his mouth landed on hers.

Brief, yet he lingered a second too long.

"See you in the fall." And then he turned, grabbed his luggage.

"We'll be talkin'," she replied faintly. Pushing the words past the knot in her throat was hard.

She watched him disappear into the terminal, still hugging herself. Shit, shit, shit. This was worse than selfies. It was worse than heart emojis. It felt like a tie she didn't want. Or need.

Her throat tightened further. No, she definitely didn't want it.

Chapter Thirteen

@KahalaResort looking for the perfect destination wedding? Treat yourself and your guests to a relaxing, five-star getaway on the white sands of Ka'anapali Beach, and make memories to last a lifetime.

Kahala Resort, Hawaii, two weeks later

Laurent strode up the stone path toward the seaside patio. A rainbow of flowering bushes lined a manicured lawn, before giving way to a white beach and turquoise waters. As far as destination weddings went, it didn't get much better than this. Gorgeous views over three-hundred sixty degrees, refined dining, a fully equipped gym, and half a dozen tropical swimming pools on the property. Hell, he'd even been doing yoga on the beach every morning, watching the sun rise over the ocean. What more could a guy ask for?

Someone to share it with. He shook his head. No, he

wouldn't let those thoughts ruin his evening. Tonight, he was here to celebrate his buddy Max and his future wife, surrounded by all their friends. This was not the time to get down on himself just because Lorelei hadn't dropped everything to fly off to Hawaii with him.

She was right. It would've been weird. So, he should just forget about that particular conversation. He should stop at the night that had preceded it, because no way in hell could he wipe those images from his mind.

He spotted Colby and Gabby standing by the entrance to welcome guests and approached. "You guys on duty tonight?"

"Unfortunately," Colby grumbled.

Gabby plastered a performative smile on her face, like a journalist switching it on in front of the camera. "You bet."

"You coming in for a drink soon?"

Colby snorted. "I sure as fuck hope so. I'm going to need hard liquor if I want to get through this evening."

Laurent raised an eyebrow. Crisse, who'd pissed in his cornflakes? Last time he'd seen Colby and Gabby in the same room together, they'd looked about two minutes away from tearing each other's clothes off. "All right, tiger. How about we try to make nice for Max?"

"I *am* being nice," he snarled.

Gabby pressed her lips together. "Go on, Gilly. A bunch of the guys are inside already."

"Catch you later."

He wasn't sorry to step away from that situation, whatever it was. The air around them buzzed with tension. So which one of them had fucked it up this time? His bet was on Colby, but no way would he bring up the topic with his teammate.

Inside, the tables were laid in crisp, white linen, dripping in floral arrangements in tones of pale yellow. The bay windows overlooked an even more breathtaking vista of beachfront with breakers rolling over pristine sand. But his growling stomach distracted him from the view. Thank God uniformed waiters were offering trays of artfully arranged appetizers to go with the champagne.

After stocking a small plate with tenderloin sliders and tiny skewers of curried shrimp and snagging a champagne glass, Laurent looked around at the assembled guests. Hand in hand, Max and Addie were chatting with an older couple. Glued at the hip. Max met his gaze and gave him a grin and a nod.

No point in butting in now. He made his way toward a table in the back. Eddie, the team captain, and Jayden were shooting the shit, while Cait and Eddie's wife Hailey waited by a second buffet table for freshly seared salmon sushi. The Steelhawks top pair, Eddie and Jayden were often the last line of defense in front of his net. Maybe they'd have his back tonight.

"How are my two favorite d-men on this fine evening?"

Jayden smiled. "Don't let Rocky hear you, or he'll leave you out to dry next season."

Laurent pulled out a chair. "Nice set-up, huh? But then Max has always had fancy tastes."

Eddie stroked his short brown beard. "Oh, I can guarantee you he had nothing to do with any of this. He's probably seeing it for the first time and is just as stunned as you are."

"Speaking from experience?" Jayden asked.

Eddie slapped his shoulder. "I guess you'll be finding out soon enough, bud."

Jayden shrugged and took a sip of champagne. But he didn't contradict Eddie either.

Laurent bit into the shrimp skewer. A perfect blend of ginger, cumin, turmeric, cardamom, and hot pepper melted on his tongue. Yeah, Jayden was definitely planning on putting a ring on Cait's finger. Smart man. He glanced over at Cait and Hailey. Both of them gorgeous, smart, accomplished ladies. What kind of idiot *wouldn't* want to have a woman like that by his side for the long run?

Though maybe it wasn't that simple. Maybe there was some sort of it factor that made you one hundred percent certain *she* was the girl for you and no one else.

"When did you know, captain?" he blurted.

Eddie frowned. "Know what?"

"That Hailey was the one?"

"Aw, you getting sentimental, Gilly?"

"I always get sentimental at weddings. Must be the food." He tore the last piece of shrimp from the toothpick. "But seriously, when did you know?"

Everyone on the team knew that Hailey and Eddie had been high school sweethearts, and their marriage was rock solid. Meeting that young and staying together.... Still, Eddie couldn't have known in juniors that he was going to marry her.

"Actually, we broke up after I made the show," Eddie said. "The pressure got to me. I was supposed to play in Vancouver while she finished her studies, but I don't have to tell you the league doesn't give a shit. I got traded here, and the distance was too much. But then I realized I was miserable without her. Like a part of me was missing and no amount of partying or winning games made it better. I think that's when I knew."

"So, you didn't grow apart? That's got to be rare when you get together in high school."

"We were just teenagers, yeah. But Hailey knows me

better than anyone. I mean... If she loved you when you were a dumb, awkward, zit-faced kid, she'll stick with you to the end."

"I hear that," Jayden said.

They clinked glasses. Laurent shook his head. "What the hell do you mean? You and Cait have been together for a year."

Jayden rubbed the back of his neck, his biggest tell that he was uncomfortable. "She's my sister's best friend from middle school. She knew me back in the day and, well... She had a massive crush on me, but I had no clue."

Laurent nearly spit out his champagne. "Are you serious? Tabarnak, I've always known you were only firing on three cylinders, but..."

"Shut up," Jayden shot back, though he was trying not to laugh himself. "And you can never tell Cait I told you this, all right? Yes, I was a total idiot, but at that age, who isn't?"

Who, indeed? Laurent tapped the end of the toothpick against the plate as he sank into his own memories of that time. What hadn't he seen? What had he missed that was right in front of him?

Lorelei.

She knew him better than anyone. During his third year, when Laurent had confronted the other vets over the way they'd punished the rookies after a blow-out loss, they'd threatened to have him benched for not being a team player. They'd claimed it would be good for team bonding, but that was a load of bullshit.

And only Lorelei had seen that. When he'd sneaked into her window and broken down, she'd gathered him close, soothed him with her words, then somehow it had escalated into more. They hadn't slept together since before

Sandrine, but he had broken up with her, specifically because Sandrine didn't understand why he was making such a big deal out of the situation.

And nothing had stopped him and Lorelei from acting on their raging hormones.

After that night, he'd known he wanted more than friendship with Lorelei. But the end of the school year hadn't been far off. Hockey pulled him one way, and she'd been bound and determined to leave to see as much of the world as she could. Their paths were diverging, only to converge, in the following years, at unpredictable intervals.

Now that they were once more in each other's orbits, Laurent was right back where he started. Confused. Frustrated. Afraid he might blow everything up in the end simply because he couldn't keep his feelings in check.

Eddie eyed him. "You're awfully quiet all of a sudden. Something on your mind?"

Damn it. There was a good reason Eddie was their captain. He could read every single guy on the team in a glance.

He set his toothpick down and drained his champagne glass. "Nothing I can't deal with later."

———

Hamilton, two days later

Lorelei took a bottle of kombucha from the fridge, then leaned against the counter while she cracked it open. Her gaze fell on the small, pink Pokemon plushie that stood out against the gray upholstery of the chesterfield. The plushie itself was cute, but it hid a secret, something she'd stuffed under there to remove temptation four hours earlier.

Her phone. On off days, it had pretty much become her

worst enemy. Her shifts at The Daily Grind were almost a relief because of Theo's strict no phone policy—even during breaks.

She took a sip of kombucha, gaze still fixed on the pink critter that seemed to be taunting her with its big smile and huge sparkling eyes. She knew she couldn't avoid it forever, but still...

A jangle of keys and the soft thud of the latch distracted her momentarily.

"Lorelei?" David called.

"In the kitchen," she replied.

Her roommate appeared with two cloth bags filled with groceries. "I tried calling you all afternoon!"

She bit her lip and rushed to take the bags from him. "Oh God, I'm so sorry. I thought we were doing the shopping tomorrow. Here, let me put all this away."

She fished out a net of lemons and a sack of chickpeas. David wiped his forehead with his forearm. "That's why I was calling you. I went today because tomorrow, we're leaving for Kingston"

She raised an eyebrow. "Kingston? Doesn't your sister live there?"

"She does, and she just had her baby."

Lorelei stopped to stare at him, chickpeas still in hand. "Oh my God. I thought that wasn't until next month!"

David gave a little bewildered laugh. "Yeah, well, the little rascal decided to come early!"

"Aw, congratulations." She went to give him a hug. "The kid is going to have the best uncles ever. How's the baby? And your sister?"

"They're fine, but they'll be in the hospital for a few days. Since Mason doesn't have a lot of work lined up next week, we thought we'd go and keep my brother-in-law company, help out if we can." He rolled his eyes. "My mother's coming in too. Someone has to stand guard twenty-four seven so she doesn't harass the nursing staff."

"Sounds like fun." She dug in the bag for a pair of avocados. "How long will you be gone?"

"About a week. Sorry to leave you all alone."

She shrugged. "I'll be working anyway."

"Making coffee, or something more stimulating?"

Lorelei pressed her lips together but didn't answer. David's sharp gaze followed her as she put the avocados in a large ceramic fruit bowl on the counter.

"Lore, please tell me you replied to that person who wanted to buy a design from you."

"Well..."

David crossed his arms in front of his chest. "Okay, that's it. Where is that damn phone?"

Lorelei cringed. "Would you believe me if I told you I lost it?"

David glared at her and tapped his foot. Probably what he used to intimidate unruly third graders.

She sighed. "All right. I left it under the pink cushion thingie on the chesterfield."

"You used Jigglypuff to hide your phone? For shame." He stalked toward the chesterfield to retrieve it. "Three missed calls, hmm, I wonder who those were from. Okay missy, let's see that post."

She held out her hand and unlocked her phone, then braced herself before opening her social media feed and tapping on the post David was referring to.

An image of Laurent sprung up. He was standing on the dock at his lake house in his Tabarnak tee-shirt, a wide smile on his face and the blue sky behind him making his eyes even more striking. Her gut clenched. He'd done more than send her a pic, he'd posted the image to his official account and tagged her.

Which had result in a veritable deluge of comments and views on her page, and made her follower count balloon at an alarming rate.

"What was the comment they left?" David pressed.

Lorelei scrolled through the hundred or so replies. "Hey, are you taking commissions?" she read. "Your DMs aren't open."

"Right. So open your fucking DMs already."

Lorelei's eyes widened. "Imagine. You said fuck. I think it's the first time I've heard you curse."

"I'm serious, Lore. I'm not leaving for Kingston until you do. Would you really want to deprive a cute little baby from seeing his uncle for the first time?" His tone softened and he squeezed her shoulder. "Look, what are you so afraid of? This is great news for you."

She nodded slowly. "I know. I know. It's just..."

How could she even explain this to him? Social media had a unique way of messing with her head. And getting so much attention from Laurent's fanbase was great for business, yes, and that was why she'd created an account in the first place. But it was also downright terrifying. It meant people would potentially search online for whatever information they could find, not necessarily with the intent of buying her art.

If she and Laurent had just been friends, she wouldn't care what his fans found out about her. But this weird, messed up gray area they inhabited made everything more complicated. That was the part she couldn't voice out loud. Not to David, not to anyone. And especially not to Laurent, though she'd barely heard from him since he'd left.

He was enjoying a holiday in paradise surrounded by

friends. She was probably far from his mind, and a good thing too.

"People on social media can be total asshats," she finally said. "I like talking face-to-face."

"Great, but your art show at The Daily Grind isn't until next month," David pointed out. "You can't put your side hustle on hold when opportunity knocks because you're afraid of a few idiots."

"Guess not. Can I call you if things get really bad?"

David smiled. "Of course, sweetie. And tonight, I'm going to make some of my world-famous guacamole so we can celebrate your success."

Future success, or so she hoped. She'd never been closer to accomplishing her goal. So why did it feel like she was standing on the edge of a cliff?

Chapter Fourteen

@LAURENTGILL1 THE BEST PRESENTS ARE
HOMEMADE AND A LITTLE NAUGHTY. THANKS TO
@LORELEIWESTCOTTART FOR THE EXCLUSIVE
DESIGN!

Lorelei rolled her shoulders and stretched before setting down her pens. She rose and unclipped her phone from the tripod she'd set up next to her desk, then switched off the camera. Time to edit this reel before packing it in.

These last few days, she'd filmed time-lapses of her paintings and drawings as she worked on them. Twenty-second clips, but they'd gotten quite a lot of views and likes. Yesterday, she'd tried a short video of herself at her desk, which had gotten even more positive reactions. Apparently, people liked to see the artist behind the work.

It might be worth it. Her first client had just commissioned a design for a craft beer label, of all things, which was going to bring in a few hundred dollars. But now she needed to register herself as a business, fill out government paperwork... It was overwhelming. Thrilling. Kind of terrifying, too.

Lying on her bed, she quickly edited the video, chose a sound bite and posted it. There. Now she could finally relax.

She put her classic rock playlist on shuffle, set down her phone and stared up at the ceiling. God, this early-seventies blues stuff hit hard.

Oh yeah, love hurt.

It wasn't even ten o'clock, and though her feet were still killing her from her shift at The Daily Grind, she wasn't tired. No point in going to bed now. She'd only toss and turn for two hours.

The house was too quiet. And she was too restless. Damn it, relaxing was easier said than done in these conditions.

At a ping from her phone, she glanced at her screen. And sat up immediately.

@tanya_sull just followed you!

Oh God. Tanya Sullivan. Mum, only she refused to answer to that title. That couldn't be a coincidence. Though how had she even found Lorelei's account?

She clicked on the handle, and a feed of colorful pottery and stunning mosaic work popped up. Yup. That was her mum, all right.

Shit. She couldn't let this slide. How long had it even been since they'd talked? Maybe this was a sort of peace offering. With a sigh, she unlocked her screen and scrolled through her contacts before pressing the call button.

The tone rang only once. "Lorelei?"

"Hey. What are you sayin'?"

"It's good to hear from you. How've you been?"

Tanya's voice hadn't changed. Deep and slow, as if she chose every single word with intent, even with chit-chat.

"Fine, I guess," she replied. "I spent some time in Cape Breton when I got back from Australia, but I'm in Hamilton now."

"Yes." No expression of shock. No question of how or why Lorelei might go back. Just simple affirmation. "Rich told me."

Her *father*? What the hell? Her parents didn't even send each other birthday cards. After Tanya had moved out when Lorelei was nine, her only interactions with Dad had been on a strict, need-to-know basis. "You and Dad talked?"

Tanya laughed lightly. "Can you believe it? But I cleaned out the house before moving and I realized I'd kept some jewelry his mother had given me when we got married. It was lying in a box somewhere, and I haven't worn it for years, so I called him to see if he wanted it back. For the girls, maybe."

The girls, as in her stepsisters, Evie and Alex. Lorelei rubbed her hand over her face. "You were going to give them Nana's jewelry?"

"Well, yes. I didn't think you'd be interested in dusty old lockets and pearls. But your father told me it should go to you."

Not even a minute into their phone call, and Lorelei already had something to feel aggravated about. Why wouldn't Tanya even ask her first? True, Dad had married Evie and Alex's mother seven years ago. And yeah, on the rare occasions Lorelei wore jewelry, she did prefer fun, flashy vintage pieces.

But she'd been close to Nana. Her grandmother had

become her confidante after Tanya walked out, the only motherly figure she could count on. At the very least, Tanya had to know how much her death, a year before Lorelei had left for Australia, had affected her.

Lorelei clenched her fist around her phone and willed herself to breathe. If she flew off the handle now she would only end up crying with Tanya treating her like a child. God, she'd had more than enough of that last time they'd fought.

She settled for a more practical observation. "Did you say something about moving?"

"I moved to Saint-Jean-Port-Joli three months ago," Tanya replied breezily, as if it was no big deal to pack up her whole life in New Brunswick only to plop it back down somewhere else. But that was Tanya for you.

"You live in Quebec now? Jesus."

"I was offered a wonderful position in a craftsman's circle. It's done wonders to improve my French, and it means I can help out with the occasional English tourist."

Lorelei nodded slowly. So her mother was making a fresh start. Again.

"Enough about me. Rich told me about the art you've been creating and your social media account."

"I didn't even know he was aware of the account, to be honest. Evie must have mentioned it."

Lorelei got along fine with Alex, but she was closer to Evie even though they were a few years apart. Evie loved art, and often asked Lorelei what she was working on. The same couldn't be said about Dad.

"In any case, I'm proud of you, Lorelei. You have so much creative potential. It would be tragic if you wasted it. We've always been alike in that way."

No arguing there. Lorelei had always taken after her.

She even looked like Tanya, with her reddish curls and dark eyes.

"I try my best," she said simply.

"Keep at it. But don't ever compromise your vision."

Lorelei almost laughed. Typical Tanya. "That's such a you thing to say. I feel like I was still in grade school when you first told me that."

"Oh, that reminds me, I still have a box of your old art supplies. What should I do with them?"

Lorelei's cheeks burned. All things considered, it had been pretty shitty of her to dump all that stuff at Tanya's house with no plans to retrieve them. "You should have told me you were moving."

"You weren't anywhere close by. I didn't see the point."

"Well, I'm still not close by. I don't know if I can take time off work to come get them..."

"Work? What do you mean?"

"Dad didn't tell you that part, huh? I have a job at a coffee shop."

Silence on the other end. Of course. Tanya didn't have to tell her she disapproved of her daughter serving lattes and scrubbing toilets instead of creating. Lorelei bit the inside of her cheeks. Fuck, she hated this need to justify herself.

"Gotta pay the bills somehow," she grumbled.

"I suppose," Tanya said with a little sigh. "Well, let me know. It would be a shame to throw those supplies out. And you can sort through your grandmother's jewelry."

Was this her mother's way of inviting her over? She'd never say anything like "I miss you" or "I want to see you." Emotional blackmail, Tanya called it. Imposing your feelings on someone else and curtailing their freedom. The very reason why she'd left her husband and daughter without so much as an apology or even a real explanation.

But that was over and done with now. Water under the bridges and all that. Why stir up painful memories?

"I'll see what I can do," she said. "We'll be talkin', Tanya."

After hanging up, she stared at the blank screen of her phone. Something tightened in her chest and weighed down her stomach. Fuck, she wished David and Mason were there. She needed to clear her head, rather than let her thoughts become even more tangled.

She went down to the living room. No better time to crash on the chesterfield, watch *The Office* for the hundredth time and scroll on her phone until she was numb.

With the soothing hum of her favorite comfort series in the background and random images of art and exotic holiday locations popping up in front of her eyes, her mind wandered toward Laurent. He hadn't posted any pictures of the wedding or Hawaii, and he hadn't liked any of her posts either. Maybe he was on a self-imposed social media break. But shit, she missed the regular reminder of his presence.

She missed him, period. When was he even coming back?

Her phone pinged again, a new DM from someone she didn't know replying to her post.

> @user222907: stay away from Gilly fatass

She stared at the message. Read it twice. Her thumb moved to the block button before she even really registered it.

Fuck this. She resisted the urge to throw her phone across the room. As if it hadn't been enough to talk to her mother, the only person in the world who managed to make her feel like a silly, stupid teenager all over again.

But shit, she wasn't going to let some troll on the Internet send her down that sort of spiral all over again. Self-loathing, wondering if she would ever be good enough.

Laurent wanted her. *Her*, not some jealous stalker fangirl. And maybe it was petty and dumb, but she needed to make sure that he still did, to see it in words, to feel it in the way he touched her and stripped her naked and fucked her like he couldn't get enough.

She opened their conversation and started typing.

> Hey you, hope you had fun in Hawaii. LMK when you get back.

"Did you have pleasant stay, sir? I hope you found everything to your liking."

Laurent forced a smile. God, his head felt like it was going to split in half. "Great."

That would have to do. Objectively, the stay had been fantastic, and the wedding, as well. Fancy, yet casual to fit the tropical setting. Colorful, exotic flowers contrasted with linen. Gilded chandeliers hanging from rough wood embellished with gauzy fabric that floated on the ocean breeze. Max in the center of the dance floor, gathering his new wife in his arms spinning with her while she pretended to protest. He'd never seen his teammate so happy.

If only all that shit with Colby and Gabby hadn't gone down.

He dug into his pocket for his key card and slipped it

over the counter to the desk clerk. She glanced up from her keyboard to thank him and kept typing away. Good thing she wasn't taking too close a look at his face. Beyond a splitting headache, the bruise on his jaw where Colby had landed one throbbed like a mother. Tabarnak, at least the fucking idiot would spend the rest of the summer with a shiner.

As for what would happen when the season started again...

Fuck. He didn't even want to think about it. The last thing the team needed was bad blood messing up the room, but he sure as hell wouldn't make nice and reach out to Colby. Not after Colby had all but accused him of moving in on Gabby. It was friendship, pure and simple. Comfort. Because she'd needed a shoulder and he'd been there. If he thought about it, the scene had probably looked bad from Colby's point of view, but shit. Colby was the reason behind Gabby's upset in the first place.

As for supposedly sneaking around with his girl, Colby ought to know Laurent better than that.

"You're all set, sir," the clerk said with a smile. "We hope to see you again soon at Kahala."

He nodded. "Have a good one."

Grabbing the handle of his suitcase, he moved to one of the large white chairs grouped in the waiting area. He needed to order an Uber, though his flight wasn't for a couple of hours. A few guests were crossing the lobby to go to breakfast, but it was early enough that he wouldn't risk running into any of his teammates given how late they'd partied last night.

Once seated, he took out his phone. He'd switched it to airplane mode on arrival in Hawaii, a sort of digital detox to clear his head. Not that it had done him much good.

Because he hadn't stopped thinking about Lorelei for a second. Missing her. Wishing she was here.

That was why he and Gabby had grown closer this week. She knew what it felt like to be head over heels for someone who kept their heart locked up tight.

That girl who you're fucking, the one who sends you dirty pics, isn't she your friend too? Does she find it comforting to climb on your cock?

God, just a few words and he'd completely lost his shit. And not only because Colby was acting like a dick. In fact, his teammate had voiced the very thing Laurent didn't want to accept—that Lorelei might see their relationship differently. That maybe she was really just a friend who wanted to scratch an itch.

Enough of that bullshit. He didn't want any more of this friends-with-benefits crap. Seeing his buddies with their girls had made it painfully clear. He wanted to be with Lorelei. *Really* be with her.

So what now? Well, now, he had to go back to reality. And switch his phone on.

"Good morning, Laurent."

He looked up. Shawntelle Alexander was heading his way, heels clicking across the marble floor. Even though it was technically the offseason, her crisp, white blouse and linen slacks were sharp and professional as ever.

She eyed his suitcase. "You checking out already?"

"I figured I'd get to the airport early. No use hanging around here."

Shawntelle raised an eyebrow, and her gaze landed briefly on his bruised jaw. "Put a hockey player in a fancy tux, he's still a hockey player. I trust you'll put the rest of the month to good use in training."

"I plan to. What about you, are you back at work already?"

"I'm on my way to breakfast," she said with a smile. "But now that you mention it, I'd like to talk to about opening ourselves more to the francophone media."

He chuckled. "Tabarnak. You sure about that?"

"That's another thing." Shawntelle took a seat next to him. "That tee-shirt of yours got quite a positive reaction online."

His throat suddenly constricted. "Yeah. I saw that."

"You know the artist who made it. Do you think she'd be open to selling us the design so we can do something with it?"

No fucking way, that was *his* tee-shirt. Lorelei had made it just for him. It wasn't a novelty item to be mass produced, sold in the team store and worn fans for a season until some other fad caught on. He hated the idea. And if he did, Lorelei would absolutely despise it.

Or would she? Would a generous offer change her mind? After all, she was trying to get her business off the ground.

"I don't know, to be honest. You'd have to ask her."

"Right. Could you give me her contact info?"

He unlocked his phone. A notification popped up on the screen. A message from Lorelei. His heart leaped in his chest, but he swiped it away to give Shawntelle the information she needed.

"Thank you, Laurent." Shawntelle stood and smoothed her blouse. "I trust you'll tell Ms. Wescott we want to contact her?"

Jesus Christ. His head pounded even harder. He managed a small nod. "Sure thing."

"Have a good trip home."

Yeah, twelve hours with nothing to distract him from his thoughts but inane movies and booze. Perfect. Though it would be far worse when he actually got to Hamilton.

Seeing Lorelei again would tear him apart. He couldn't pretend everything was cool. And he definitely shouldn't sleep her with her before telling her how he really felt. But shit, how was he supposed to resist her if she wanted him? Through pain and confusion and anger, the hunger was still there, nagging him, growing stronger with each passing day.

Fuck it. He opened her text.

> Hey you, hope you had fun in Hawaii. LMK when you get back.

Sydney, Nova Scotia, ten years earlier

The keyboards of an old Queen song blasted in her headphones, the synthesized tones upbeat and catchy. Yet Lorelei frowned at her sketch pad. Maybe she should just give up on humans altogether.

Or faces, at least.

What ought to have been Freddie Mercury—she'd put on *A Night at the Opera* for inspiration—looked like someone else entirely. Giving him a mustache had changed nothing. The face staring back at her had heavy brows, piercing eyes, and a strong chin.

She suppressed an urge to scribble over her work. Her art was trying to send her a message, and she didn't like what it was telling her.

Best friend like the song said. Best *friend*. So why couldn't she get him out of her head? Maybe she just needed to indulge her whim and draw Laurent. Intentionally. With her luck, he might turn into someone else. Someone less complicated.

She swiped at the page, a shadow here, a highlight there. Nope. She still had a goalie and not a rockstar.

A muffled scraping sound broke through the music. Her pencil point snapped on the page, and a jagged line marred the portrait. Heart hammering, she looked toward her bedroom window for the source of the interruption.

Her eyes widened. Shit.

As if her thoughts had summoned him, Laurent was folding his body under the sash. Over a year had passed since the last time he'd tried this. He was bigger now, his shoulders, and chest filling out to catch up with his limbs, until he barely fit.

Mindful of her dad snoring in the other bedroom, she ripped off her headphones and jumped to her feet.

"What do you think you're doing?" She fought to keep her tone low.

He straightened. "I didn't mean to scare you. I texted the password."

Her phone was buried somewhere in a corner under a pile of clothes. She barely paid attention to it anymore. He hadn't texted the password since Sandrine... God, Little Miss Perfect. The last person Lorelei wanted to think about.

"I'm going to be in deep shit if my dad catches you in here."

"I'm sorry." He looked up at the ceiling for a moment. "You... you don't happen to have any weed on you?"

Something about the way he was carrying himself was off. His shoulders were rounded, and his back kind of curled in on itself. She remembered that stance. The last time she'd seen it he'd been lit up like a Christmas tree. But his team hadn't played tonight.

"Can't help you there. I'm all out. Is... Did something happen?"

His expression solidified into something so bleak, a shiver passed through her. "No." His tone was as dull and lifeless as his gaze. "It wasn't just one thing. It was many things. I... I don't know where to start."

She moved closer, not quite touching him, but within arm's reach. "What sent you over here? Just now, I mean."

"Sandrine."

Oh shit. That felt like a dagger stabbing her in the chest. "What about her?"

"We broke up."

Oh God. Oh God. Why was he here to tell her this?

He doesn't know.

He didn't because she kept certain things hidden away in the farthest corner of her heart. And she wasn't about to confess anything now of all times.

"Were you in love with her?" She asked the question carefully. She didn't want to hear the answer, but she also had to know, because she couldn't find any other reason for how distraught he was acting.

"No."

She let out a breath, hoping he didn't notice. "Then why?"

"She couldn't give me what I need."

"She couldn't give you..." Hot rage boiled up inside her. "Get out. If you think you can come over here for a pity fuck, and I'll happily lie down and give you whatever you want..."

He flinched as if she'd struck him. "*No!* Tabarnak!"

She froze, one ear cocked for any sign of her dad stirring. "Keep your voice down," she hissed. "Do you want to get caught?"

"Maybe I do."

She shook her head. "I don't have the slightest fucking clue what you're talking about."

He turned to one side and stared up at the ceiling. "When I said she couldn't give me what I needed, all I meant was I need someone to talk to. Someone who will listen. Someone who gets it."

Some of the tension drained out of her. "I can do that."

She sat on the end of her bed and patted the space beside her. "Sit. We'll talk."

He remained where he was. "It's all so fucked up."

"What is?"

He muttered something under his breath. French. Incomprehensible. But then he jumped into his story. "Last weekend we played in Moncton."

"I remember." She hadn't asked him for the grim details. Word had gone around school on its own. The Screaming Eagles had suffered a blow-out. Opinions were divided over who was at fault. She'd overheard comments about that frog goalie and how bad he sucked, but the performance of some of the rookies had also been sub-par.

"We played like shit." He delivered that in a monotone. Just the facts ma'am. "Some of the older guys decided to fix it."

"And?"

His lips moved, but he didn't go on. Couldn't he find the right words or had the scene been that bad?

"You don't have to pretend in front of me," she said gently. "Whatever you need to let out... Your secret's safe with me. Your secrets have always been safe with me."

He swallowed. "This kind of shit isn't supposed to happen anymore. Do you know what the hot box is?"

"No." But she definitely didn't like how he'd said that. Or spit, more like. The same way he said *tabarnak* when he was really, really pissed off.

"It's an initiation thing."

"But—Wait, don't you do that shit at the beginning of the season?"

"Usually, yeah." He pushed a hand through his short hair, making it stand on end. "We did this year, too."

"It's all so stupid." She'd heard rumors of shark piss in cheap motel rooms and making the young guys walk into the store in their underwear to buy two-fours.

"It's supposed to teach the rookies to respect the vets. It's supposed to bond the team." An edge of sarcasm cut through his tone. "Anyway, on the trip back, a couple of them decided we didn't do a good enough job this year. They said the kids were soft. That we needed to toughen them up. That we didn't break them in."

"Break them in," she echoed. Holy shit. These were boys, not animals.

His gaze turned upward, and he blinked. Hard. "Do you know how many hours it is to Moncton?"

She did a quick calculation in her head. "Five? Something like that?"

"When the roads are good." He blinked again. "Now imagine doing most of that locked in the toilet on the bus with four other guys. With the heat turned all the way up. And you're naked."

"That's..." She twisted her fingers together, searching for the right word. "That's barbaric."

Fuck, she *couldn't* imagine what it might be like for a guy, but if she put herself in their shoes... Hugging herself, trying not to let her boobs touch anyone else. Or her ass... Nausea turned her gut over.

"No shit." He crossed to her dresser, picked up a stray pen, put it down.

"And no one said anything? Where were the coaches?"

"At the front of the bus, ignoring it."

Jesus, it was just getting worse. "What about the other guys?"

"Nope."

She tried to hold onto his gaze, but he looked away. "I don't believe that."

"That's what hockey teaches you. Didn't you know that?" Again, that hard edge of sarcasm. "Respect the vets. Don't make waves. Team above everything else. And fit in."

She knew all about fitting in—or more accurately, not fitting in. But she also knew Laurent. He still wouldn't meet her gaze, even though she ducked her head to meet it. "You spoke up."

He blew out a stream of air. "For all the good it did. They wanted to shove me in there, too. I told them they'd have to fight me. They backed down."

"Cowards." But she didn't blame them, if the emotion radiating from him meant anything. She couldn't imagine how enraged he'd been in the moment.

He pulled in a deep, shuddering breath. "It wasn't enough." His voice broke. "I didn't do enough. I couldn't stop them. I—"

A sob cut him off.

She launched herself off the bed and pulled him into her arms. His face settled into the crook of her neck, and for a long moment, he convulsed in her embrace. Ignoring the sting in her own eyes, she ran her palms down his back. Over and over. Soothing. She hoped.

He raised his head and swiped at his eyes, leaving only hard, glittering anger. "I want to quit this fucking sport."

With that statement he sent her back two years ago, when he'd told her how his dad had passed on. How he'd been unsure he'd done the right thing. How his family had talked him into seeing it through.

While she didn't blame him now, she couldn't let him throw his future away. "Don't you think you should play out the rest of the season? The year's almost over."

"And after that?" he snapped. "It brings out the worst in people. It attracts girls who only chase the guys for their status."

Oh God, they were back to Sandrine.

"Do you know what she said?" he added. "She said it was no big deal."

Bitch. Lorelei only just stopped herself from saying it out loud. Sandrine shouldn't be the focus here. "You know what the sport needs if it's going to change? It needs good people sticking with it. Nothing's going to change if those who are willing to fight this shit drop out."

"That's the problem. I didn't fight. Not enough."

"But you'll be there to fight another day." She could bring up so many other reasons he shouldn't quit. He was going to the draft in the summer. His family had sacrificed so much to get him here, and they'd tell him to keep going.

She threaded her fingers together at the back of his neck. "Your team sucks. It *sucks*. And I'm not talking about your play. I mean the other guys. Your coaches. But you're not always going to be here."

And, thank God, neither would she. Only a few more months. Graduation couldn't come fast enough. Even if it meant saying good-bye to Laurent.

"You're going to be on a new team, eventually. With better people. And you'll make the most of that. I know you will."

He touched his forehead to hers, eyes closed, and inhaled—like he was breathing her in somehow. Lorelei's heart pounded against her ribs. God, his body, so close, his scent... The feelings she'd managed to bury deep inside resurfaced, igniting a familiar fire.

They held onto the moment, not talking, but the silence crackled with possibilities. Was he waiting for her to make a move? The pounding in her veins accelerated. If she gave in...

Just this once. You both need this. You both want it.

She leaned in and pressed her mouth to his.

Chapter Fifteen

@SHSlut Why does offseason always last forever?
@killerwallofsex Every year. Same thing. I miss the boys.
@lilygilly I'm so tired of pictures of them playing golf. I want to see saves.
@timmytank Want saves? Follow another team.

Hamilton, two days later

Laurent parked his car in front of a yellow townhouse with a tiny, immaculately cut patch of grass in front. Number seventeen. This was it.

He took a deep breath and exited. He could do this. Crisse, he'd once managed a fifty-save shutout against Edmonton. McDavid *and* Draisaitl stopped stone-cold. How much harder could one conversation be?

He made his way to the door. At least this was new

territory. No ghosts of past trysts lurking at every corner. Lorelei had suggested meeting at her place—a return to old habits in a way, given the amount of time they'd spent in her room back in high school.

Still, every time they'd met up at his, they'd ended up with the headboard banging against the wall, so this couldn't be worse. If her roommates were in, he might have a shot at saying his piece without giving in to temptation.

He rang the bell, and a few seconds later, Lorelei swung the door open. Wild red curls, dark eyes, plump lips stretching into a big smile... God, he'd missed her so damn much, and it hadn't even been three weeks.

"Hey, you." His voice was hoarse. Should he hug her like he always did?

She was wearing that damn romper again, the one with the buttons. Fuck, he felt like he was sixteen, gangly and awkward, never knowing what to do with his arms. Finally, he leaned in and sort of hugged one side of her.

"Hey, you." Though her smile never faltered, a line etched itself between her brows. "You look tired. Still jet-lagged?"

"Yeah, I guess."

Taking his hand, she led him inside. "How was the wedding?"

Incredible. Awful. Uplifting. Heart-wrenching. "Great."

Her gaze landed on his bruised jaw, but she simply pulled him down the hallway.

"David and Mason aren't home. They went to Kingston because David's sister just had a baby. Not that you care about any of that, but anyway." Her tone was breathless, almost nervous and rambly. "Shall I show you the house?"

Alone.

That single word was all he could focus on. A few more threads escaped the fraying edge of his nerves. With no one else in the house, he couldn't hold back thoughts of how easy it was to rip that romper off.

She gestured to the left. "So this is what David calls his study, but it's basically an extra room where we store random stuff. And here we have the living area and kitchen."

He stopped for a moment, eyes wide. "Why are there so many plushies in here?"

"David and Mason collect them. They're Pokemon, mostly."

He had to laugh. At least a hundred colorful creatures sat in various poses on shelves or random pieces of furniture. "Now I've seen everything."

She nudged his shoulder with hers. "It's not any weirder than those mancaves filled with Steelhawks memorabilia."

"Guess not."

Her grip on his hand loosened, and he resisted the urge to squeeze her fingers tighter. "Can I get you something to drink?"

"I'm good, thanks."

She nodded and bit her lip. "You want to see my room then?"

Her room. *Tabarnak*.

He should sit her down now and start talking. There was no way he'd fuck her with those freaky plush toys watching. But shit, curiosity poked at him. He remembered the tiny bedroom in Sydney where she'd listened to classic rock, smoked up, and created art. Had she done something to this room, like paint another mural? Either way, it was *her* space, not David and Mason's.

He forced a smile. "Sure thing."

She led the way up the stairs. Crisse, the way that flimsy cotton molded her ass was criminal. *Resist. That's not what you're here for.*

At the top of the stairway, she tossed a glance over her shoulder. Caught him looking. And put an extra swing in her step. His breath caught in his throat. Fucking shit, they weren't even in her room yet, and his resolve was already nearing breaking point.

She opened the first door off the top of the stairs. "So, this is me."

Yeah, it was her. A smile, a real one this time, fought its way to his lips. Sunshine filtered through the tree leaves outside and poured in the window. A striking pattern of red, orange and royal blue striped the bedspread, and a few art posters brightened up the white walls. Opposite the bed was Lorelei's desk with her computer and tablet and a rainbow stack of markers in a plastic tray.

"It's not so different from your room back in high school," he noted. "Though you've gotten better at organizing your markers."

She sat on the bed. "I have to. Drawing and painting is serious business now. Some guy hired me to design something after I posted the Tabarnak tee-shirt."

He turned towards her. "Seriously? That's great."

"Yeah. It's for a beer label."

He laughed. "Making honest money. I'll be sure to ask the team caterers to stock your beer instead of Molson."

"Don't joke around. I'm trying not to have conniptions, and you know how much I hate social media but..." She took a deep breath. "I mean, it's something. Plus, I have my art show at the coffee shop in three weeks."

Finally, her talent was being recognized. About damn time. "Lots happening for you, then. Speaking of which,

Shawntelle Alexander is in charge of PR for the Hawks, and she asked me for your number."

Her eyes widened. "She did?"

"Yup. So I guess they'll be calling you soon. That's exciting."

"It is. But it's still work. There are other things I find a lot more exciting." Her gaze locked with his. "Aren't you going to sit?"

No need to guess what was on her mind. His heart beat against his ribs. Right. He wasn't going to do this standing, anyway.

He sat at the opposite end, far enough to avoid contact. Confusion clouded her gaze for a moment before she scooted closer. Oh fuck, he needed to stop her, stop *this*, because already the heat from her body, her scent, the way her teeth pulled at that plumb bottom lip, all of it was making blood rush from his brain to his cock.

"Lore, I..."

She lifted her hand to graze the side of his jaw. "How did you get that bruise?"

"Got in a fight with one of the guys." He shook his head. That didn't even begin to cover it. Throwing punches was one thing, but at a teammate's wedding? And with someone he'd been playing with for years? "It's a long story."

She frowned. "Oh fuck. You mean with a teammate? Things must have been really bad if you came to blows."

"Yeah, Colby... He's got his own shit to deal with. He thought I was hitting on his girl."

She gently cupped his jaw. "Does it still hurt?"

He closed his eyes and leaned into her warm palm. God, that sensation alone could completely undo him. He hadn't felt that sort of touch since that fateful night in high school, the last time they'd slept together before he left, when he was hurting so badly, and Lorelei had offered him comfort.

Yeah, it fucking hurt. Not his jaw, everything else. And shit, he knew it would hurt even worse if he didn't push her away, but he couldn't. *Just one last time, if it comes to that. Just a few more minutes.*

He caught her hand and pulled her to him. Their lips met in a slow, deep kiss, and she moaned into his mouth, arching her back to press against him. His palms found their way up her smooth thighs, over the curve of her waist, down to her ass. She moaned again and slipped her fingers under his tee-shirt to skate over his chest. Lifting the hem with every stroke until he broke the kiss and raised his arms to get rid of it altogether.

Her clouded gaze roamed over his chest before she leaned in to kiss him again, more hungrily this time, licking and nipping his bottom lip. He could no longer think, no longer speak. She was everywhere, around him, in him, permeating his senses.

More. He needed more. More skin, more softness, more heat. His fingers fumbled at the buttons of her romper and popped them open.

Finally, her breasts spilled free and he caught the pointed tip with his mouth, teasing it with his teeth.

She threw her head back with a whimper. "Yes. Yes, yes… Oh God…"

He wrapped his lips around it and sucked, eliciting another string of breathy cries. He could never get enough. Tasting her, hearing how much pleasure he gave her, feeling her go higher and higher and taking him with her, every damn time.

He let the wet, swollen peak fall from his lips and

switched his attention to her other breast. She raked her fingers in his hair, urging him on.

"Please, Laurent... Please, I need you..."

She pushed him back to wriggle out of her romper and underwear, then lay back on the bed. Fuck, she was so beautiful, all creamy skin and curves, he was going to lose his goddamn mind just looking at her.

"Touch me," she panted. "Please, I'll do whatever you ask. I'll be good."

"I know how good you can be."

Fuck, he could live a hundred years and never see something more erotic than Lorelei leaning against the wall, hands tied with his leather belt, slick with his cum. It was almost unbearable, this hold she had on him. Even when he was the one calling the shots.

He slid his hand to the reddish curls between her legs. "Right now, I just want to give you all the pleasure you deserve."

―――

Lorelei gazed up at Laurent. His muscles were tense, his face flushed, his blue-green eyes searing with desire. It knocked the breath straight out of her.

Something had changed, some kind of subtle shift. But what? Lust fogged her thoughts, clouded her senses, pushed any shred of reason away.

And then he thrust a finger inside her, and there was nothing beyond the delicious sensation of being filled and stretched. Her hips jerked to meet his hand, and when he added a second finger, her hands twisted in the sheets.

"Keep going," she moaned. "Oh God, that's so good. Make me come."

He thrust deeper, faster, and burning ripples of pleasure spread throughout her body, pulsing then receding. She bucked her hips to take him deeper still, but somehow, she couldn't reach her peak. Not like this. Not when he was still half-dressed.

She stilled his hand. "I need all of you. Now."

"Lorelei..."

She traced her hands along the waistband of his jeans, then stroked his erection through the thick fabric. "Fuck me. *Please*. You know I'll beg, if you want me to."

"Beg?" he growled. "No games this time. I'm fucking helpless when I see like you this. You think I could deny you? I'll do anything, ma belle, anything to make you cry out my name, even if it kills me."

He unbuttoned his jeans, and she grabbed a condom from the drawer in her nightstand, ripping it open and rolling it down his cock as soon as he'd freed himself. Fuck, she was so desperate for him that the deep, aching throb in her core made her wince and sent her limbs trembling. She couldn't wait another second. He positioned himself over her, and she wrapped her legs around his waist, hips rising to meet his cock. He plunged in one forceful stroke, and stars exploded in her field of vision. Her eyelids slammed shut.

He stopped. "No, look at me."

She opened her eyes again. "What?"

He leaned down to kiss her and started to move again, hitting deeper. Something lit his gaze; something soft and burning and painful...

"Look at me, Lorelei."

Oh God, what was happening? She lost herself in his eyes, in the slick, sweaty friction of their bodies, and with each powerful thrust she was getting closer, spirals of pure pleasure unraveling until they reached further and further inside. Finally, they gathered in her core in a burst of pure bliss, and she cried out, but still Laurent never tore his gaze away, even as his movements grew more frantic. At last, a hoarse groan tore from his throat, and he collapsed, grasping her hips, fingers digging into her skin.

For a few moments, nothing quick shallow breaths filled the room. Then Laurent rolled away and took off the condom. She stared up at the ceiling, not daring to move or speak. It had never been this intense before. They had connected on another level, beyond mind-blowing pleasure. They'd stripped each other bare.

And Laurent... He simply lay there too. No cuddling, no kissing her. Just covering his face with his hands, his chest heaving.

Lorelei turned toward him, inching her hand closer, not daring to touch him yet. "Laurent, what's wrong?"

He waited a few moments before wrenching his hands away. Lips pressed together, brows furrowed. "I can't do this anymore."

Her entire body went cold, inside and out. "What... what are you talking about?"

Shit. Was he about to tell her he'd met someone else? Maybe there'd been something behind that fight with his teammate. Some girl, he'd said. What if Laurent really had gone after a teammate's girlfriend?

Her throat tightened. Why had she thrown herself at him like some pathetic idiot when she felt something was off?

Indulging in their mutual desire was supposed to make things better. For him, and for her. Because she needed it just as much as he did.

"The whole friends with benefits thing," he said. "It has to stop. It's fucking with my head."

She wrapped herself in the bedspread and tried to make sense of the situation. "Okay. So you're saying you want us to stop having sex and go back to being just friends."

God, just voicing it out loud was like plunging a dagger into her gut. She'd have to respect Laurent's decision, but giving up the incredible, mind-blowing connection they had in bed...

But then what the hell had she been expecting? It had to end sooner or later. It had before. Twice. And the first time, another girl had come between them. Shit, maybe this time, too. Being someone's fuck buddy was never a long-term arrangement.

Laurent straightened and shook his head. "This was more than just sex. And I can't just be friends with you. Not anymore. I want us to be together, Lore. For real this time."

Her heart froze in her chest. Then started beating again, hard, as if it was warning her that danger was imminent.

She gaped at him. "Wait. Wait, when did this happen? When did you change your mind?"

"I've been thinking about it for a while, but the wedding..."

The wedding he'd sort of invited her to, blithely unaware that she would stick out like a sore thumb. And now he'd come back with a change of heart and a busted jaw.

"Jesus, Laurent, what the hell happened in Hawaii? It must have been more than that one fight."

He looked at her, finally. And his blue-green eyes burned with defiance. "It just clarified things. I'm tired of fucking around, and I don't want to waste any more time."

The words hit her like a slap in the face. "Fucking around and wasting time? Is that what we've been doing?"

He swung his legs over the side of the bed and grabbed his boxer briefs. "Come on, you know I didn't mean it like that." He looked at her over her shoulder, his gaze almost angry now. "Calisse, do I have to spell it out? I want to take you on dates and have you wait for me in the family lounge after games and introduce you as my girlfriend. I've waited long enough."

His girlfriend, who would wear his jersey and attend Steelhawks events. Smiling with the other wives and girlfriends at charity events for the photo ops. Like she belonged with them. Play the part she was supposed to play. Get hate online from angry fans who didn't like the way she looked. Panic seized her and sent her pulse into overdrive until her head swam.

"Look. Slow down for a moment," she said in a shaky voice. "You just got back from a wedding. Seeing your friends with their wives and girlfriends and fiancées, maybe that tricked you into thinking..."

"Tricked me?" He stood and yanked his jeans back on. "Tabarnak, you think I'm still some fucking confused teenager? I told you what I want, plain and simple. Do you want the same?"

She wanted to be with Laurent, yes. When they were together, just the two of them, she could truly be herself and still feel cherished. But being his official girlfriend came with a whole lot of extra baggage. It wouldn't be just the two of them. Not anymore. "I... I..."

He grabbed his shirt. "Right. I get it."

Her eyes stung, and her chin wobbled. Fuck it, this was all wrong. A few minutes, they'd been so close, closer than she thought she could be to anyone, and now it was like the earth had opened up, creating a massive gulf between them.

She wiped furiously at the tears that threatened to spill over. "What the hell do you want me to say? You spring this on me right after sex, and I don't even have a second to think. You're pushing too hard. Just... give me some space."

"Space. Yeah, that's all you ever wanted." He clenched his jaw and nodded. "Well, you know where to find me."

He turned and left. She wanted to run after him. To tell him to stay. Because sitting alone, naked in bed, staring at the empty side of the mattress Laurent had occupied not a moment before, was tearing a hole through her heart.

But how could she blame him for leaving? He was giving her exactly what she'd asked for.

Chapter Sixteen

@THEDAILYGRIND ICYMI NEW ART EXHIBIT COMING SOON. STOP IN AND TRY SOMETHING DIFFERENT.

"Order up for Chrissie." Lorelei handed the cup to a brunette with oversized glasses hiding half her face. "Here you go. Enjoy."

Fucking useless. The woman didn't even look up from her phone. But an unfailingly friendly tone was company policy.

Lorelei went back to her station next to her coworker, one of the only people she'd met at The Daily Grind she actually got along with. Deidre had bright multicolored braids, and they'd bonded over their love of the Pantone color chart in the break room.

"You here until closing?" Deidre asked.

Lorelei sighed and wiped a drop of oat milk off the counter. "Only five hours to go, but I'm off tomorrow. You?"

"Clocking out in an hour. You got this, girl."

Lorelei smiled. She didn't want to tell Deidre that no matter how much she hated working at The Daily Grind, the thought of having an entire day off at home filled her with cold dread. Because a day off meant a day of glancing at her phone every ten minutes, wondering if she should call Laurent, talking herself into doing it before backtracking. Lather, rinse, repeat.

Was this what teetering on the edge of sanity was? This going in circles in her head, unable to get in the zone to tap into her creative energy and produce art? She wanted Laurent, yes, but she would undoubtedly fuck things up for both of them if she became his girlfriend, and where would that leave them? On the other hand, she missed him like crazy, and the thought of him blocked everything else.

The whole thing was toxic and messed up and just too much to deal with. Unlike making lattes and selling vegan muffins.

"Excuse me, you messed up my order."

Or maybe not. Lorelei turned. The woman with the sunglasses had returned to the counter with her cup. "This isn't almond milk."

Lorelei switched on her customer service smile. Neutral. Polite. Something designed not to ruffle feathers. "I'm sorry, I must have misunderstood. I thought you asked for oat milk."

The woman snorted and plonked the cup down. Coffee sloshed from under the lid onto the clean counter. "I never get oat milk. It's always almond milk. Now make me another one. God, I don't know why I keep coming here. You're always fucking up my drinks."

Lorelei inhaled, every muscle tense with the effort to keep her smile intact. "I'll get right on that for you."

Hands shaking, she turned to make another drink. All the while she could feel *Chrissie*'s gaze on her back. God, she had the perfect name too, so close to crisse. Laurent would get a kick out of that.

Don't think about him. Just don't.

"Jesus, could you move your fat ass?" the woman snapped. "I'm in a hurry."

Lorelei's fists clenched. Enough was enough. If she finished this drink, it would end up straight in the bitch's face.

Deidre placed a hand on her shoulder. "Take a break," she muttered under her breath. "I'll handle it."

Lorelei whipped around and stomped into the break room, blood pounding in her head, face blazing, chest tight with suppressed rage. *Breathe. Just breathe.* She collapsed onto a plastic chair, leaned her head against the wall, and closed her eyes. *Inhale. Exhale. Count to ten.*

"Lorelei? Why are you in here? You know the rules, no unscheduled breaks."

She opened her eyes again and straightened. Theo. Her pulse kicked up a notch, but she forced down her anger. Getting into it with a customer was one thing, but if she got mouthy with Theo...

"A customer insulted me. Deidre stepped in before it got out of hand."

Theo rolled his eyes. "Good grief, Lorelei. What have we talked about multiple times during briefings? If you want to make it in this business, you need a thicker skin. You can't let the small stuff get you down."

Lorelei clamped down on a laugh. She had zero intention of making it in this business. In fact, as soon as her exhibit was over, she'd be out the door like a rocket.

"You're right, I should focus on what's important," she

replied. "Speaking of which, mind if I come in early to set up for my art exhibit tomorrow?"

Theo raised an eyebrow. "Your art exhibit?"

"Call it whatever you want. I have seven paintings total, but they're small to medium format."

"Oh, right." Theo nodded slowly, but the expression on his face set off warning bells in Lorelei's mind. "Well, I have a friend who's been asking me to display her work for a while, and she's going out of town soon, so I gave her the coming slot. You can put up your stuff next month."

Lorelei blinked. It took a few seconds for Theo's words to work their way through the rushing in her head. Then reality hit, and a strange calm washed over her. Maybe it was liberation. Like a weight had been lifted.

She stood, untied her apron and let it fall to the floor, then headed toward her locker.

"What are you doing?" Theo spluttered as she dialed the combination on the lock.

Without a word, she grabbed her bag from the hook, and marched toward the exit.

"Wait, where the hell do you think you're going?"

"Go fuck yourself, you pathetic asswipe," she shot over her shoulder as she yanked at the doorknob. "I quit."

The metallic door hit the wall with a loud bang, and she was gone. Out past the preparation area, past Deidre who stared at her wide-eyed, past the bitchy customer who was still waiting for her fucking almond milk macchiato with a shot of caramel, past the tables she'd scrubbed clean and those damn green plants and that stupid swirly neon sign hanging on the brick wall that read *Win The Day*. God, another second in this shithole was one too many.

Out on the street, she kept moving. She couldn't stop, couldn't look back, couldn't even wait for the bus to take her home. Fuck staying in one place, fuck waiting, fuck taking a chance thinking that this time, it might just work out.

Tears rose to her eyes. Every time she'd tried to do the right thing, to be patient and mold herself into someone more amenable, it had blown up in her face. Like it was impossible for her to simply find a place where she could be herself and fit in at the same time.

Sure, she did fit in with David and Mason. They made her feel welcome, like she finally had a home of sorts. But since they'd gotten back from Kingston, she couldn't face them snuggled up together on the couch, scrolling through pictures of David's nephew, without feeling like a third wheel. And it would be even worse if she hung around the house all day.

She kept walking, eyes fixed on the pavement in front of her. Bollocks, what was she going to do now? Spend her days stuck in her room, sending out CVs and waiting for replies, trying to land commissions? God, she couldn't even look at her bed spread, couldn't lie on her mattress without thinking about the feel of Laurent's body on hers, couldn't close her eyes without seeing his face, the intensity of his gaze while he was driving her to her peak, and the expression he'd worn when he'd stormed out.

Space. She'd told him she needed space. But she would never have enough as long as she stayed in Hamilton.

And now that she'd burned this particular bridge, nothing was holding her back.

Steelhawks practice facility, *a week later*

Legs stretched in front of him on the gym mat, Laurent bent forward and reached for his toes. His lower back protested, and a twinge of pain made him wince. Crisse, his muscles were too damn tight. Even after a full yoga session.

"You okay, man?" Colby stood next to him, patting his face with a towel.

Laurent straightened and rolled his shoulders back. "Yeah, why do you ask?"

"Usually, I'm the one who makes faces when the poses get too bendy."

Not surprising for someone who had just started yoga. Colby had returned to Hamilton with the intention of making amends and getting Gabby back. And he'd enlisted Laurent's help, starting with basic poses and breathing exercises to try to cool that damn temper of his.

And it was working.

Sure, anyone who didn't know Colby well enough wouldn't see it—he was still the same aloof, unsmiling, no bullshit guy he'd always been. Laurent could sense it, though. Colby was calmer. More grounded.

A good thing too, since his teammate had recently learned that he'd gotten Gabby pregnant. If impending fatherhood didn't mess with a guy's head, Laurent didn't know what would. They were both going to have to put in extra hours to get their focus back before the season started.

Not that Laurent's situation compared. Colby was trying to navigate a new relationship on top of having a kid on the way. Laurent was trying to navigate... nothing. Way too much nothing, since Lorelei had asked him for space.

Three weeks. Three fucking weeks, and she hadn't called or texted. How much damn space could she need?

"Guess I'm not feeling it today," he grumbled, and got to his feet. "You did fine, though."

"Sorting things out with Gabby helped for sure," Colby

replied. "Remember what you told me? Can't loosen your muscles if your mind is tied in knots."

"I stand by those words." And his head was about as tied in knots as it had ever been.

Colby nodded slowly. "So, um... You know, if you ever want to talk about it or something..."

Laurent almost laughed. "Tabarnak. Never thought I'd hear Colby Shelton say that."

His teammate smiled. "Gabby's rubbing off on me, I guess."

"Remind me to send her a thank you note. But I'd rather not bore you with the state of my life right now. The most exciting thing I have lined up this week is a haircut."

"If it makes you feel better, my evening plans are taking Gabby to Whole Foods and cooking dinner with her. We're making asparagus risotto tonight."

We. Something else he'd never thought he would hear Colby say in reference to anything other than the team. The word echoed in his mind as he hit the showers. Things were moving too fucking fast. Max was married, Colby would be a dad in a few months...

Whereas he was contemplating spending the season as Rocky's last remaining wingman.

Laurent shut off the shower and grabbed his towel. No way. Fuck that noise. He would do whatever it took to convince Lorelei they could make this work.

She felt something for him. Something that went beyond friendship, beyond physical need and gratification. He'd felt it when they'd made love in her room, the way she clung to him, drew him deeper, stripped herself completely bare in front of him—literally and figuratively. You couldn't fake or misread that kind of intimacy.

But she was scared, and how could he blame her? As far

as he knew, she'd never had a serious relationship, though he didn't exactly have a lot of experience in that area himself. And yes, the public scrutiny that would come with being his girlfriend wasn't helping. He just needed to show her that they didn't have to spend all their time in his world.

They could live in hers, as well.

No better time than the present. Once he was dressed, he took his phone and checked Lorelei's feed. Ah, there it was. A painting of hers, posted six days ago. *Drop by The Daily Grind to see this and more, starting tomorrow!*

Surely it wouldn't hurt to drop by the coffee shop and check it out. If she was working, he'd play it cool and let her lead. If she wasn't, he could send her a message to congratulate her. Either way, it would prove that he didn't need an invite to take an interest in her accomplishments. And little by little, he might make her more comfortable with the idea of actual dates.

One endless drive later, he arrived in front of The Daily Grind. Just his luck it was on the other side of town, so he had all the time in the world to ponder what he'd say to Lorelei—if she was actually there—beyond a simple hello. On entering the coffee shop, he scanned the counter for familiar reddish curls, his heart pounding. But there was only a tall skinny guy manning the coffee machine and a girl with rainbow braids at the register.

His gaze landed on the wall. What the fuck? The only frames he could see were black and white pictures. Not Lorelei's warm, swirly, colorful paintings.

Something wasn't right.

He walked to the register and glanced at the girl's name tag. Deidre. "Hi there. Would you mind telling me if Lorelei's working today?"

She blinked at him. "Lorelei? Lorelei Wescott?"

"Yeah. I came to see her art exhibit. Is it in the back?"

Deidre hesitated. "She doesn't work here anymore."

The statement hit like a slapshot, straight in the solar plexus. "Are you serious? What the hell happened?"

Deidre cleared her throat. "Let me take your order first, sir."

Right. Whatever the explanation was, the girl probably couldn't chitchat on the job.

He pulled out his wallet. "Medium plain white for Laurent."

"Right away, sir."

He waited for his drink, his fingers tapping a rhythmless staccato against the counter. Had Lorelei quit, or had she been fired by that shithead manager? In any case, she should have told him. He could have been there for her.

"Order up for Laurent." Deidre leaned forward as she handed him his cup. "Lorelei quit. The manager had it out for her."

"Yeah, so I heard."

She lowered her voice to a whisper. "The asshole canceled her art show. I called her, and she told me she'd left Hamilton anyway. She was off to Saint John something or other."

The words carved a hole in his chest. Saint John, New Brunswick? Last he'd heard, that was where her mother had settled. No, this couldn't be real. She couldn't just have up and left town without so much as a goodbye. She couldn't have simply disappeared again.

Again. Yeah, she'd done it before. But things were different this time. Unless...

He nodded, dazed. "Thanks. Have a good one." To his own ears, his voice sounded hollow, distant.

He walked out of the coffee shop, took his phone from

his pocket, and scrolled to Lorelei's number, his throat tightening in a swirl of panic and anger and confusion. He pressed call.

Lorelei's voice immediately sounded in his ear. Cheery and musical. What he wouldn't give to hear it for real. "Hi, I can't pick up right now…"

He hung up.

Gone. She was simply gone. Sure, maybe her manager had pushed her until she quit, but she'd only have left Hamilton for one reason.

Him.

He'd come on too strong, spilling his guts right after sex, leaving in a huff when she didn't give him the answer he wanted. Tabarnak, he'd been giving Colby advice on managing his emotions and communicating better, and he'd gone and acted like an overbearing dick.

Shit, if the preseason wasn't starting, he'd go to David and Mason's house and ask if she'd left a forwarding address. Then he'd be off to wherever the hell she'd gone. And he'd convince her to come back.

Only… that would just be more of him imposing his decisions on her. When it came to Lorelei, he couldn't follow his own advice and remain patient and level-headed. He loved her too much for that.

Well, he didn't have a choice now. There was nothing left but try and get over her.

He dumped the untouched coffee cup in the trash. He was going to need something a lot stronger.

Chapter Seventeen

@Hamiltonsteelhawks You've been patient. You've been good. And at long last it's here. Don't miss the first game of the preseason when we take on Ottawa. A few tickets still available. Get 'em before they go.
@SHSlut God I thought today would never get here.
@Eddie4prez IKR?
@Lilygilly Finally, new hockey.
@timmytank Finally, new suckitude

Steelhawks barn, two weeks later

The roar of the crowd echoed into the tunnel. Preseason but the adrenaline rush still hit Laurent like a wave. With a roll of his shoulders, he tightened his grip on his stick, focusing on the game ahead. The ice in front of him glowed red in the swirl of overhead spotlights.

"Let's fucking go, boys," Rocky bellowed behind him. "Show us what you got, eh, Hammer?"

"Come on, Hammer, you fucking beauty!"

Laurent didn't turn to see who'd said that. No doubt some of the guys were giving Drake Hammersmith the usual high fives and fist bumps, trying to include him in their pre-game rituals. The standard welcome for a player who'd just been traded into the team.

Laurent wasn't part of it, at least not tonight. He had other shit to deal with. Besides, he didn't feel like slapping the back of a guy who had put three pucks past him during scrimmage.

Hammer had been lethal in Winnipeg, and he was lethal now. Good for the Hawks and tough shit for Ottawa, but fuck if it hadn't messed with his head to see Hammer in a Steelhawks jersey sailing one past his shoulder. Yeah, that would take some time getting used to.

Focus. Don't think about the scrimmage. There's new guys in camp every year. Each game is a fresh start. Past is past. Nothing left but the present.

"Let's go, Gilly!"

He flipped his mask down, trudged through the tunnel, and skated onto the ice. The feeling of a fresh sheet under his blades, the pucks flying, his muscles heating up and his limbs stretching, nothing else mattered in that moment. His shoulders still felt a bit tight, but it would be fine. Just a bit of preseason rust, nothing more.

Max paused in front of him to line up a shot. Glove side, nice and predictable. Laurent caught it easily. Max grinned and sent another one flying top corner—caught again. Nothing like an attempt in the middle of the action with three goons screening, but the puck smacking against his palm still felt good. It infused a dose of much-needed confidence.

"Atta boy, Gilly."

Laurent gave him a nod. Tabarnak, he'd missed this. *This* was what he was all about. What he was good at—one of the very best. Sure, as much as he hated to admit it, Kovy had had a better camp. His backup had managed to stop Hammer cold, for one thing.

But only because he had let all of his personal crap mess with his head, because the emptiness had been eating away at him.

The empty space *she'd* left. No way to fill that.

But the ice didn't have room for any emptiness. A full sixty minutes where every second counted when you were a goalie. Which was exactly what he needed.

And then the puck dropped.

Minutes ticked down in the first, between whistles and face-offs with not a lot for him to do but watch the action down at the other end. Shots and rebounds and red-jerseyed Hawks trying to jam one in, but nothing was getting past Ullmark.

Before Laurent knew it, a pair of white jerseys were bearing down. Odd-man rush. His gaze followed the puck. His instinct honed in on the angle of the opponents' sticks. A shot when he was banking on a pass, and the puck whipped past his ear.

The crowd groaned, and he swiped the frozen bit of rubber out of the back of the net.

Fuck. What a way to start. More than half a period to go, though. *Focus.*

But focus was elusive when he kept losing track of the puck.

In the corner.

No, in front.

Tabarnak.

By the time he was down in his butterfly, the shot was past him. Wide, thank fuck. But that was another one that would have gone in.

Come on. Shake off the rust.

Shit, what else could he expect when he'd barely slept over the past few days? Something was going to have to give, and fast—before the games got serious. Because yoga wasn't cutting it, not by a long shot, and neither was weed. In fact, he'd been going a bit overboard on that front.

Like the other night, at Jayden's barbecue? What the fuck was that?

He shook the thought away. *Not with a game on.*

Shit, they were coming again. He crouched.

They passed. Tic-tac-toe.

The shot pinged off the post and went in.

Laurent sucked in breath. No good. His lungs felt like pair of hands was squeezing the air out of them. He tipped up his helmet and reached for his bottle. Cool water squirted to the back of his throat, but it didn't help.

During the TV timeout, he went for a skate, but his cheeks burned despite the cold air in the rink. He eyed the bench, but shit, he didn't even want to go over there. The guys would all give him encouraging looks and tap him with their sticks but...

No. Waves of nerves were already settling into his stomach. Sympathy would only make it worse.

He grabbed his stick and got back in his crease, hunched over. Another face-off in his end. The play went into the corner. He followed from over his shoulder. The boys were battling.

An Ottawa player hit the ice. Stützle. Fuck, he loved

nothing more than trying to trick the refs into sticking an arm up. Tonight, at least, they weren't buying.

Neither was Rocky. "Hey, shithead! You go down faster than your mom!"

A rumble of laughter floated from the Hawks' players on the ice. And yeah, maybe that would help with the tension. A second later, one of the Ottawa guys rammed into Rocky, and the struggle for possession was back on.

The puck came out of the corner on an Ottawa stick. Another pass.

Boom.

That one went in five-hole.

Calisse.

Behind his visor, the shooter grinned. "Nice save, bud. You'll be up for the Vezina this year for sure."

The little shit skated past until Laurent could read GREIG on the back of his jersey. A second later, Max plowed into him and started a shoving match.

Laurent pulled in another breath while counting to ten. Fucking hell, time to pull it together. Right fucking now. No way could they let Ottawa win on home ice. No way he could afford to let any more shots in.

Shut the door.

Thank God, the boys took over the game for a bit, letting the seconds tick down. Five minutes left. Maybe he could get out of this.

Maybe.

But then a bad line change had Ottawa attacking again. A faked shot, a pass, a whiffed one-timer sent the play into the corner. Tkachuk elbowed his way to a spot just outside the blue paint, ready for the tip in.

His teammates closed around the net like wagons circling as Giroux came up with the puck. Shoving in front of him obscured his view. The next thing he knew, he banged into the side of the net, and pain shot through his shoulder. Then his ass hit the ice.

Out of the corner of his eye, he caught the red glow of the goal light.

Laurent flipped his helmet up. That fucking did it. Anger and frustration broke through the dam and swept over him, pulsing through his veins and shivering through his limbs. That stupid fuck was going down.

"You wanna go, you piece of shit?" He drove the point home with his blocker. "Let's go right now."

Tkachuk spun to face him, and his gloves hit the ice. Laurent popped him another one.

A twisting yank on his arm sent another bolt of pain searing through his shoulder and separated him from the Ottawa captain.

Black spots floated in front of his vision. "Osti de calisse de tabarnak."

A red jersey waded in, pulling his opponent away, landing a punch straight in his jaw. Presto. On unsteady legs, Laurent skated away from the scrum and tried to shake off the pain. But it pulsed like an electric current all the way down his right arm. Fuck, fuck, this was really bad. Supporting his arm with his left hand, he headed for the bench, a trainer meeting him halfway.

Coach Reed's red face and his teammates' wide-eyed stares barely registered. Kovy had already donned his mask and blocker, ready jump into the crease. Even without the injury, Laurent's night was already over.

But it was more than tonight. The throbbing told him he'd be out a hell of lot longer than that.

Dirty Puck Buddies

Laurent's apartment, two days later

"And it's a long drive to deep left field. This ball is outta here! Home run Vladdy! That's gonna bring in two runs."

Whatever.

Laurent slumped on his sofa and stared at the flatscreen on the wall, watching but not really seeing the game he'd randomly landed on. The meds were just starting to set in, but the shooting pain in his shoulder turned the slightest movement into agony, even with a sling. The MRI hadn't picked up any labrum damage, thank God, because that would have meant season-ending surgery. Just a bad sprain, but shit, a sprain shouldn't hurt this much. It was like his muscles had gone through a shredder.

Four to six weeks. That was the prognosis.

He'd miss the start of the season. He wouldn't be on the ice with the boys when they started that eighty-two-game marathon to make the playoffs. He'd let them all down.

Maybe he hadn't fucked up his shoulder on purpose, but the way he'd been playing the other night had almost opened the door to an Ottawa bloodbath. He'd let his anger get to him and lashed out when the only person to blame for those four goals was himself. It didn't matter that the Hawks had come back for the win. He should never have put them in that position in the first place.

And now he couldn't erase the images from his mind, like a video session running through his brain on permanent loop. One goal after another. And with each replay he blamed himself more.

What else could he do? The one person he needed fill this empty hole in his chest was halfway across the country.

You stupid fuck, you're your own worst enemy.

He looked away from the baseball game to the coffee

table. The bag of weed he'd left there a couple of days ago still sat untouched.

He'd brought it home from Jayden's barbecue. And hadn't that been a shit show?

He hadn't even wanted to go, because he'd have to see all his buddies with their girls. Alone. Solo. Still raw and reeling from Lorelei skipping town.

But Jayden had only wanted to get the boys back together, perhaps celebrate getting engaged in his own way. How could Laurent say no to beers and steaks and a chill, lowkey party?

Except Chase Barret, one of the younger guys on the team, hadn't gotten the memo. He'd shown up with party favors, and Laurent had sampled the goods until his head was lost in a haze so thick Rocky had seen him safely home.

Fucking *Rocky*. If that wasn't the lowest of the low…

No. *This* was the lowest of the low. He glanced at the weed again. He could dig the hole a little deeper. Maybe he could smoke enough to erase that replay in his head.

A beep sounded from the other side of the couch.

His phone, right where he'd tossed it. Out of reach. With a groan, he leaned over, grabbed it, and looked at the caller.

Luc.

Shit. His little brother had texted twice this morning already, but Laurent hadn't bothered to reply. He'd already talked to Maman and figured she would pass on the basics, because he didn't feel like repeating the sob story to anyone else. Not today.

But Luc *never* called. And if he was calling now, it had to be important.

He swiped to accept the call.

"Salut, frerot."

"Hey, nice of you to finally give me a sign of life," Luc grumbled on the other end.

"I was resting."

"And I was fucking worried, you ass."

"Worried?" Laurent sat back down. "It's just a shoulder injury."

Luc was silent for a moment. "Four to six weeks. Maman told me."

He leaned back and stared at the ceiling. "What else do you want me to say? It is what it is."

"Yeah, but... It's not just the injury. You've been acting weird lately."

Laurent almost wanted to laugh. "Did Maman ask you to grill me? You know she does the same thing with me when she's fretting over you."

"Maman didn't say anything," Luc shot back. "She didn't have to. I noticed on my own. You didn't text me before my first game to wish me luck, and that was four days ago."

Laurent opened his mouth to reply but his words caught in his throat. Tabarnak. Luc was right. He'd always texted his little brother before the first game, every single year since they'd both had their own phones. This time, it had completely slipped his mind.

Just like everything else.

"I'm sorry, frerot. Really."

"It's okay." Luc sighed. "I just want to know you'll be all right, whatever the hell is going on."

"I will be. Eventually." God, he hoped this wouldn't be the first time he lied to his brother. "I need some time to think things over. To get my head straight."

Time and space. Wasn't that what Lorelei had wanted too? Well, if she could up and go, so could he. He couldn't start rehabbing this injury for at least ten days. More if the swelling didn't go down.

"I'm going to the lake house."

"By yourself?" Luc spluttered. "Are you nuts? You can't even drive!"

"Yeah, I know, but that's what car services are for. Besides, it's better than staying in Hamilton staring at the wall and having angry fans yell at me if I try to go out."

Luc sighed. "I guess so. But you better fucking call or text to let me know how you're doing. I'm serious. Or else I'm telling Maman to come make you a batch of chicken soup."

Chapter Eighteen

@ClassicRockRoundup Today on the podcast, we take a deep dive into the make-love-not-war era. Look at how songs like "Fortunate Son" pair with "Love the One You're With" to define a generation.

Saint-Jean-Port-Joli, Quebec, that same day

Daylight filtering through the curtains roused Lorelei. She stared at the ceiling, breathing in deeply. Those few first minutes after waking up were the best part of the day.

She could hold onto hope that today would be better. Still convince herself that, rather than wasting the hours, she'd be productive and come up with a plan for the next few weeks, maybe even the next few months. Get organized. Get her shit together.

But it was all downhill from there. A ball of lead dropped into her stomach the moment she came down for breakfast and bit into a scone. It would remain there, weighing her down and making her sluggish, until she went to bed.

She glanced around the small, cozy kitchen. Warm, yellow walls, and wooden cabinets painted a burnt orange with a colorful collection of mismatched bowls and mugs piled behind glass panes. In front of the window, a wind chime tinkled softly. Tanya's new digs were the perfect escape. For one, they were far from Hamilton—fifteen fucking hours on three different buses far. For another, Tanya would be the last person on the planet to update her on anything hockey-related.

The best spot for a full detox, pure and simple, where she could completely cut out thoughts of Laurent and the mess she'd left behind. As long as David and Mason left her alone. They insisted on checking in via text on the regular. God forbid she didn't send a prompt reply, or they'd bombard her with messages.

"And don't think for a moment we'll rent out your room to someone else," David had told her before she left. "We know you'll be back."

True, she'd paid two months in advance, but what the hell would she come back to? Contemplating that shit only raised a painful, confusing whirl of thoughts and images in her mind. Things she'd rather block out for now —if not for good. Only one problem. Since her arrival at this so-called perfect haven ten days ago, nothing had gotten better.

In fact, it had gotten worse.

She pushed her half-eaten scone aside. It was flavorless and hard as a fucking hockey puck. Store-bought. Nothing like the fresh-baked delicacy Laurent had made her that morning...

Tears welled in her eyes. Bollocks, not *again*. Why did

every little fucking thing remind her of him? It was like the entire world had turned into a minefield.

"Good morning, Lorelei." Tanya breezed into the kitchen wearing a flowy cotton dress, her curly hair swept into a knot and large turquoise earrings hanging from her lobes. "Tea?"

"Thanks, but I just had coffee."

Tanya smiled. The calm, easy smile she always wore, as if she floated above such mundane trifles as hot beverages. Her demeanor never failed to get on Lorelei's nerves.

"Whatever you prefer," Tanya replied. "Have any plans today?"

She shrugged. "I'm not sure."

Her standard reply. And so far, Tanya hadn't said anything, but then Lorelei's plans were probably another mundane question. When she had called to say she wanted to visit, Tanya hadn't asked how long or why, thank God. For once, she didn't mind her mother's lack of curiosity about her own daughter's life. In fact, she'd counted on it when she decided to come.

"Well, I'm off to visit a few antique sellers in the area. See if I can find some old pots and china for the mosaic I'm planning. I'll be back in time for dinner."

"Okay. I can cook us a zucchini loaf or something."

Tanya plugged in the kettle. "Yes, that would be wonderful."

Least she could do. She just hoped she had all the ingredients on hand, because a trip to the grocery store was its own brand of torture. Riding the bus out of Montreal had been bad enough, with most of the passengers speaking French all around her. She hadn't understood a word. Despite Madame Campbell's best efforts, she could still only say things like bonjour and merci—and tabarnak.

But on her first day here, the guy behind the counter at the corner store had come to her rescue and ventured a few words of heavily accented, rusty English. Still, he'd sounded too much like Laurent for comfort. A simple, halting question asking if she wanted a receipt had felt like a dagger.

She should be glad her mother's house didn't overlook the St Lawrence—or as they called it here, the St-Laurent. She never thought the sight of a river could make her want to cry, yet this was her life at the moment. A pathetic shitshow.

Get it the fuck together. Stop wallowing. God, she needed to keep busy if she didn't want to go insane.

"You know, I think I'm going to go through my old art stuff," she said. "See what I'm keeping."

She'd been putting it off long enough. She owed it to Tanya to sort through her crap, and she had to take the plunge sooner or later. Though she had managed to sort through the box of Nana's old jewelry without completely falling to pieces.

Her finger grazed the small pendant at her collarbone, hanging from a thin chain. A small disk of resin, brown with age, encasing tiny multicolored flowers, recalled from childhood afternoons when she'd come home from grade four or five to the scent of baking cookies. Nana had always greeted her with a smile, a glass of milk, and fresh treats, ready to hear about her day and help with homework. Lorelei hadn't taken it off since clasping it around her neck days ago.

Tanya poured boiling water into her mug. "Great. There's a large cardboard box in the garage with your name on it. You can't miss it."

"Well, thanks for not throwing it all out when you moved."

Her mother tutted softly. "Lorelei, I would never do that. The tools of art are our most precious possessions."

Lorelei nodded. "I can't argue there."

Though an hour later, when she finally pulled the dusty box from its corner, she had the distinct feeling of digging through an ancient garbage pile. Paint and markers didn't exactly hold up over time, and God only knew what else she'd stuffed in there.

Taking a deep breath, she opened the box.

Dried up tubes of paint, boxes of markers, everything haphazardly dumped together ... At least she'd gotten better at organizing her supplies. Maybe there was hope for her yet.

One by one, she consigned items to the trash, but then she uncovered a bag of brushes. Clean, some of them brand new. Those were keepers. She set them aside.

The red cover of a sketchbook caught her eye.

Her pulse quickened. Oh fuck. She'd had that in high school. Blood pounding, she dug it out of the mess of supplies and flipped it open.

The penciled face of masked goalie stared back at her.

She pressed her lips together. A shiver raised the hairs on the back of her neck. Shit, that wasn't just any goalie. Face in shadow, drawn in monochrome graphite, but the eyes were clear and glittering. And her mind pictured their color as blue-green as in real life.

Laurent.

She flipped to another page. Another goalie—but not really—the full body this time, crouching in front of the net. She'd been trying for generic, a study of poses and complex details like padding, but every single attempt turned into *him*.

Flip. This time Laurent stood in profile. Strong brow,

high cheekbones, defined jaw. No mask. Just him. Done on the sly after he'd snuck into her room to hang out.

A tear rolled down her cheek, and she hugged the sketchbook to her chest. This was torture. A knife to the heart. Because she couldn't look at these sketches and pretend that she hadn't been head over heels for her best friend back then.

Just like she was in love with him now.

And she'd never had the guts to tell him. She'd pretended that sex wasn't that big a deal, that she wasn't jealous of his girlfriend, that she didn't sketch him over and over because she couldn't get him out of her mind.

Denial then. Denial now. Pretending this entire trip wasn't a huge cop-out, like she didn't miss Laurent so much that it made her sick to her stomach. That getting through each day wasn't an ordeal.

Eleven years. Eleven years from those sketches to now. And nothing had changed. Laurent said he'd waited long enough. So why was she still running? What was she afraid of? Because anything had to be better than this perpetual no-man's land where she simply existed.

―――

"The zucchini loaf is divine. Where did you get the recipe?"

Lorelei tapped her fork against her plate. She'd managed to eat half a slice, while Tanya had wolfed down two. And acted like she didn't notice Lorelei was toying with her food.

"My roommate, David. He's a great cook."

Tanya nodded. "I'm so glad you've connected with some people in Hamilton. Even if some friendships don't always stand the test of time, they're the healthiest relationships a person can have."

Right. And her mother would definitely categorize whatever Lorelei had with Laurent as the exact opposite. And maybe she'd be right. Family relationships and romantic love were doomed to end in drama. That's how she'd viewed those relationships, or so it seemed to Lorelei.

Which was the root of their original falling-out. Lorelei had ended up at her mother's house after a few years of rambling from one place to another, doing whatever odd jobs she could find to pay for food and lodging before moving on. But then her landlord had wanted to raise the rent and the second-hand clothes shop she'd been working at had gone under, only a few months after Nana's death, and she'd needed somewhere to crash until she could get back on her feet.

Except Lorelei had expected Tanya, for once in her life, to act like a mother, someone who would comfort and ask the tough questions. Someone like Nana. But Tanya had no intention of doing so—or perhaps she'd never learned how. She was kind and easy-going, yes, but she treated Lorelei as she would any other house guest breezing through her life. And because of that, confiding anything really personal to her had always felt... weird.

"How long are you planning on staying?" Tanya asked.

"Is there a problem?"

"No. Take as much time as you need. But I'm going to a ceramics retreat next week so I wanted to know if you'd be here to water the plants."

Lorelei sunk her teeth into her lower lip. "I'm not sure yet. I'm kind of... confused about a lot of things. As you may have noticed."

Tanya hesitated before answering. "Confusion is a

result of wanting to break free of something, only fear is holding you back."

Lorelei almost laughed. Leave it to Tanya to sound like a self-help book. "No shit."

"You did the right thing coming here, then." Tanya smiled and refilled their water glasses. "You're still struggling to let go of whatever you let behind. You need to send it out into the universe. Have you thought about writing everything down and burning it?"

Her mother was right, in a way. But fuck, from where Lorelei was standing, *she* was holding herself back. And it wasn't like she could launch herself into the sun. After all, Laurent had given her the space she'd asked for. He'd called once and hadn't even left a message.

He wasn't the problem. *She* was.

And maybe her mother had been the problem, too, way back when she'd noped out of their family without so much as an explanation.

"Is that what you did when you left Dad?" She hadn't meant to ask the question. It had just come out on its own. But her mother's serene, detached attitude was snagging at something deep inside. Something that was tangled with the pain of having feelings for Laurent but being unable to act on them.

Tanya sighed. "Lorelei... I don't want to get into this. That was my path. You have yours. Your father has his. I've let it go, and it's gone." She fanned out her fingers like she was releasing a butterfly. "I've nothing more to add."

"Well, I need to know why you decided to leave instead of trying to work things out." She set her fork down and pushed her plate away. "I don't want to hear an apology or whatever, just the facts."

Her mother tensed. "I have no need to apologize. No one should ever say they're sorry for living their truth."

This was exactly what they'd fought over last time. But Lorelei had no intention of rehashing it. That wasn't why she was asking. "Again, I only want the facts. I think you owe me that much."

Tanya sighed. "Is that what you're carrying around, then? This antiquated idea that I owe you an explanation for choosing what was best for me?"

Lorelei slapped her hand down on the table. "Best for you? What about what was best for me? Jesus, I was nine years old."

"Old enough to understand that it was better for all of us if I didn't stay," Tanya insisted, her voice hardening. "I was miserable. I would have transferred that energy to the rest of you."

"Yeah. If only you'd taken the time to explain it to me. Did you think I would come to that conclusion by myself? Or were you hoping an after-school special would clear things up?"

Tanya paused and inhaled. One of those re-centering exercises. Lorelei could almost count along with her. "All right. If you want the facts... Rich is a good man. Sensible and solid. We met at a point in my life when I needed reassurance and material comfort after bouncing around for too long. But after a while, I realized that I missed the freedom to follow my own calling, wherever it took me."

Freedom. Yes, Lorelei remembered that siren's call. All through high school it had beckoned to her until all she could think about was getting the fuck out of Sydney. She'd found it in a way, and for a while it had been enough.

But now? Now her mother's words no longer resonated.

"I thought he would understand," Tanya continued,

almost wistfully. "All those old records we used to listen to. Protest songs. Free love. Breaking the bonds of society's dictates…"

Lorelei could almost picture them, young and holed up in some tiny bedroom, smoking dope, and playing record after record on an old stereo.

"At the time he said it expanded his horizons. But I guess the lyrics never sunk in. Or they never spoke to him the way they did to me."

Oh, but she was wrong there. Dad had listened to those records even after her mother was gone. Night after night, he'd come home from work, put on his music, and grab a beer. By the time she was ten, Lorelei could name the groups and sing along. At the time, she figured it for his taste in music. Hell, it became her taste, too.

But maybe, somewhere in there, he was reliving moments with Tanya. Moments he could never get back except through memory and song. Some nights, when he was feeling particularly maudlin, he'd play "Angie" over and over.

Pathetic, maybe, but right now Lorelei could relate.

Fuck, so much had gone straight over her head back then—the way the meanings of a lot of those old lyrics had.

But she saw things clearly now, like a bolt of lightning suddenly illuminating a darkened room.

Dad's job may have been boring. He may have worked all his life for the man and fallen into a rut. But in his own way, he'd genuinely loved Tanya. You didn't have to be an artist to feel things keenly on the deepest level.

And being an artist didn't require you sacrifice everything on the altar of creation. Separating herself from Laurent wasn't freedom, or following her calling. It was a decision she'd made because she was scared shitless, and it had torn her heart to shreds.

Tanya took her empty plate to the sink. "We're the same, you and I. I could always tell you took after me more than your father. You'll never be happy being a wage-slave for some idiotic boss or tying yourself to one man who doesn't care that the grind he's gotten into stifles all your creative spark."

"No. You're wrong. I'm not like you."

"Believe me, I understand it's not an easy thing to accept, being outside of the norm and desiring freedom above everything else..."

"Will you stop it?" Legs wobbling, she stood. "Just stop it, okay? I'm an artist, yes. I like to travel and explore new places, yes. But that doesn't mean that when I meet the right person, I'm going to throw that all away in the name of some nebulous ideal."

"Lorelei..."

"You didn't leave Dad just to be free and live your truth. You left him because you didn't love him anymore, and I would have been a shitload better off if you'd just told me that. If you'd loved him..."

As much as I love Laurent. The words were screaming to get out, but she clamped them down. This belonged to her and Laurent. Not to her mother.

"... you'd have found a way to make it work, no matter what."

Tanya stared down at the sink. Lorelei couldn't stand being in the same room with her another second. "Excuse me."

She barged out of the kitchen into the tiny living room, then out the front door. The cold air took her breath away, yet it refreshed her, like a dip in a stream on a hot day. Clean and pure as it filled her lungs.

Holy shit, had that conversation been an eye-opener. All this time, the consequences of tying herself to Laurent had paralyzed her. But they were already tied together—in so many more ways than the literal, physical sense. They had formed their own unique bond, and their feelings hadn't come out of nowhere.

He always accepted her for who she was, and she had always accepted him. *Everything* about him, even stuff a lot of people would think was dark and twisted. She'd never been afraid of what their games would lead to, because he'd always given her the power. A single word would stop anything they did, and she trusted him.

With her body, anyway. Trusting him with her heart was another issue entirely. Laurent made her feel too much, and it was terrifying. A serious relationship would mean leaving herself open and raw and vulnerable for an extended time.

Was she strong enough to handle that? Oh God, could she face it?

Her heart pounded. She needed some time alone with her realization. And then she needed to figure out what the hell she was going to do about it.

Chapter Nineteen

@HamiltonSteelhawks The Steelhawks have placed goaltender Laurent Gill on long-term injured reserve. He is expected to miss four to six weeks with an upper body injury.

Hamilton, a week later

Robert Plant's voice resonated in Lorelei's earbuds, singing about smoking and drinking, heartache and making a fresh start. And maybe that's what she needed now, but not before she finished her old business first. Her brush slid over the canvas, and tracking a fine swirl of bright red. Perfect. Just a few more here and there...

"Lore! Dinner's almost ready!"

She glanced over her shoulder.

David poked his head through the garage door. "Mind if I take a look?"

With a smile, she switched off the music. "Go right ahead."

David stepped in for a better look. "I love it. The contrast between the black and white portrait and all the touches of color in the background..."

She kept the inspiration to herself—the profile of Laurent from her old sketchbook. She'd redone it with Laurent as he was now, ten years older and wearing his Hawks jersey. Sharper, more handsome, with the shadow of a beard on his jaw, though the intensity of his gaze was the same. All it needed was a bit more color around him, perhaps even dabs of Steelhawks silver, but not to the point where it would overpower the subject.

"I'm not quite done yet," she said. "But soon."

David raised an eyebrow. "Any news from the recipient?"

With a deep sigh, she set her paintbrush down. "Nope. Nothing yet."

She'd learned of Laurent's injury and the hellish game that had preceded it four days ago when she'd returned from Tanya's. God, just imagining what Laurent had gone through... He'd always gotten down on himself when he didn't play well, and an injury on top of that?

And this time, she hadn't been there to comfort him. Take him in her arms, hold him tight, let him express whatever he was holding back. It didn't matter how much time had gone by. They could still lie on her bed, listen to music, and drift off together if that was what he needed. The same way she had back in high school, when he'd told her about his dad or that whole mess with the rookies. He'd opened up then.

But now, he had closed himself off, gone silent. Was that why he wasn't answering his phone? Three calls had gone directly to voicemail. He'd left her texts unread. Was he avoiding everyone, or just her? David and Mason had done their best to cheer her up, but the only thing that soothed was working on Laurent's portrait.

"Come on." He squeezed her shoulder. "Let's go have a drink while Mason finishes the tomato sauce."

She put her phone in her back pocket and followed him to the kitchen. David took out two kombuchas and a beer for his husband.

Lorelei took a sip and sat down. "I don't know what to do. I don't even know if Laurent is in Hamilton or at his lake house. For all I know, he's in Montarville."

"He'll be back at practice eventually," Mason said as he stirred the sauce. "But it might be a while. The team only said upper body injury and four to six weeks. He must have sprained something."

David shrugged. "Well, that makes sense, he's probably just resting. I'm sure he'll call you soon, Lore."

A vibration from her back pocket made her jump in her seat. "Oh fuck." She whipped it out of her back pocket. "Unknown number."

David let out a breath. "Damn it. That would have been so cool."

"Local call, though." She swiped at the green button. "Hello?"

"Ms. Wescott?" The voice over the line was smooth and quiet. Something about it screamed culture and taste. "This is Chloé Taylor-Wallingford." Yeah, and so did that name. "I'm calling on behalf of the Hamilton Steelhawks PR department."

Shit. Laurent had mentioned that the last time they'd seen each other, but with her mind in such turmoil, she'd completely forgotten about it.

She went into the hallway. "Um... hi. Laurent said he gave you my number, though it was a while ago."

"He did. Shawntelle Alexander, VP of Communications, expressed significant interest in the tee-shirt you designed for him. Would you be willing to discuss the possibility of selling us your design?"

"What, you mean like for merch?"

Oh God, the ultimate sell-out. Teenage Lorelei would point a finger and call her a traitor, but then teenage Lorelei didn't have bills and rent to pay. Surely this was several steps above selling eight-dollar lattes at The Daily Grind.

"Yes. There was a lot of positive feedback online after we posted that video." The woman sighed. "I would have gotten back to you sooner but things have been quite busy this pre-season. We're thinking of releasing it when Mr. Gill comes off the long-term injured reserve list. If we come to an agreement with you, of course. Perhaps we could set up a meeting?"

Lorelei pressed her lips together. A deal like this could bring in a decent sum, but more importantly, the public exposure would be a godsend for her business. Yet she felt wrong giving the go-ahead. Because yeah, she'd come up with the design, but she'd made it for Laurent and nobody else.

The silence stretched out, and she could almost picture Chloé Something-Something's manicured fingernails tapping on a datebook.

"I'm interested," she finally replied. "But I need to discuss it with Laurent first. You get it, right? That word is like his trademark."

"Of course," the woman said. "And I imagine that this is a challenging time for him. Just let me know when you've come to a decision. You can reach me at this number during office hours."

"All right. Thank you."

She leaned against the wall and stared up at the ceiling for a moment. Bollocks, how was she supposed to discuss anything with Laurent with him so aggressively incommunicado? Maybe she should have asked the woman on the phone if Laurent had told the team where he could be reached, but she couldn't take the humiliation. She was his friend, supposedly. She should know.

And she needed to find out, somehow. She couldn't just wait around forever—and not just because she didn't want to leave the Steelhawks PR department hanging indefinitely.

She could hardly blame him for not wanting to speak anyone at the moment. But in a not-so-distant past he still would have turned to her. And fuck, she had so much she wanted to tell him, to show him, if only he was willing to give her another chance and listen.

She glanced back at her phone. There was one thing she hadn't tried yet, because she didn't want to pry if Laurent needed privacy. After all, when she'd asked him for space, he'd respected her wishes.

Screw it. Desperate times and all that. It couldn't hurt to ask for a little help.

―――

PORT CARLING, *three days later*

Laurent's eyes shot open. Fuck, what time was it? He shook away the last remnants of sleep, but his head still felt like it was stuffed with cotton, but something had woken him with a start. He lay in silence, staring at the deep blue sky, but only the soft sound of the water lapping at the lake shore broke the surrounding silence.

Damn it, he'd only come down to the waterside to catch some rays, lie in his deckchair, and scroll on his phone. The air got chillier every day, but the afternoons were still warm with Indian summer, enough to make him drop off, phone still in hand. *Tabarnak*, it was like he was still on painkillers. Though he'd cut way back on the meds, his energy levels hadn't returned.

He sat up and gently rolled his shoulder the way the physiotherapist had shown him. Pain pinched at his muscles, but it no longer rippled all the way down his arm.

A distant ringing tickled his ear.

The doorbell. Shit, was that what had woken him? He checked the time. Four-thirty. The grocery delivery wasn't supposed to come until six, but maybe they were early.

He stood and trudged back up to house, crossing through the kitchen and the living space toward the front door.

The doorbell rang again.

"Yeah, I'm coming," he shouted, then paused as he reached for the doorknob. "Who is it?"

You never knew. He'd never had trespassers before, other than the idiots who'd crashed his birthday party while high on coke, but if some hotshot reporter was stupid enough to try his luck...

"It's me."

Oh.

Oh fuck. His hand froze. His entire body froze. *Lorelei.*

He wrenched the door open. And suddenly, there she was. Standing right in front of him, after weeks of absence. He drank in her dark eyes, her silky curls, the red, long-sleeved shirt with a flowery pendant at her neck. Her jeans hugged her curvy figure.

Say something, you dumbass.

"I... um... What are you doing here, Lore?"

She bit her lip. Dark smudges marred the skin under her eyes. "Luc told me you were here. I tried calling you a few times, and you didn't answer, so I reached out to him."

Fuck. If he had known she was worried for him... But then he wasn't even aware she was no longer halfway across the country.

"I thought you went to New Brunswick."

"I came back a few days ago, but not from New Brunswick. From Quebec. Turns out my mum moved to Saint-Jean-Port-Joli a few months back. I went to stay at her place to, you know... To take a break from everything."

He did know. He'd been doing the exact same thing since his injury. Blocking all calls and texts from everyone but Luc, Maman, and Coach Reed.

"Anyway, who told you I was in New Brunswick?"

"Your coworker told me you were in Saint John. She must have gotten the two mixed up."

Her eyes widened. "What? You went to The Daily Grind?"

"Yeah. For your art show."

She gave a sharp, joyless laugh. "Jesus. We've really been giving each other the runaround, haven't we?"

A smile fought its way to his lips. "Well, you didn't come all the way up here to stand in the doorway. Come in."

His eyes caught the movement of her hand. She picked up a rectangular parcel wrapped in brown paper that she'd set against the wall.

"What's that?"

Her gaze softened. "That's the reason I'm here."

Holy shit, his heart was beating so hard that breathing became difficult. He led her to the living area and sat on the couch, but Lorelei remained standing, shifting her weight from foot to foot.

"If you want anything to drink..."

"No. I need to..." Her voice wavered, but she pushed on. "I need to do this now, so... Just open it, all right?"

She set the parcel on the couch next to him. As he tore away the brown paper, a profile emerged. But not just any profile. It was him in black and white, surrounded by swirls of warm colors, dominated by red, like fireworks were going off behind him.

His throat was so tight he could barely get the words out. "You painted me."

"I found something when I was at my mother's place," she said. "My sketchbook from high school. You know the one I would never let you look at? That was because it was filled with drawings of you."

He tore his gaze away from the painting to focus on her. Oh fuck, tears were pooling in her eyes. "Lorelei..."

"I was so in love with you back then." Her tone was breathless, as if she was finally ridding herself of an anchor that weighed her down for too long. "But those feelings confused me. They scared the shit out of me. I thought... I thought that if I said anything, it would ruin our friendship, and I couldn't risk that. So I convinced myself that whatever was going on with us was the best I could hope for."

Eleven years. So much time they could have had together... But maybe this was the way things were supposed to happen. Maybe back then, they would have been too immature to make things work, too caught up in family issues and future plans to hold a relationship together.

But past was past. The only thing that mattered was the present.

He swallowed. "And now?"

She wiped at the tears rolling down her cheeks. "I'm still scared. But I'm no longer confused. I'm still in love with you. I never really stopped. And I want to be with you, and not be filled with anger and jealousy and regret if you end up meeting someone else..."

"Someone else?"

How could she even think for a second that he'd even look at another girl, after she'd just told him she was in love with him? Suddenly, the foot and a half between them felt like a mile. He reached out pulled her to him.

"Get that thought out of your head right now, because it's not going to happen." She sank down on the other side of him, and he wrapped his arms around her. Closer. He needed her closer. Even that wasn't enough. He buried his nose in her hair and breathed in the sweet, exotic scent that was uniquely her. "You're the only one I want, Lorelei. Ever since you left, I've been walking around with a gaping hole in my chest, and fuck, I never want to feel that again. Do you understand? From now on, I'm not letting you go."

She nodded against the crook of his neck. "Me neither. Being away from you hurts." Her fingers clutched at his shirt. "So fucking much."

He loosened his embrace and bent to kiss her. So soft, so warm. He was starving for her, and she responded in kind, her mouth opening as she arched into him. He raised his arms to bury his hands in her hair...

He winced. Dammit, he kept forgetting... too quick a movement and.... "Ow. Tabarnak."

She bit her lower lip. "Oh shit. Your injury. Is it that bad?

"It's getting better, but I have to be careful." He grinned. "No athletic sex for a while, unfortunately, and you're probably going to have to do most of the work."

There was that smile, that bright Lorelei smile that made all his problems melt like the last snows under the spring sun's rays.

"I'll be gentle, I promise," she said, and kissed him again. "There's no rush. This time, I'm not going anywhere."

A RAY of sun worked its way through gray damask curtains. Laurent had been staring at that sliver of light on the hardwood floor for the past few minutes, but he didn't want to move. Basking was so much better. Simply lying there, not caring what time it was, with Lorelei breathing softly next to him... Bliss.

He rolled to his side and ran his palm down Lorelei's bare back. She shifted in her sleep, and turned her face toward him. Her lower lip poked out, and her brows furrowed, almost like a pout. Not the first time he'd seen that expression.

Not the last, either, thank God.

A rippling energy billowed through his chest. He grinned, though impulse pushed at him to jump out of bed and bounce off the walls. No more wondering when their next hook-up would be. No more going months without seeing her. No more pretending that he wasn't desperately in love with this woman, and ready to go all in.

They'd talked long into the night, confessing every one

of their hopes and fears. The knowledge that they both felt and wanted the same thing was like the ultimate safety net for pure intimacy—not the physical kind, the emotional kind.

Although emotion had given way to physical expression. They'd retreated to his room and made love. The memory of her slowly grinding down his length, drawing every ounce of pleasure from him made his cock twitch, but that only served as additional motivation to grit his teeth and push through rehabilitation.

With the back of his hand, he brushed a stray curl from her forehead. Lorelei stirred and a few moments later, she opened her eyes.

"Hey, you," she murmured with a sleepy smile.

"Hey, you."

She turned onto her back and stretched, letting the sheets fall away. The sight roused his cock.

"What time is it?" she asked.

"Who cares? I left my phone downstairs."

"Well, I'm starving." She bent over to retrieve one of his old Steelhawks t-shirts from the floor. "I'm going to make breakfast. Lunch. Whatever."

Damn it, if he were a hundred percent, he wouldn't let her get away so easily. "Why are you putting that on? If you're cold, might as well come back to bed."

She stood and shot him a teasing look over shoulder as she walked to the window. "I can't just walk around the house naked. It's not good for you while you're recovering."

Easy for her to say. Besides, she was just as sexy wearing his t-shirt. More, even.

"So, what do you say? Breakfast in bed?"

"Careful. I could get used to this."

She pushed the curtain aside and peered at the

sweeping view on the lake. "Me too." She sighed. "Although we'll have to go back to Hamilton sooner or later. Back to reality."

He sat up. "Hey, come here."

Lorelei lingered by the widow for a moment longer before crossing back to the bed, taking her time while his gaze roamed over her curves. The hem of his t-shirt was just long enough for decency, but as she moved, it offered teasing glimpses...

He reached for her hand and intertwined their fingers. "Does this feel like a dream to you? It's not. This is reality. Our reality."

She squeezed his hand, her grip solid and sure. "It is. And it's way better than any dream."

Epilogue

@HamiltonSteelhawks Huge welcome back to our favorite goalie. Let's get the dub!
@lillygilly WOOHOO (ps: get stuffed @timmytank)

Steelhawks barn, mid-November

"Oh God, I'm so nervous. I feel like I'm going to throw up."

Lorelei glanced at David, as they, along with Mason, made their way to the lower level of the arena. Damn, his face *had* paled to an ominous shade of white. He'd been jittery the entire game, but the chips and pop he'd consumed threatened to make a second appearance.

She linked her arm through his. "It'll be all right. Promise."

Pretty ironic that she should be the one comforting her

friend with her own stomach tied in knots for the past two days. Laurent's first game back, and her first official outing as his girlfriend—enough to keep her staring at the ceiling for hours at night. Though in a weird way, it helped that she wasn't the biggest nervous wreck here.

Thankfully, Laurent hadn't shown the slightest sign of nerves. In fact, she'd never seen him so pumped, though once he was between the pipes, he'd exuded nothing but calm and confidence. And that had kept her awake, too. Her cheeks flushed. When he climbed into bed that surplus of energy needed an outlet, and she was more than happy to provide one.

Big Steelhawks victory tonight, six to one against Boston. At least with an off-day tomorrow, they could celebrate as late as they wanted.

In front of the guarded door, the security goon stepped aside without any trouble. A pass hanging from a lanyard around her neck granted her access the secured area open to the players and their families.

David patted his hair as they continued down a wide corridor. "How do I look?"

On his other side, Mason squeezed his shoulder and kissed the side his temple. "You look fantastic, babe. You'll do great."

"Yes, what gorgeous t-shirt you're wearing," Lorelei added in a teasing tone. "Wherever did you get it?"

In front of the entrance to the family lounge, David struck a pose. "Do you like it? It's limited edition, you know. Ethically sourced and part of the proceeds go to charity. You should get one."

Yeah, they were joking around, but the Tabarnak tee-shirt really did look good on him. The silver letters on red had come out fantastic. Thank goodness the Steelhawks had agreed to her conditions, including Laurent's approval.

She took out her cell. "Hang on, can you do that again so I can film you?"

David swatted the phone away. "Enough nonsense. This is a serious, solemn moment." He took a deep breath. "Okay, let's go."

Lorelei pushed the door open. The walls of the family lounge were painted Steelhawks red and decorated with pictures of former players. A few padded chairs were scattered here and there, and on her left was a large table laden with plates of cold cuts, finger food, cakes and cookies, with an assortment of drinks on ice.

And all around, the wives and girlfriends chatted in groups, dressed in expensive clothes and hair done to shiny perfection, while a handful of kids giggled over a makeshift game of tag. Oh God, there was Véronique. Lorelei's pulse ticked up. Was she supposed to socialize with her now? What the hell would she even say to her? Ask to be added to their Whatsapp group? She tamped down the rush of dread and started her mantra. *You look great. Everything's fine. You belong.*

Yes, she could only look great wearing Laurent's jersey. A brand-new one that he'd given her last night over dinner at Hamilton's trendiest vegetarian restaurant.

"Look, there she is," Mason murmured, just as Lorelei spotted Addie in a corner, typing a message on her phone.

David tensed and let out a little whimper. Lorelei gently nudged him forward. "Come on, I'll introduce you."

Addie looked up and smiled. "Hey Lorelei."

"Hi Addie. How've you been?"

"Busy. It's been madness since the season started.

Anyway, it's great to see you. We're so happy Gilly's back. Oh, and congrats on the tee-shirts."

"Thanks. We came as a group to cheer him on. This is David and his husband Mason. I don't know if you remember when I asked for a pic that one time?"

A glimmer of recognition passed through Addie's gaze, and her smile widened. "Oh yes. Pleased to meet you."

David cleared his throat, his eyes shining. "I... I'm a very big fan of yours. I just wanted to thank you for the incredible performances throughout the years."

Addie gave a light laugh. "Oh wow, you're welcome. That's really sweet of you to say."

"Can I ask if there's one that really stands out for you? My personal favorite is your world championship performance. Your take on Romeo and Juliet was so unique."

Lorelei tiptoed toward the buffet. Mission accomplished. And now time to see which of those yummy treats was vegetarian-friendly. Her stomach hadn't settled enough for arena food during the game, but now her appetite had returned to life with a vengeance.

She was taking the last bite of a delicious chocolate chip cookie when a hand lightly tapped her shoulder. "Lorelei, right?"

She turned and immediately recognized the cheery blonde. She swallowed and nodded. "Cait. Yeah, we met at Laurent's party at the lake house."

"God, that feels like a hundred years ago."

"Sure does. It's been a whirlwind these past few months." She shook her head. "I can hardly believe I'm here."

Cait gave a deep sigh. "I know exactly what you mean. It's kind of terrifying, right? I was in France all last season so I'm pretty new at all of this. And I'm not used to the limelight like Addie or Gabby. I mean, they were both figure skaters. They know how to handle media attention."

So Gabby was a former figure skater too? Laurent had explained everything that had happened at Max's wedding, but he'd failed to mention that detail. Lucky she wasn't here tonight or David might have fainted.

"And here I thought I was the only new girl," she said. "Not going to lie, it's a relief to know I'm not alone."

"Same. We can stick it out together." Cait smiled and nodded toward the buffet. "How are the cookies?"

"Absolutely insane." Though not quite as good as the ones Laurent made. "You have got to try one."

The door banged open. "Let's go, boys!"

Laurent appeared, a huge grin on his face, followed by a bunch of his teammates. Everything around Lorelei melted away. Holy shit, that suit made him so incredibly handsome. Snug across his broad shoulders, and that tan color made his dark hair stand out even more. Would her heart ever stop fluttering when she saw him?

He lifted her into his arms for a kiss. "Enjoy the game, ma belle?"

"I sure did. Solid presence between the pipes."

He set her down gently. "You're starting to talk the talk. Let's see if our lessons have been paying off. If I saved thirty-two out of thirty-three shots, what's my save percentage?"

Damn it, she'd always been shit with numbers. "Um... Really, really good? Almost perfect?"

He raised an eyebrow. "I think you need a few more lessons, before we get into the advanced stats."

She grinned and tugged at his tie. "Do I? Better start tonight then."

"You know what, screw the shutout." He bent down and drew her into a longer kiss. "This is what I call perfect."

END

Read on for a sneak peek at the next book in the Hamilton Steelhawks series, *Getting Bodied*, coming in 2025.

Getting Bodied Sneak Peek

CHAPTER ONE

Stockwood, Ontario, early September

Maisie Kelly put her foot against the pitching rubber and breathed in. Runners at first and third, winning run at the plate. Two out. Full count. A single pitch might decide the outcome—either way.

The softball twisted under her grip until her fingers found the seams. Just like that.

She eyed the batter forty-three feet away. Tall and broad-shouldered with tawny blond hair that curled under a red Steelhawks cap. Like any hockey player, possessed of freakish hand-eye coordination, which only meant she had to place the ball in the exact location, low and inside.

"Swing, batter, batter, batter, no batter!" The rapid staccato taunt from her sister at first base stretched Maisie's lips. Time to end this.

She rocketed into her motion, arm muscles screaming, hand sling-shotting back. The ball whipped toward the plate.

Under the shade of his black-brimmed cap, the batter's eyes rounded. He stepped into the pitch and sent the bat whooshing through the air. The ball thumped into the catcher's mitt.

"Strike three!"

Maisie let the full broadness of her grin break out, as she jogged toward the dugout. From her left, a dark-haired blur thunked into her, and Rachel's arms circled her in an embrace. "You did it, sis!"

Maisie may have chased off a few demons after months of work to get back into shape, but that didn't matter here. They'd done it. Her hastily assembled girls' team had defied the odds. They'd beaten the pros. Sure, a hockey team, but when that team included your brother, you were happy to kick his ass.

No one could claim the Kellys weren't competitive.

An absolute wall nearly knocked her over. Her older brother Jayden pulled her into a sweaty hug, toppling her ball cap from her head. On purpose, without a doubt.

To prove that point, he scrubbed a fist into her scalp. "Good game, Maise."

He didn't know the full meaning of that, but she wasn't about to tell him. "You too."

The *psh-psh-psh* of the camera shutter intruded on her conscience. Great. Now she was going to be all over the team's social media, red-faced and frizzy-haired. At least, they'd already gotten the official pictures with her family and the Steelhawks posing with an enormous cardboard check made out to the Stockwood hospital out of the way before the game. Thank God for that small favor.

She plucked her cap from the ground and plunked it back on her head before exchanging "good games" and handshakes with the rest of the Steelhawks. Until she got to the end of the line and came face-to-face with one who didn't immediately thrust out a hand.

A pair of hazel eyes scrutinized her from head to foot, until she suppressed an urge to shift on her cleats. Heat rushed up the back of her neck.

"How do you do it?" he said after what felt like a full nine innings.

Another teammate—he'd removed his ball cap to reveal a truly spectacular cinnamon colored mullet complete with racing stripes shaved into the sides—shoved his buddy. "Looking for more abuse, Presto? Like you didn't strike out enough times today?"

Presto. Stupid hockey nicknames. No way was she calling him that, but all she could remember of his real last name was something long and Italian. Presto hardly applied to that even-featured face, one that was pleasing enough under a coating of reddish stubble.

"Get fucked, Rocky," he replied.

"I'd love to, trust me."

"Let me clarify. Fuck off somewhere else." Then he turned his attention back to Maisie. "How do you do it? I want to know." For some God-forsaken reason he wasn't acting like a typical member of her brother's team and taking the piss. The way he was looking her up and down...

Christ, Maisie, it's not like he's interested. She wasn't the type of girl men flirted with. A pro hockey player? Forget it. "Do what?"

"Pitch like that. How many strike-outs did you put up today?"

She shrugged. "I don't know."

Twelve. She'd struck out twelve professional athletes today over seven innings, but in her experience, most guys didn't like girls who showed them up, especially when it came to sports. So she settled for the lie.

"You don't remember me, do you?"

Oh, she remembered him all right. The previous summer, the team had come into the family pub to film a promotional feature about her brother, and this guy, this Presto, had decided to fuck around. She'd been manning the kitchen when his order came through. "Mr. Surprise-Me? How could I forget?"

"Thank fuck. I thought I was losing my touch." He made a show of rubbing his belly. Or what would have been his belly, because his abs were completely flat. Probably ripped, as well. "To this day, the best burger I ever had."

Pride bloomed in her chest. She'd sacrificed her lunch for his surprise—a combination of ingredients she'd been dying to try. At least he appreciated it. But that didn't mean she was going to turn all gooey over his compliment.

Another shrug. "Glad you liked it."

He took a step closer. "I still like surprises, you know."

Was... was that actual flirting? "Listen, Mr.... I'm not calling you Presto, okay?"

"Why not?"

"It's stupid." They called her brother Killer, after all, but at least that one made sense. On the ice, her brother was big and mean and delivered vicious cross-checks whenever he could get away with it. "Are you supposed to be a magician or something?"

"Maybe I have magic hands." God, it sounded like a pick-up line but... No, he was probably just fucking around. Again. She'd lived with her older brother long enough to know pranks ranked high on a hockey player's scale of amusements. "You could call me Magic Mike. No one else does."

She crossed her arms over her chest. "Hard no."

"Maise, you coming?" Rachel stood a few feet away, her gaze darting between Maisie and... Michael. If she was going to call him anything, it would be his proper name.

"Gotta go."

"We're all going back to the pub for a few beers," Rachel added with a nod in Michael's direction. "You in?"

Micheal grinned. "Hundred percent. A thousand, even."

Maisie held her tongue until she'd gotten into the passenger seat of Rachel's car and they'd pulled out of the parking lot. "Stop smirking."

Rachel paid extra careful attention to the traffic in front of them, but the corner of her mouth twitched. "I'm not smirking."

"Yes, you are, and I don't like it."

"Then maybe you should tell me what's going on."

"Nothing." Damn it, there went the corner of her mouth again. "I told you to stop."

"Nothing. Sure." Rachel drew that last word out as long as humanly possible.

"Do you remember who that was?"

"From when the team was filming last summer? Yeah."

"Then you remember he likes to fuck around."

Rachel glanced over, and damn it, she was still grinning. "Interesting choice of words."

"Christ, will you stop?"

"No."

Maisie narrowed her eyes. "Look, he and his buddies had a good laugh at my expense."

Not the first time it happened, either. They might be grown-ass men, but they clearly hadn't evolved since high school. Typical dude-bro bullshit. Something she'd learned about through bitter experience.

Rachel nodded, but her facial expression hadn't changed. She looked way too self-satisfied. "Uh huh. Right."

"Well, they did," Maisie pressed on. "He plays straight man for that other one. That Rocky guy. Fucking idiots. Anyway, if they didn't play hockey, they could take that act on the road."

Rachel's lips stretched even wider.

"Stop it." Rach was lucky they normally got along so well, because Maisie's palm tingled with an urge to smack someone. Hard enough to wipe any silly expressions off that someone's face. She settled for a fake punch.

"Do you want me to lose control of the car?"

"Oh please."

Rachel rubbed her shoulder for good measure. "Did you ever hear that line about protesting too much?"

"I am not—"

"Yes, you are." She flipped on her turn signal, in preparation of leaving the main drag through Stockwood. "Anyway, I think you should play along and see if something happens."

"Oh, here we go." Maisie rolled her gaze toward the sunroof. "Ever since you pushed Jayden in Cait's direction, you think you can set everyone up."

"He didn't need that big a push."

No, because Cait was blonde and gorgeous and curvy. And a total sweetheart and unpretentious, who'd overcome a lot of crap in her life. She'd just gotten back from spending a year in Paris as an au pair. She might as well change her name to Mary Freaking Poppins. No wonder Jayden had just slipped a diamond ring on her finger.

"God, he's just been disgustingly mushy ever since they

got back from France. If he doesn't watch out, his teammates are going to change his nickname to Kitten next season."

"Stop changing the subject." Rachel made a left—away from the usual route to the pub. "We're going by the house and getting you in the shower before we head over to Kelly's. Start thinking about what you're going to wear."

"If you think I'm letting you dress me up in some slinky outfit and too much makeup, think again. I don't have time for that shit. And I sure as hell don't have time for that type of guy."

"What type of guy? You don't even know Presto."

Christ, that name. "Rach, he's a hockey player. That's all I need to know. If he wants to hit it and quit it, he can find someone else."

"Our brother is a hockey player." Rachel pulled her attention from the road for a second to glance over. "You just pointed out how he's all mushy over his fiancée."

Maisie wrinkled her nose. "Look, no one is happier than me that Jay-Jay found someone willing to put up with him, but that just proves my point. After they're done partying and screwing around, they always end up with the same kind of girl. A girl like Cait, not a girl like me."

Because what Maisie saw when she looked in the mirror was a feminine version of her older brother. Tall, broad shoulders, large bones. Imposing. Not heavy so much, but big.

Big like a moose. She shoved that memory back into its compartment in her brain and slammed the door.

Rachel shook her head. "Well, for fuck's sake then, show them what they're missing."

Michael Prestifilippo took a long pull on his beer, the taste of hops and varied malts strong on his tongue before the cold liquid hit his throat. Amsterdam Boneshaker. Normally, he was one for trying something new, but since last summer he'd made this IPA his brand when he could get it. Support your local craft brewery and all that. In any case, this brew hit the perfect balance of bitterness, and he always went for something full-flavored with a strong bite.

He eyed the entrance to Kelly's. Maisie hadn't shown yet. Maybe she wouldn't. And if not, he could knock back a few with his teammates. With September already on them, training camp loomed in three weeks. It was beyond time to get serious if he wanted to lock in a place on the third line. Damn rookies always pushing for a spot meant he couldn't take it easy like most veteran players. Like every year, he expected a fight on his hands to avoid a trade or waivers.

But for tonight, at least, he might as well try to kick back.

He pushed off the bar and shouldered a path through the crowd, stopping for a second to sign some guy's shirt. It was an open secret around Stockwood that fans could run into Steelhawks players at Kelly's. With so many of them in town—though they were missing the top line and the starting goalie—for a charity event over Labor Day weekend, the pub was buzzing.

No surprise the owner, Steelhawks defenseman Jayden Kelly wore a smile tonight. Well, that and he had one arm around his fiancée's waist. A large diamond glittered on Cait's finger.

Michael exchanged greetings with her, lifting her hand to get a better look at the rock. "Nice. Someone has good taste." Then he bumped fists with Jayden. "Like what you've done with the place."

Jayden made a show of looking around. "We haven't changed that much."

His old jerseys still adorned the walls and a huge, flat-screen TV took up space behind the bar, but subtle nods to the Hamilton hockey team had replaced the bright green and shamrocks. Red, black, and silver accents stood out against the old hardwood.

Jayden nudged Cait with his hip. "She wouldn't let me get rid of the pool tables."

Two spots of pink bloomed on her cheeks. "Stop it." Clearly it was an inside joke because she changed the subject. "Menu's new, courtesy of Maisie. Have you seen it?"

Michael plucked a card from a nearby table. "Cute. Naming the fish and chips after Gilly." But then another item caught his attention. *Presto Burger*. "Wait, is that mine?"

He read the description. Pesto rosso, caramelized onions, mushrooms, and brie. It *was*.

"I think Maisie's pretty proud of that creation." Cait was watching him carefully.

"She should be."

"Did you know she gave you her lunch?"

"What?"

"Yeah, she was going to make that for herself."

"Wow, really?" Michael downed the rest of his beer. He might need it for this next part, but after what Cait had just revealed, he was going to have to go through with it. Turning to Jayden, he said, "Theoretical question for you."

"Shoot."

"Let's say—in theory—one of the guys asked your sister out. Would you have a problem with that?" Better get it over with since Jayden was the biggest player on the team.

Michael could hold his own in a fight, but taking on Jayden would be drawing way above his weight class.

Jayden's brows shot toward his hairline. "Depends on who. Are we talking Rocky? Because he's an automatic no-go."

"Let's say it's not Rocky."

"Then it depends on the sister." Jayden scrutinized him through narrowed eyes. "Two are underage, Rachel is taken, so that only leaves Maisie."

"Yeah, and?"

He chuckled. "It's not me you need to worry about. She'll take you down if she's not interested."

That reply should have brought relief, but somehow it only made matters worse. "I guess I could have figured that out."

"Just one thing." Jayden punched Michael's shoulder, perhaps a little harder than necessary. "If anything happens, no bragging. I don't want to think about any of my sisters in that context."

"Not my style, man, you know that. I know when to clam up, especially in the room."

"You'd better start now, both of you." Cait raised her hand to wave. "Over here!"

Michael glanced toward the entrance. Maisie and Rachel were making their way through the crowd.

He blinked. Holy fuck, *that* was Maisie? Damn, she looked good.

Last summer, her no-bullshit attitude had piqued his interest. Her clear blue eyes had blazed when she shut down Rocky's comments. Then Michael's teasing lunch order had sent her back to the kitchen half pissed off and half determined to take up the challenge, which she had—

brilliantly. He could still taste the way the flavors exploded in his mouth.

And after watching her pitch seven innings this afternoon, he wanted to get to know her better. You sure as hell didn't meet a girl like her every day.

But now want was fast turning into a need. Her hair tumbled over her shoulders in waves, the darkness a perfect contrast to flawless skin. And her top... Black fabric hugged her frame and crossed over the delicate swell of her breasts to loop into a bow at her side, baring a sliver of toned skin right above her jeans.

Yeah, with a body like that, she gave as good as she got on the field. And in bed? He only topped her by maybe three inches—barefoot or in those bright pink Chucks made no difference. She'd probably put him through the wringer and make him beg for more.

Get your mind out of the gutter, you maniac. Killer's right there and she still hasn't given you the time of day.

Her blue eyes met his, and her lips flattened. Yeah, he was going to have to work his ass off for this. Given who her brother was, he couldn't coast on being a pro-hockey player, but he preferred it that way. High risk, high reward.

He tapped his empty bottle. "Anyone want a refill? Ladies, what are you drinking?"

"Rum and coke, please," Rachel said.

Maisie looked away, hand on her hip. "Bud Light."

Michael raised an eyebrow. With all the craft offerings on the menu, she had to be shitting him. Anyone with her taste wouldn't settle for mass-produced horse piss. "Really?"

"Whatever you're having then."

When he returned with the drinks, Jayden was chatting with his dad, while Mrs. Kelly and Rachel buzzed around Cait excitedly. As he passed Rachel her glass, the words "venue" and "summer wedding" cut through their chatter—ah, right. Which left Maisie standing next to them, hands shoved in her jeans pockets, gaze darting toward the swinging doors to the back.

He handed over her beer. "Not a fan of wedding plans?"

Maisie snorted and took a sip. "They just got engaged like a week ago. Leave it to Mum to go off the deep end. Now that she and Dad working fewer hours, she's got too much time on her hands."

"Is that a bad thing to have?"

"I wouldn't know. I have all the hours I can handle in the kitchen." She nodded toward Jayden. "You know my idiot brother actually ordered the rest of the staff not to let me in there tonight. He thinks I need to *enjoy myself*."

He clinked his bottle with hers. "I'll have to thank him later, then."

Her blue eyes narrowed. Gauging him. Like she was trying to work out if he was shitting her. At least she didn't stalk off or cross her arms. Progress. Time to make a move before Jayden or Rocky or one of the other guys butted in.

"Cait showed me the new menu." He smiled. "Very nice. Though I don't remember agreeing lend my name to a burger, no matter how delicious it was."

The corner of her mouth lifted. "You took out a trademark on your nickname?"

"Still, I think we should discuss this. Over dinner, for example. Maybe you can introduce me to the food scene."

This time, she snort-laughed. "Food scene? In Stockwood?"

"I'm always up for trying something new."

"Right. It's thriving, let me tell you. The Tim Horton's

here only uses the best imported blueberries and fair-trade cocoa powder."

"I'm always down for Timmie's. At least, you know exactly what you're getting."

Her fingers fluttered over her beer bottle. "I guess there's that Italian place... They're pretty good." Her gaze softened into something that hinted at teasing. "It's a little place in a strip mall. Take-out only. I don't know if it's up to your standards."

"Only one way to find out."

About the Author

We are an international tag team of romance authors. We love hockey, books, and eye candy, not necessarily in that order.

Both of us publish under other pen names. Ashlyn Macnamara has written historical romance, as has Delphine Roy—if you'd like to check out something completely different.

Subscribe to our newsletter to be notified about upcoming books in the series.

Reviews are gold to authors. Please consider leaving your honest opinion of our work.

For more books and updates visit us at AC Sheppard.com

 instagram.com/ac_sheppard

Milton Keynes UK
Ingram Content Group UK Ltd.
UKHW020050181024
449757UK00011B/587